The young dinosaur leaped onto the cow's back and sank its talons into her hide. The cow bleated and began to reel. She turned in circles, her head lolling. Her hooves splashed through the brook, and she collapsed on her side not twenty feet from David.

The dinosaur gutted the still-living cow as she shuddered and became still. It scored the cow's belly and opened it even wider, pulling meat out and stuffing it into its mouth in an all-too-human way.

Finally sated, the dinosaur faced David, cocking its head to one side and peering at him from its left eye.

David's bowels threatened to let loose as a terrifying thought occurred to him: *Would the creature have hesitated to attack* him *had the cow not wandered away from the herd?*

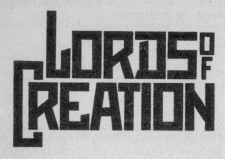

LORDS OF CREATION

TIM SULLIVAN

AVON BOOKS • NEW YORK

LORDS OF CREATION is an original publication of Avon Books. This
work has never before appeared in book form. This work is a novel.
Any similarity to actual persons or events is purely coincidental.

AVON BOOKS
A division of
The Hearst Corporation
1350 Avenue of the Americas
New York, New York 10019

Copyright © 1992 by Timothy R. Sullivan
Cover art by Joe DeVito
Published by arrangement with the author
Library of Congress Catalog Card Number: 91-93035
ISBN: 0-380-76284-6

First AvoNova Printing: April 1992

AVONOVA TRADEMARK REG. U.S. PAT. OFF. AND IN OTHER COUNTRIES,
MARCA REGISTRADA, HECHO EN U.S.A.

Printed in the U.S.A.

RA 10 9 8 7 6 5 4 3 2 1

to Ma
just like the U.S. Cavalry

to Debra, with love
after all, we've saved each other once or twice

Special thanks to
S. P. Somtow, David Bischoff and Tom Monteleone,
Bob Walters, John Horner, Roberta Lannes,
John Douglas, and Valerie Smith,
and to the late James Blish.

As flies to wanton boys are we to the Gods;
They kill us for their sport.

—*King Lear*

1 ━━━━━━━━━━━━

"It sure looks like we've got *something*," David Albee said.

David stood in a narrow excavation wiping the sweat off his face with the back of his hand. He tried to contain his excitement as he looked at the dusty object in question. Whatever this thing was, it had been buried in the Montana shale at "dinosaur level," which made it old enough to have been around at the tail end of the Cretaceous. It had apparently been waiting here at least sixty-five million years to be discovered by five beer-swilling amateur paleontologists.

"Like the commercial used to claim, 'It doesn't get any better than this,' " a sweating Charlie Terrazini said, as he carefully brushed away some of the powdered stone covering the find—if it really was a find. Charlie was grinning, but that only lasted until he had completely cleaned a patch of dirt off the thing that had stopped his chisel with such a resounding clang just a minute or two ago.

"What's the matter, Charlie?" David asked. "Is it a fossil?"

"Can't be," Charlie said. "It's . . . uh, some kind of metal."

"Huh?"

"Some kind of metal," Charlie repeated. He tapped a flat surface that did indeed possess a metallic sheen, and sneezed as dust clogged his nostrils. "Somebody must have put it here recently."

"I don't think so," David said. "That shale hasn't been disturbed in a long, long time."

Ferdy Dobkin, returning from the ice chest with a cold beer, snorted. "That's understatement if I've ever heard it. This stuff's been untouched since the days of the you-know-whats."

The "you-know-whats" were, of course, dinosaurs. David had read enough science fiction to imagine several time-travel plots about how such an artifact might come to be buried in the Cretaceous. He quickly consigned such flights of imagination to the back of his mind, however, in order to deal more realistically with the metal object.

"Get your fat ass down here and help us dig this out, will you, Ferd?" Charlie said.

Ferdy flipped him, but eased his bulk into the hole to give David and Charlie a hand, exuding an odor of beer and stale sweat. He went right to work and carefully chipped away the shale around the thing, being careful not to damage it with his chisel. Charlie continued brushing the dust off its surface with a whisk broom, until a rectangular metal surface was revealed. It was about three feet long by a foot and a half wide.

"Well, we know two of its dimensions," David said. "Let's dig around it until we find out how far down into the ground it goes before we extract it. Once we get it out, maybe we can figure out what to do with it."

"Sounds like a plan," Ferdy grunted as he worked.

"What's a plan?" Cilla MacDonald called out as she approached the dig. She was accompanied by Hiram Walking Bear. These last two members of the weekend expedition had been working apart from the others all morning at a site two miles to the north.

"*Lunch* is a plan," Ferdy said, "as soon as we get this box out of the ground."

"Box?" Hiram asked. His expression was quizzical. He walked up to the excavation with Cilla and peered down at the unexpected find. "Ugh, me no like what me see."

"It was probably buried by a super-intelligent marmoset in the late Cretaceous, chief," Ferdy said.

"More likely by some clown back in ninety-three," Charlie said. That was the year that the Department of Morality had tried to ban paleontology, calling it an affront to a Christian nation. Scientists had been worried that it would come to a decision by the right-wing ideologues on the Supreme Court, but the Congress had put it to rest for the moment, after a close vote in the Senate. Lots of things had been buried that year, but not usually in the form of metal boxes.

Everyone was silent as their labors revealed more and more of the box, Hiram and Cilla taking turns with Ferdy and Charlie in the narrow trench; there was only room for three people at one time, but David knew he couldn't climb out of the excavation until the job was done. From time to time he touched the smooth metal, which was warmed by the late morning sun. It was very hard, and he wondered if it was titanium, or some dense alloy he wasn't familiar with. He finally admitted to himself that he had no idea what it was.

At Ferdy's insistence, they broke for lunch about a half hour later. A couple more hours' work would probably free the metal box, unless it went down deeper than they anticipated. David sat on a rock munching a chicken salad sandwich and drinking a Bud. He didn't say much as he stared across the Montana plain and tried to imagine how the box came to be where it was. The others were conducting a lively conversation about the peculiar find.

"It's like that old Firesign Theater album," Ferdy said. " 'Everything You Know Is Wrong.' "

"Fireside Theater?" said Charlie, with his customary New York skepticism. "What the fuck is that?"

"A comedy group that was around when your parents were young and fucked up on acid."

"You mean like the Three Stooges?" Charlie pronounced it "Tree Stooges."

Ferdy rolled his eyes.

"Leave it to you to come up with something obscure," Charlie said, annoyed. "Isn't this thing weird enough?"

"Well, it's pretty weird, all right," Cilla agreed. "Could somebody have put it there as a joke?"

"How could they have packed the shale around it like that?" Hiram asked. "It looks perfectly natural."

"It *is* perfectly natural," David said, swallowing a bite of bread and chicken and washing it down with beer. He hadn't expected to say that, but there it was.

His comment shut them all up for a moment. Ferdy's eyes widened, and Charlie's jaws failed to close on his sandwich for a moment. Cilla looked at the plastic tub of potato salad in her hand. Only Hiram showed no surprise.

"That's what I think, too," Hiram said.

"Okay, so we're in a Spielberg movie, right?" said Cilla. "E.T.'s gonna come down and say he left his little metal box here back in the age of dinosaurs, right?"

"Dave didn't say he knew where it came from, or who left it here," Hiram pointed out. "He just said he thinks it's been here awhile."

"Awhile!" Ferdy bellowed. "Since the *Mesozoic?*"

At seventeen minutes past two they lifted the box out of the excavation and moved it toward the smaller of their two tents, known as "the honeymoon lodge," since it was traditionally used by romantically involved couples on digs. David felt a drop of sweat slowly trickle down the bridge of his nose and onto the tip, where it dangled annoyingly all the while he and Ferdy were carrying the box to its designated spot. They were very careful, but he didn't really think it was necessary. The box had survived sixty-five million years buried under a shale anticline without so much as a scratch or a patch of rust marring its flawlessly geometric surface. What could they possibly do to damage it?

"Doesn't weigh all that much," Ferdy said as they set it down on the flattest piece of ground they could find.

"Thirty pounds, tops. One of us could easily carry it alone."

"Maybe we should cover it with canvas or something," Cilla said.

"It'll be okay there, hon," Hiram said, as though he'd been thinking the same thing as David. "If it's lasted this long, we sure as hell can't hurt it."

Cilla nodded. They all knew that this was crazy, but here it was right in front of them. David thought about what he had said before and decided that it was ridiculous. This thing couldn't have been there more than a few years—a few decades at the most. He shook his head. "How the hell did that box come to be here, guys?"

Nobody answered, because they all understood that the question was purely rhetorical. None of them knew anything about it, any more than David did. No matter how much they wanted to laugh it off, or explain it away, they couldn't do it.

"This one's sure got our studio audience stumped," Ferdy said in a comic game-show host voice. "Maybe it's time to call in our panel of experts."

"Maybe so, Ferd," David agreed. He looked out over the brown grass across the plain and imagined, as he had countless times before, an inland sea stretching down through the Midwest. Who the hell could have put this box here back in those days, when mosasaurs and plesiosaurs swam just miles from where he stood, and pterosaurs soared overhead hunting for fish in the crystalline waters? The box was a thing of precise right angles, and the right angle did not exist then, except perhaps for a rare accident of nature. Who could have tooled its perfect, metallic shape? Dinosaurs didn't operate lathes, for Christ's sake.

"Only question I have," he said, "is who do we call in a case like this? CIA, FBI, Ghostbusters, Doc Savage, Pee-wee Herman?"

"David," Cilla asked, "who's Doc Savage?"

* * *

They decided to call Professor Robert Pierce at the university. David phoned Billings from McCullers' Rock Shop, the nearest pay phone, located some twelve miles from the dig. He thought that maybe Bob Pierce would have some ideas about what to do. Maybe Pierce, his former paleontology professor, would tell them that the shale could have fallen back around the box, making it look as if it had never been disturbed. He certainly hoped that Professor Pierce would offer such a supposition, but unfortunately he didn't say anything like that at all.

"Is this some kind of gag?" Bob Pierce demanded, his voice querulous as it came through the handset of the pay phone at McCullers' Rock Shop.

"No."

A long pause. "Well, why don't I come out and have a look around?" Pierce said.

"I was hoping you'd say that, Bob," David said.

"How do I get there?"

David gave him careful directions, said good-bye, and hung up. Jack McCullers, co-owner of the rock shop with his wife, Emma, called to him from behind the counter, "Find something interesting, Dave?"

"Just an old box."

"A box?"

"Yeah, it was buried at the dig. We can't figure how it got there."

Jack shrugged. "Strange world."

The bell over the front door tinkled as two customers entered. Jack warmly welcomed the middle-aged couple, who were attired in Hawaiian shirts and Bermuda shorts, and he began to chat them up. David was relieved, because he really didn't want to talk about the box anymore. It was all just a little bit too odd. He thought that he'd look around at the shelves bearing stone eggs and fossil imprints for a minute or two before going back out to his jeep. McCullers' place was twelve miles from the site where they'd found the box, and he'd been in here hundreds of times to buy a cold beer and gaze at the fossils

Jack and Emma sold to tourists. David was pretty sure they made more money on drinks and cigarettes than on dinosaur eggs; this shop was one of the last of its kind. There had been dozens of them between here and Choteau twenty years ago, but they had been put out of business—not from lack of interest, but from a surfeit of interest—by the Christian Millennialist movement, a coalition of religious-right groups that believed the millennium was nearly at hand, and that paleontology was the work of Satan. When the threat of being jailed for selling fossils had become imminent, the last owners of the rock shops had closed their doors. All except for Jack and Emma.

Paleontology had only been a small part of the Millennialist assault, of course. Art deemed offensive to "community standards" was under attack throughout the nineties, followed by the sciences that conflicted with the views of the religious right. In other words, anything that logically argued against creationism—the notion that God had created the earth and everything on it four thousand years or so ago—was fair game for fundamentalist fanatics after they had managed to foist a weak administration into creating the Department of Morality—good old D.O.M., the bane of secular humanists everywhere. Somehow Jack and Emma had survived the witch-hunt, and the furor had died down a little until recent months. After all, this was 1999. Things were bound to get a little peculiar between now and New Year's Eve.

David sighed and turned to leave. Just then the bell tinkled again, and he stood face to face with his ex-roommate, ex-lover, Liz Tomlinson.

2 ───────────

"Hi," David said. The word came out choked and high-pitched, he thought, but Liz showed no sign that she'd noticed anything out of the ordinary.

"David," said Lizaveta Tomlinson, as if he were the last person in the world she expected to see. Her green eyes were opened wide and she hesitated on the threshold.

"Don't let the flies in, Liz," Jack shouted from the back of the store. The two tourists in Hawaiian shirts chuckled, and the mildly embarrassed Liz came inside.

"Sorry," she said to Jack. And to David: "Just stopped in for a cold drink."

"Let me buy it for you," David replied.

"No, that's okay."

"Really, I'd like to." David went to the old-fashioned Pepsi-Cola tub and stuck his hand into the refreshing cold. "Diet Coke?"

"Lemonade, if there is any."

David groped around in the icy water until his fingers got numb, trying to think of something to say. "What brings you out this way?" he asked as he found a clear bottle with yellow liquid in it and handed it to her.

"Kraul family's got a heifer with a virus."

"Oh." He couldn't help noticing the firm line of her jaw, which seemed perfect to him, as she held up the bottle.

"This is apple juice," she said.

"Huh?"

"It isn't lemonade, David."

"Oh, sorry. The light's not good in here."

"That's okay. I'll look for myself."

As she put back the apple juice and fished in the cooler for lemonade, he thought about how emblematic this little scene was. David screwing up by playing the white knight to Lisaveta's princess. But those were the wrong job descriptions; he was a guy who drank too much, and she was a self-sufficient veterinarian. She knew this deep inside her, and he didn't. Intellectually he was aware of it, but he still labored under delusions of grandeur, a romantic at heart. Not Liz, though. Not anymore. Not after living with David for two years.

"Ah." She rose from the cooler with a carton of lemonade, opened the top seam efficiently with the nail of her right index finger, and took a sip. "Wonderful."

David smile. He still liked to see her enjoying herself.

"You look good, David," Liz said, "nice and tan."

"Thanks. I'm on a dino dig."

"I figured."

"Yeah, we found something this morning."

Liz gaped comically, the lemonade carton poised at her lips in an exaggerated attitude of astonishment. "Honest to God?"

"Yep." He laughed, appreciating how goofy she could be. This was what they'd always said when a dinosaur bone was found, in mockery of the Millennialists. "Honest to God."

"Well, you know me, David. These days I'm more interested in living animals than dead ones."

He nodded. "Ah, yes, the quick and the dead. Therein lies the crux of our problem, right? Romance died and you were quick to get out of it."

"Let's not get into it here, David. It's over and that's it."

Liz took her lemonade to the cash register as the couple, each clutching a brown paper bag, went outside to face the harsh prairie sunlight.

David watched Liz buy the cold drink, and realized that

he still loved her. He was not entirely convinced that they were really through. Maybe it was wishful thinking, but it seemed to him that they'd been through breakups worse than this. Besides, he had never been known to keep going back to a woman before, but he felt differently about Liz. If only they hadn't fought all the time when they were together, their relationship would have been great.

"Jeez." He laughed, thinking how ridiculous he was. A guy with an opinion about everything, no steady job, no master's degree, no nothing, expecting a woman like Liz to want him.

Liz turned and glared at him as Jack glanced from her to David. "What's so funny?" she demanded.

"I don't know." David shrugged. "Guess I better get back to the dig."

"Good idea," Liz said. "I've gotta get going, too."

She turned and looked at him, and he thought she might still feel something for him . . . or was he dreaming?

"Bye, Liz," he said. "See you, Jack."

A moment later the screen door slammed behind him, and he was sitting in the jeep. Why was his heart pounding, and why was he breathing so heavily?

"Must be the heat," he said, turning the key in the ignition and cranking up the jeep's motor.

Robert Pierce, known as "Hobbit" to an earlier generation of students, stood at the dig site, staring down at the box. He was sixty-one years old, and had been tenured as full professor for nearly twenty years. This "sinecure," as he liked to call it, had not come easily to him, since he had a reputation as something of a curmudgeon. Bob Pierce was not the sort of man who didn't speak his mind if he thought it was important, and he didn't care who was offended in the process. David liked that about him.

"David," Bob said, squinting and adjusting his horn-rimmed glasses as he examined the box, "are you fucking with me?"

"No, I'm not."

Bob's fleshy, gray-bearded cheeks swelled, and he blew out air to exhibit his frustration. "Well, I'm no metallurgist, but I'd say this is impossible."

"I was afraid you'd say that, Bob."

"I'm no geologist, either," Bob said as he wiped sweat off his pink neck with a handkerchief, "but I'm pretty sure I can get one to come out here and have a look at this thing."

"You don't think we ought to take it to the campus?" Cilla asked.

"Not just yet." Bob turned toward the excavation. "In fact, I almost wish you hadn't taken it out of the ground. Might make things a little more difficult for us."

"Won't they be able to see that it came out of that hole?" Ferdy said.

"Not necessarily. You guys could have dug the shale out to fit the dimensions of the box."

"But we wouldn't do that—" Charlie was sputtering indignantly.

Bob raised a plump hand. "Hold on, Charlie. I didn't say *I* don't believe you. But you're going to have to handle a good deal of skepticism before we can get anybody to believe this."

"Well, there's the box, and there's the excavation. What more do they need?"

"The box doesn't look like it's ever been underground, wouldn't you agree?" Bob turned and patted the gleaming metal as though it were a poodle. "How can you expect anybody to accept such a thing at face value?"

"Okay, then," Charlie said. "Fuck 'em. We'll just use the box for a footstool."

"Good idea," Ferdy snorted. "Better still, maybe we can pry it open and use it as an ice chest."

"All right, all right, I get the idea," Bob said. "I don't want the box to be ignored any more than you do, but we'll have to go about this logically if we want to get anywhere."

"Shit," Charlie said.

"Listen to the man," David said. "He's been working inside the state bureaucracy for a long time. He knows how to get things done."

The murmuring died down, and the wind whipped along the prairie. Bob's baggy suit rippled like a flag. "I'll get Pat Duvic out here from the geology department. I know I can trust Pat to keep this quiet for now. Might even be able to give us some idea of how old this thing really is."

David nodded. "I guess it can't be all that old, but it sure is weird that it was buried in that shale."

"Yeah, and if the one-in-a-trillion chance that it dates to the Cretaceous is verified, then the whole world will be buzzing with the news. And not just the scientific community, either."

"National Enquirer?" Ferd inquired.

"The government," Bob said solemnly. "That includes the Department of Morality, Supreme Court, Millennialist congressmen. The works."

"Christ," Hiram said, "those assholes aren't gonna like this one bit, are they?"

"No, and they're gonna like the people who discovered it even less."

"Well," David sighed. "I guess we know who the good doctor means by that remark, don't we, kids?"

Bob slapped him on the shoulder. "I just want to let you know what we're in for. There are some strong negative forces at work, reactionary groups trying to get paleontology and physical anthropology removed from the curriculum, for Christ's sake. These people are denying facts that have been known for a century or more. Just imagine what this little tidbit is gonna do to them."

"I see what you mean," David said.

"This has got to be handled, if you will, with kid gloves," Bob said. "I appreciate your impatience, but it won't do in the present political climate."

"Okay, Prof, we'll do things your way," Ferdy said. "Everybody agree on that?"

They all said that they did, and David was relieved to

have someone take charge of a situation that he hadn't been prepared for. Nobody had ever been prepared for something like this, of course, so that meant Bob was flying blind, too. But at least he was approaching the problem methodically and logically.

"Well, we can be thankful for one thing," David said. "At least we don't have to encase *this* fossil in plaster."

At about half past seven the next morning, they saw a blue car kicking up a trail of dust on the dirt road in the distance. Hiram was just emerging from the smaller tent; he shared it with Cilla, who was getting an iced coffee from the chest. David had first met them the previous year at a paleontology seminar where Hiram, a full blooded Crow, had worn a name tag that said "Chief," and the blonde Cilla had worn one saying "Squaw." It was well over ninety degrees already, and there wasn't a cloud in the sky.

"Who's that?" Ferdy's voice came from behind them as he wandered out of the other tent. Neither of them turned to look at him. They continued to watch the approaching vehicle. "That's not Bob's car, is it?"

"No," David answered. He was just coming out of the big tent, rubbing the sleep from his eyes.

But as it came closer, they saw that the passenger in the front seat was indeed Bob. The driver was a middle-aged woman wearing sunglasses.

"Who's driving?" Charlie asked.

"I think it's Professor Duvic," said David.

"I thought Pat Duvic was a man," Cilla said, delighted.

The blue car, streaked with prairie dust, pulled up to the site, and two doors slammed as Bob and Pat Duvic got out. Pat was a stately woman with gray hair and strong features. She looked them all right in the eye as she shook each hand.

"I remember you from an introductory course some years back," Charlie said in his Brooklyn brogue. "I enjoyed the class."

"Thank you," Pat said.

Cilla frowned at Charlie. "Why didn't you guys mention that Pat's a woman?"

"Why, Cilla, what a sexist thing to ask."

They all had a chuckle over that, including Cilla. But Pat got down to business immediately. "I take it that's the offending artifact, over there?"

"That's the McGuffin," Bob replied.

As Pat moved toward the box, David noticed the tight fit of her jeans. She was slender and moved with remarkable grace. He'd seen her around the campus back when he was taking graduate courses, and had often wondered what this striking woman was like. He'd wondered what a lot of women were like in those days, before he'd met Liz.

Pat squatted by the box, running her fingertips over the smooth metal. Then she moved over the excavation and took a look at it.

"This shale was undisturbed when you first cut into it?" she asked.

"Yeah, that's right," said David.

"That pile is what you dug out?"

"Pretty much."

"We better take it in for testing," Pat said. "There's nothing we can do out here."

"I just wanted to show it to you in as close to its original state as possible," Bob said, "to give you an idea of what we're up against."

"Thermoluminescence is probably out of the question, at least for the moment. So is electron spin resonance analysis. Potassium argon dating is probably the quickest method to figure how old this thing is."

"Potassium argon dating! Electron spin resonance analysis!" David was astonished. As he recalled, the former method compared the relative amounts of the two elements potassium and argon, which changed over lengthy but quantifiable periods. The latter sounded so high-tech that he didn't know what to make of it, though he had heard of it before. "Isn't that going to be a little hard to arrange?"

"Yes," Pat said, "and it'll be a considerable expense. So if this *is* some kind of hoax, you better tell me now, before you get us all in trouble."

"It's no hoax," David said emphatically.

Pat nodded. "That's what I thought."

3

Of course, they weren't allowed anywhere near the box once it got on campus. The government moved in so quickly that Bob was left apologizing outside his office as a group of grad students and amateur paleontologists assailed him angrily with indignant shouts and accusation. David, Cilla, and Hiram were in the forefront.

"I didn't notify the D.O.M., David," he said. "You know me better than that."

"Somebody did." David tried to control his anger and outrage. This building, with its bulletin boards on pale green corridor walls and its cubbyhole offices, was a sacred place to him. He simply couldn't believe that Dr. Robert Pierce, one of the world's greatest paleontologists and his close friend, could do this to them. "Was it Pat?"

"No, I think it was somebody in the lab who got nosy, or maybe the geology department head himself. It wasn't Pat, though. I'm sure of it."

"What's the difference?" Cilla said. "The D.O.M.'s got it now, and they'll make sure nobody ever finds out the truth about it."

"I don't know if they can hush it up that much, Cilla," Bob said. "But they may very well try."

"They'll discredit everyone who tries to tell the truth about this," Hiram said. "Everybody knows how they operate."

"Tell me about it," Bob said. "I've been on the right wing shit list since—"

16

"I know, I know," David said, repeating the familiar refrain, "since we were babes in arms."

"You're *still* babes in arms," Bob said. "If you weren't, you wouldn't think we can do something about this bullshit."

"I guess that's true," David said.

"Damn right it is, but you'd never forgive yourself if you didn't try," Bob said. "David, I can't fit all of you in my office."

David glanced behind him and saw that the corridor was milling with dozens of students who had caught wind of what was going on. Some of them might have been genuinely interested, but most were just the idle curious.

"Go ahead, David," Cilla said. "Hiram and I have got to go, anyway."

David watched them shoulder their way through the crowd. As soon as Cilla and Hiram were out of sight, he stepped inside the office, which smelled of rich coffee. Bob closed the door.

"Just how long you been on that ole gummint shit list, Bob?" David asked as he plopped himself down in a leather-backed chair next to Bob's desk. The room was too small for the guest's chair to be placed elsewhere.

"Ever since I directed an off-campus production of *MacBird* back in the sixties, maybe even before that," Bob said, waddling toward a little table supporting a coffee pot and four mugs. "Cup o' joe?"

"Sure."

After Bob had poured him a cup and David had sweetened and whitened it with powders from packets, David sat looking around at the shelves of books, several written by Bob himself, and fossil teeth that crowded the tiny office. A cursor blinked on a computer screen. On the walls were framed paintings by the great dinosaur artists—Knight, Walters, Manly, Kish. He'd always loved this cramped little space, the domain of a man who had passionately loved dinosaurs all his life. David realized that Bob probably never would have dreamed, when he first took his degree, that one day his job might be taken away because of religious pressure on politicians.

"Dinosaurs," Bob said, stroking the serrated spine of a toy tyrannosaur, "can't live with 'em, can't live without 'em."

David chuckled. "So when are they gonna carbon-date the box, Bob?"

"Not carbon dating. Not potassium argon dating, either. Thermoluminescence, to start. Carbon is, if you'll pardon the expression, dated."

"I knew that," David joked. "But when are they gonna do whatever it is they're gonna do?"

"Oh, I don't know. I imagine they'll use a number of different methods for comparison. They're hushing it all up over there now. Flanagan has sent his own boys down to keep an eye on all the wicked secular humanists."

"Jaffrey Flanagan?" Flanagan was the Secretary of Morality himself, the bête noir of scientist and scholar alike. "This is really getting out of hand. Jaffrey Fuckin' Flanagan."

"The very same. I guess he thinks we might cheat on the dating tests."

David shook his head and took his first sip of coffee. It burnt the roof of his mouth. "Sheesh."

"Pat slipped me a little nugget of info this morning, though," Bob said, guzzling his black coffee. "The X-rays showed something inside the box."

David set down his mug on the edge of Bob's desk and leaned forward. "Don't leave me in suspense, Bob. What is it?"

"Eggs."

"Eggs?" David felt a thrill that almost made the coffee come back up. "What kind of eggs?"

"Medium-sized for a dinosaur, like a dromaeosaurid's, maybe. Hard to tell for sure."

"A box full of eggs." David stated this flatly. It was a little too much to take in all at once.

"Yeah, five of them. And they're all intact, so far as anybody can tell without opening the box."

"Which they *are* planning to do, right?"

Bob shrugged. "Sooner or later, I suppose. They can determine the box's age after it's been cut open."

"Wow!"

"Hey, that's what we used to say in the sixties. I feel very nostalgic, hearing you make such a pronouncement on the eve of the new millennium."

"The new millennium won't start until January first, twenty-oh-one, Bob. You know that. We've got almost a year and a half to go before the end of all life as we know it."

"Tell it to the Millennialists." Bob took another swig of coffee, and then looked back at David. "There's something else in the box, too."

David frowned, frightened for some reason. "What is it?"

"They don't know. Some kind of mechanism, Pat says, but unidentifiable."

David could think of nothing to say. So he said something inane: "This can't really be happening."

"No, I don't suppose it can."

The two men looked at each other, bonded not only by their friendship, but by this great mystery that they had stumbled upon, as well. Their lives were being changed ineluctably by a metal box that had been dug out of the earth a couple of days ago, and they both knew it. Along with a sense of wonder, there was an almost palpable sense of regret hanging in the air. Nothing would ever be quite the same again.

"How about the metallurgist?" David asked.

"Says that the alloy was blended so flawlessly that it couldn't have been done on Earth."

"I don't understand."

"Well, on Earth the denser mineral will sink to the bottom. In space the minerals'll blend perfectly, if they're far enough away from any planetary-sized body."

"So they're saying it was blended in space."

"No, they're just saying it couldn't have been done on Earth, which is not the same thing."

David laughed nervously. "Sure sounds like the same thing to me."

"Never were one to put too fine of a point on a thing, were you, David?"

The phone on Bob's desk rang. Taking one last slug of coffee, Bob sighed, set down the drained mug, and picked up the handset. He punched the button next to the blinking light.

"Pierce," he said.

David was still trying to take in what he'd just heard when he noticed a subtle change in Bob's expression.

"What . . . ?" The wrinkles in Bob's forehead deepened; he was clearly shaken. "Are you sure?" He glanced at David without seeing him. "Okay, I'll be right over."

He hung up. For a moment he didn't move, just sat staring at the silent phone.

"What is it, Bob?"

"The box." He swung his head to reveal his haunted gray eyes. "They've opened it."

They were inside the Earth Sciences Building within five minutes. The place seemed strangely dark and silent except for the glare on the marble floor reflecting light from high windows, and the echoing murmur of voices. Pat was waiting for them, surrounded by three dour men wearing dark suits. One of the men stepped forward as though to block their way, but Pat said, "They're the ones I need."

The D.O.M. agent hesitated, and Pat took Bob by the elbow. "This way."

David followed, but turned to look back at the agents, and thought that such a thing shouldn't be happening on a university campus. How easily these people just took over, disrupting higher education, ordering the easily cowed university administration to do their bidding. It just wasn't right, but it was happening.

They entered a lab on the north side of the building, away from the classrooms. More agents were posted there, but they let Pat, Bob, and David pass. A group of men and women with goggles hanging on their chests and wearing lab coats were inside.

David quickly got an idea of what was going on, even though there wasn't much light to see by. On a long table was the box, one end cut off cleanly. There were some machines he didn't recognize, including something that looked like a microwave oven—perhaps the thermoluminescence gizmo or the electron spin resonance analysis thing, he thought—six computers, and a laser for cutting the metal. As Bob and Pat conversed rapidly in low tones, David walked around to get a look inside the box, trying to be as unobtrusive as possible.

Five yellow ovoids, mottled with pale blue, were set in recessions in the bottom of the box, just as though they had been placed in a refrigerator door's egg tray. Behind the eggs was a delicately curved protrusion from the box's wall, three or four inches in diameter.

Two guys in lab coats looked familiar, one of them playing with his glasses, the other studying something on a clipboard. They were professors David had seen on campus from time to time. He didn't recognize anybody else.

"What happened?" David asked the two men. Pat and Bob were talking softly behind him.

"We started by just cutting off a tiny sample for testing," said the guy playing with his spectacles, "but then we got the go-ahead to open the box. Something blew the laser when we cut it open, and all the power in the building went off. It was a surge that you could actually feel, sort of an unpleasant wave that went right through you. It only took a fraction of a second or so, and then it was over."

"They should have the power on any time now," the other guy (Sosnowski?) said. "I don't think there's anything wrong with the laser, but its power cells seem to be drained.''

Whatever the source of that energy surge was, David thought he knew its purpose. ''Those eggs are alive,'' he said. ''They've been in stasis.''

The two scientists looked at each other.

''That's right, David,'' Pat said. ''And we want to hatch them.''

David turned and saw an expression of mingled hope and anxiety on Bob's face that told him this was no joke.

''We need an incubator real fast,'' Bob said. ''Or they'll die.''

''I know where there's one just a few miles from here,'' David said.

Bob and Pat looked relieved, but David couldn't help wondering how Liz was going to react to having her veterinary clinic taken over by a lot of people she didn't know.

4

"David, I thought you gave up drugs a long time ago," Liz said angrily. She stood behind the screen door at the front of her house, looking more enraged as each government vehicle pulled into the yard, one by one. A buzz-cut D.O.M. agent named Burles stood behind David, as if he didn't trust David to ask the right questions. Bob hadn't arrived yet, and that was disturbing.

"I know it sounds insane," David said, "but it's true. Remember I told you at McCullers' that we found something? Well, this is it. You've got to help. Besides, these guys are gonna use your incubator whether you want them to or not, so you might as well give in gracefully."

"Let me see the eggs," Liz said.

"What?"

"You heard me. I want to see the eggs."

"Well, I don't know if it's gonna be all that easy to arrange, Liz. They're probably going to want somebody of their own to take care of this."

"I'm a trained vet," she said coolly, pointing at the shingle next to the door that read "Lizaveta Tomlinson, Veterinary Medicine." "Can any of these people make that claim? I mean, who's going to run the incubator?"

"Good point." It was Pat, walking up to the house with the two lab-coated guys in tow.

Burles said, "Let her see the eggs. We're wasting time."

"Okay." The bespectacled lab coat, whose name was Fine, ran back to a van parked at the side of the driveway under an elm tree. His partner was right behind him. They

23

emerged a few moments later with the box, which was still open on one end but otherwise intact. Pat was right behind them.

Liz opened the door for them, and they carefully carried the box inside, through the reception area and a hallway, and set it on the kitchen table. David followed Agent Burles inside, and watched from a vantage near the sink. He felt odd being here, though he had lived with Liz for over two years. Many was the time he had eaten scrambled eggs and toast and drunk juice and coffee in this little room.

"We left it in the original, uh, container," Pat said. "There's some sort of suction that holds the eggs in place. They come out easily enough, but it seemed wise to keep them in there for the time being."

"Can I take one out?" Liz asked.

"Go ahead," Pat said, smiling. "You're the doctor."

Liz nodded and reached inside the box. David held his breath as she carefully clutched an egg and withdrew it. This was a *dinosaur* egg, for Christ's sake.

Liz laced her fingers and cupped the egg in both hands. She carried it to the window and held it up to the light. After a moment she said, "Let's get 'em into the incubator."

Somehow David got to the table first, just as Liz set the egg back inside. He picked up the box by himself. When Burles stepped forward to object, David said, "The back door is narrow, and the steps are rickety. I know the way."

"Better let him do it," Pat said.

Burles backed off. David hefted the box and started toward the rear of the house with it, and Liz ran ahead to open the door for him. Dogs started barking as soon as he stepped outside, and other birds and animals twittered and squawked in the cages behind the house. He descended the three steps and started toward the shed where Liz kept the incubator.

Again, she was ahead of him to open the latch. He carried the box inside and set it down on the floor planks.

Liz snatched the chain over her head and snapped on the light.

The incubator was revealed as a structure composed of three infrared lights inside a corrugated iron frame a little smaller than a Subaru. One side was lined with panes of glass, so that observation was possible. Liz opened the hatch, piled up some straw on a shelf inside, and placed the eggs carefully on the straw. Then she shut the hatch, and snapped a switch to turn on the heat lamps.

"Is that it?" said Burles.

"That's it," Liz said. "My dad built it over twenty years ago, and it's always worked fine on a variety of mammals born prematurely, as well as birds' eggs."

"Will it work on dinosaur eggs?" Pat said. "That's the question."

"We have no evidence that these are dinosaur eggs," Burles said.

"Have you ever seen eggs like those before, Dr. Tomlinson?" Pat asked.

"No."

"I have," David said.

They all looked his way.

"But not in this condition. These appear to be the eggs of a dromaeosaurid, perhaps dromaeosaurus itself, or deinonychus, or velociraptor . . . or a cousin of theirs we don't know about yet."

"What do you mean," Burles asked suspiciously, "not in this condition?"

David caught the smirks on Pat's and Liz's faces while he answered as earnestly as he could. "I mean that they were fossilized, sir, not fresh like these."

Burles scowled. All this was undoubtedly opposed to his religious principles. If his bosses had sent him to uncover a hoax, he must have been sorely disappointed by now. Still, David was sure that Burles would keep trying in his single-minded—not to mention simple-minded—way.

"Well, there isn't gonna be much to look at for a

while," Liz said. She turned off the overhead light and they went back to the house, caged animals woofing, meowing, and cheeping after them.

"Would anybody care for a cup of coffee?" Liz asked. Everybody but Burles said that they would, including Fine and Sosnowski. The clipboard was set down carefully on the sideboard as Liz handed its owner a steaming cup.

"I'm expecting a patient in a few minutes," Liz said. "A German shepherd."

"I'm afraid that'll be impossible, Dr. Tomlinson," Burles said. "Only authorized personnel will be allowed on the premises for the time being."

Liz looked at David as if she wanted to kill him, and then turned to Burles. "What about my patients?"

Burles didn't answer.

"Look, the eggs aren't in the house," David said quickly. "What harm can it do to allow Liz to go see her patients? She has a business to run here."

"That's right, Burles," Pat said. "You can cordon off the back, and just let Liz go in and out and tend to the animals. If you close down the place entirely, you not only prevent her from making a living, but you arouse the curiosity of the ranchers who depend on her. Pretty soon everybody will know that something's going on back there, because somebody always talks. Why run things like this is the Cold War when you can get what you want without stepping on Liz's toes?"

Burles thought it over. "I don't want to be unreasonable," he said at last. "But the back of the house has to be off limits to everybody but you, Doctor, at least for now."

Liz nodded solemnly. "You've got a deal."

The phone rang.

"Excuse me." Liz went to the kitchen wall phone and answered it. "Professor Pierce!" she said in mock surprise. "We're having a party. Why don't you come out and join us?"

She paused. "Hold on. It's for you, David. Your former paleontology professor."

David took the handset. "Bob?"

"David, I'm having a hell of a problem here."

"What's the matter?"

"Somebody's arrived from Washington, and I think he's going to make life difficult for all of us."

"Who is it?"

"Jaffrey Flanagan."

David glanced at Burles out of the corner of his eye. So Burles was sent to Billings just to hold the fort down until the big cheese showed up—the Secretary of Morality himself.

"What, uh, what does he intend to do?"

"He's on his way out there right now, and he's loaded for bear."

"Well, I don't think Liz has got any bears," David replied. "But she might have some dinosaur hatchlings before long."

"I just hope Flanagan doesn't make *huevos rancheros* out of those eggs," Bob said. "This campus is crawling with government people. Is it the same there?"

David glanced out the window. He saw several men in dark suits standing around. "Yeah."

"Just because you're paranoid, that doesn't mean they're not out to get you."

"Is that one of those sixties expressions, Bob?"

"Yeah, but don't laugh. The good old days are coming back."

"Sure."

"I'll try to get out there, but I don't know if Flanagan will let me. He's had a security check done on me by now."

"He might have even seen you in *MacBird.*"

"The price of stardom."

"Thanks for calling, Bob."

"See you later—I hope."

The receiver clicked, and a dial tone ensued. David

looked at the handset for a moment before hanging it up. He thought how insane this was. They were being treated like enemies of the state, when they should have been celebrated for one of the great scientific finds of all time.

"Is Bob coming out here?" Pat asked.

"Maybe." David looked at Burles. "Your boss is on his way, Agent Burles."

He thought he detected an expression of relief on Burles's pug face, but he couldn't be sure. If so, it was the first sign of emotion the guy had shown. Probably saved it all for holy rolling at Sunday go to meetin'.

There was a knock at the front door.

"That's probably my patient," Liz said, excusing herself to answer it.

As soon as she was gone, David began to feel very disoriented. Four strange people sat with him in a house he had thought of as his home until a few months ago. They were all here because of five dinosaur eggs sitting in the incubator a few yards from Liz's kitchen, while Liz conducted business as usual in the front room.

"Don't worry, Mrs. Johnson," he heard her say through the wall, "Rocky will be as good as new in a few days."

Liz got rid of Mrs. Johnson as quickly as she could, fending off questions about all the vehicles parked in front of her house. She soon returned, leading a German shepherd on a leash. The dog seemed frightened, and refused to enter the kitchen. Liz tugged at his leash until he couldn't fight her any longer. Whining, he finally allowed himself to be led out the back door. The German shepherd's canine odor lingered in the kitchen.

While she was gone, somebody else came to the door. Burles and the lab coats both looked up, but David was one step ahead of them.

"I'll get it," he said. "Liz's customers know me."

He made his way through the hall, glad to get away for a few moments. He went to the front door and flung it open. He didn't find a rancher with a sick puppy standing there, as he might have expected, but a man familiar from television and magazine covers. But it wasn't the celebrity David expected, either.

"Hello," the man said in a resonant voice, "I'm Charles Margolis."

5 ━━━━━━━━━━━━━━━

David could only gape for a moment. This was the White House Chief of Staff, reputed to be the man who *really* ran the country. Then he chided himself for being a sucker; this guy was a media personality and politician, so why should David—who didn't even own a TV, and who sneered at *Time* and *Newsweek*—be impressed?

"How do you do?" he said, opening the screen door and extending a hand. "I'm David Albee."

Margolis stepped inside and grasped David's hand firmly. He was taller than David by a couple of inches, was slender, and had a healthy, tanned complexion. It was hard to tell how old he was; maybe forty-five to fifty-five. "You're the young man who discovered the artifact, aren't you?"

David realized that this wasn't really a question. Coming from this guy, it might be more of an accusation. He decided to act as if it were a compliment. "Thank you, but there were five of us, actually. I didn't do it all by myself."

Margolis smiled, seeming to be quite reasonable and friendly. It was hard to believe that this was the guy who had, in concert with Jaffrey Flanagan, single-handedly almost destroyed several rather important branches of scientific endeavor in the United States of America these past few years.

"Everyone's in the kitchen," David said, gesturing and leading the way. "Except for Dr. Tomlinson, who is tending to her charges in the back at the moment."

"I think a veterinarian is an inspiration to us all," Margolis said, as if he thought a TV camera were lurking somewhere in the shadows. "It's a very fine thing to care for dumb animals, the innocent creatures of the world."

David thought he was going to be sick, but he didn't say anything. They were in the kitchen already, and Margolis was greeting Burles, who seemed genuinely surprised to see him. "Good to see you, Jim," he said.

"Thank you, sir," Burles said, an admiring look on his craggy face. They shook hands, and then Burles introduced him to the two lab coats. "This is Dr. Fine, and this is Dr. Sosnowski."

David thought that Sosnowski was the one with the clipboard and Fine the one with the glasses, but he wasn't sure. Maybe if they stuck around long enough, he would figure out which one was which for certain.

"This is Professor Duvic, from the geology department at the university. And this—" He turned toward David.

"Yes, Mr. Albee and I have already met," said Margolis.

Burles nodded. Just then the back door swung open, and Liz entered. She looked at Margolis without seeming to recognize him.

"Well," she said to David, "Rocky's got worms, and the eggs are about the same."

David almost smiled. She had spoken to him in such a familiar way, he almost felt as if he'd never left. He used to help her with the animals, which she had appreciated greatly, but not enough to keep him around when things got bad between them. It would have been terrific to be here with her now—had they been alone.

"This is Charles Margolis, Dr. Tomlinson," Burles said in a reverential tone, "the White House Chief of Staff."

"Oh," she replied, looking straight at Margolis. "I thought you were taller."

Burles gaped, and the lab coats looked uncomfortable. Margolis was taken aback, too, but he recovered quickly.

A phony smile arranged itself on his handsome face, and he said, "The tricks of the media, Doctor."

"I see." Liz walked past him to pour herself another cup of coffee. Margolis waited respectfully for her to speak. She seized the opportunity. "I don't appreciate your turning my home into a military camp."

"I'm sorry, Doctor," he said smoothly, "but we really have no choice."

She slammed her mug down on the counter so hard, David thought it would shatter, but it didn't. "What do you mean, you have no choice?"

"Due to this extraordinary discovery, we feel that an investigation is required, so that incorrect information doesn't leak out to the public and cause panic."

"Panic? Incorrect information? What do you think this is, a fifties sci-fi movie?"

"I'm not sure what you mean."

"I mean that this discovery upsets your political apple-cart, Mr. Margolis." She looked straight at him. "You don't want this getting out, do you? You want to hush it up, so that nobody knows the truth. That wouldn't jibe with the beliefs of the Millennialists, would it? The best you can hope for is that this is a hoax, but I assure you that it isn't. Those are living eggs, and they weren't laid by any bird or reptile living today, nothing that's been on this planet for millions of years. And that's hard to rec-oncile with Jaffrey Flanagan's teachings, isn't it? I mean, how do you answer somebody who asks you if this is com-patible with Creationism, which says the earth is four thousand years old?"

"The Lord our God has given us all the answers," Burles declaimed stridently, his face red with fury. "They are to be found in the Holy Bible."

Liz shook her head as Margolis put his hand on Burles's shoulder. "It's all right, Jim," Margolis said. "She knows that. Everybody knows it, down deep inside their hearts and immortal souls."

David wished with all his heart and soul that Liz would

keep her mouth shut. Antagonizing a powerful man like Margolis was not wise, as far as he was concerned. He doubted that Margolis believed the crap he was spouting, but he had to act as if he did for political reasons, and that was just as bad, maybe even worse. A surprising calm had descended in the room now that Liz had spoken her mind, however. She clearly remained unimpressed by Margolis's rhetoric, and she didn't care who knew it.

"Let's not allow rancor to divide us," Margolis said. "Let's work together instead, and perhaps we can learn the truth."

Liz rolled her eyes. She was not ready to make peace with these people.

"I understand how you feel, Doctor," Margolis persisted. "I'd be distraught if a lot of strangers took over my home, too. But don't allow that to color your judgment."

"Oh, *come on,*" David said, the words seeming to escape his mouth of their own volition. "Are you implying that she's too emotionally overwrought to think logically, when in fact it is *you* who have nothing to answer her with except platitudes?"

An expression of pure malevolence came over Margolis's even features, but it was almost instantly transformed into the benign look that had served him so well on television and in politics, if those two could fairly be separated anymore.

"One man's platitude is another man's truth," Margolis said.

A stillness descended, broken only by the howling of a cat coming from outside the house.

"Would you care for a cup of coffee, Mr. Margolis?" Liz asked. "I'm afraid I forgot my manners."

"Thank you. Do you have decaf?"

"Yeah, I think I have some free samples somewhere." Liz opened the cabinets and rummaged around until she came up with a tiny orange packet. She turned on the burner under a teapot and tore open the packet to pour its powdered contents into a mug. David found himself staring at the blue flame under the teapot, wondering how the country could have come to this. He knew how, actually. The moderates had been stifled by rampant jingoism during the Gulf Wars of the early nineties, and as the economy continued to decline, the right had needed the fundamentalists and the growing Millennialist movement to stay in power. Thus the promise of a new cabinet post as a sop to the religious right—the Department of Morality. Its architect and spokesman had, of course, been none other than the famous, telegenic Christian Millennialist Jaffrey Flanagan. The Christian Millennialists' candidate had needed Margolis to win the presidency, but Margolis's price was high.

David never thought he'd be standing in the same room with the White House Chief of Staff, telling him off, but it had just happened. The consequences were yet to be seen. Was Margolis big enough to shrug it off?

"Differences of opinion are healthy," Pat said cautiously, "but let's not get too worked up. We've got an important job here."

"Well, some of us do." Margolis turned his silky charm on Pat. "Those who are qualified will be asked to work with us on this complex and vexing project."

David knew what this meant. No amateur paleontologist would be welcome in these parts. Margolis didn't want him and Liz double-teaming him all the time, so he had decided to split them up. "That means I have to leave, right?"

"You understand that we have certain obligations and duties to uphold," Margolis said.

"I think you should say you have certain pious obscurantisms to mouth," Liz said, her eyes narrowing. "That would be a little bit more accurate."

David looked at her with something like astonishment. He'd seen her get her back up before, but never like *this*.

Well, maybe on one or two occasions when he'd pissed her off, but rarely. "Liz, that was great," he said.

Pat smirked, Burles reddened, and Margolis pursed his lips. Liz looked at Pat, and began to laugh. David snickered, snorted, and threw his head back to roar with wild mirth.

"Jim, I want you to escort this young man off the premises," Margolis said.

"Wait just a minute," Liz said. "This is my house, not yours. I decide who stays and who goes."

From the expression on Margolis's face, it was clear that Liz was living in the past.

"Forget it, Liz, I'll go." David wiped away tears of laughter. "Anyone can see that I'm a disruptive influence."

David waved good-bye to Pat and Liz, and headed toward the reception room. He slammed the screen door and, still chuckling, smartly saluted the nearest guy in a gray suit as he walked to his car.

He was thinking about Bob as he started up the jeep. Maybe the old beatnik really was in trouble. The feds could make life difficult for him, waving grants in front of the right noses—or threatening to take grants away—unless Bob was fired.

"You're an incurable paranoid," he said as he eased out onto the two-lane road and stepped on the gas. "You romantic fool."

He'd gotten a lot of these ideas from Bob, who believed that every government agency and a number of megacorporations were spying on him. Lately Bob had been obsessed by the *MacBird* thing, and had been dwelling on the days when he claimed to have first gotten onto the ole gummint list. *MacBird* was a mid-sixties play that had been considered dangerously radical in its day. Still, Bob might have been right . . . or maybe not.

"Brain-damaged Bob," David said, remembering Bob's disclaimer about not having to be paranoid to know that people are after you. The arrival of Charles Margolis was only the tip of the iceberg.

Maybe it was silly, but he headed toward the campus just to make sure Bob was all right.

6

While David was searching for his former professor, he wondered if the first of the five eggs had begun to crack. It would be wonderful to see that, but it didn't look like he would. Maybe Liz would, though. A firsthand description would be fascinating.

He found Bob at the second place he looked. The Ale Odyssey was an off-campus beer joint for the thirsty student. Bob was the only faculty member who frequented the place, but that was because he enjoyed a certain rapport with his students. After the last afternoon David had spent in grad school, Bob had taken him out for a few parting beers. Unlike most of Bob's students, though, David hadn't gone on to other things. He might not have been able to afford to get through graduate school, but that didn't mean he couldn't still find dinosaur fossils on his own without a master's degree. He worked construction jobs the rest of the year, while the summer was reserved for digging bones.

He'd been on a dig every summer since he'd left school, six of them in all. Liz had been on the second one, and they ended up sharing the honeymoon lodge that summer. David had never been so happy in his entire life. Fossil-hunting with his best girl; you couldn't beat that with a stick.

Squinting as he walked into the dim interior of the Ale Odyssey, he looked around until he saw Bob sitting with a pitcher of beer in the booth all the way in the back. Bob waved at him, glowing cigarette lodged between index and middle fingers.

"Have a seat, David," Bob said affably as David approached.

"Thanks," David replied, and slid into the booth.

"Bring us another glass, will you, Tom?" Bob shouted to the bartender.

"Bob, do you think it's a good idea to sit here getting smashed while all this is going on?" David asked.

"What the hell *else* can we do?" Bob slammed his glass down on the cracked Formica, much as Liz had done with her coffee mug a few hours earlier. "David, we're the ones who should be in charge of this thing—not Jaffrey fucking Flanagan, for Christ's sake."

"I know, Bob. I know. And Charles Margolis got there before Jaffrey Flanagan."

"Christ," Bob groaned. "It's not just an ego trip. If they brought in somebody like Dodson from Penn, or even Bakker, it would be all right, but a bunch of goddamn politicos and Bible bangers are going to muck this up but good. And there's nobody to stop them, because the Millennialists are practically running the government nowadays."

"Oh, come on, Bob," David said as the bartender walked over and handed him a clean glass, "it's not that bad, is it?"

"Let me have a tuna salad sandwich, will you, Tom?" Bob asked the retreating bartender. "You want one, David?"

David shook his head. "We have to fight them, Bob."

"David, we're not on the ramparts," Bob said, carefully filling David's glass from the pitcher. "We're on the ropes."

"For the moment, Bob, only for the moment." David took a sip of beer. "The truth has a way of getting out."

"They can't very well let people know what's happening, can they, my naïve young friend?"

"They can't stop the truth from getting out." But David

wasn't so sure about that. "And I'm afraid I'm not all that young anymore, Bob."

"Oh, they won't try to stop *us* from telling the truth. And our claims will be published in those same periodicals that claim Madonna didn't die in that accident, that alien big-game hunters stole the president's brain, and that bigfoot is a nuclear physicist working for the Arabs. Just like those poor, benighted souls, we won't have a shred of hard evidence."

"Bob, you give up too easily." David downed the glass of beer and started to get up. "I gotta go."

"Wait a minute, wait a minute." Bob waved his plump fingers in the air. "What are you going to do?"

David hesitated. "I have to admit that I don't know, Bob. I'm just as frustrated as you are, but I feel I have to do *something*. Maybe I'll just go and make camp as close to Liz's place as I can. I don't know. But I'm not just gonna sit here and get plowed."

"You're a better man than I am, Gunga Din." Bob poured himself another beer, pausing to admire its perfect head before tossing it down.

David thought of something. "Bob, do you know a Dr. Fine, or a Dr. Sosnowski?"

"Sosnowski's in physics. He was at the geology lab today."

"Physics. They're trying to figure out how the stasis field works."

"Or how it doesn't work anymore."

"That must have been what blew the power in the building," David said. "What I don't understand is why it sent out a surge of energy and shut down when they opened the box."

"Must have damaged it." Bob removed a pack of cigarettes from his herringbone jacket pocket and lit one up.

"I don't see how that could have happened. The mechanism was at the other end of the box."

"Maybe the field had to be contained," Bob said,

warming to the subject. "The alloy the box was made from might have been specifically blended for that purpose too."

"What alloy was it?"

"Pat didn't say, but she did say that it was only the durability of the blend that was unusual. It must have been treated with something before it was buried. Better than simonizing. Common enough metals, though. Flanagan and his boys didn't care about any of that. They just wanted the eggs."

"What do you suppose they've done with the box now that the eggs are safe in Liz's incubator?"

"Probably using it as a laundry hamper, as Charlie and Ferd might say."

David sat with Bob through another pitcher, and by the time that one was empty, he was feeling pretty good. He almost forgot about the box and the curved mechanism inside it. Almost.

"Mind if we join you, Professor Pierce?" It was one of two young women speaking, a blond coed with a big chest. Her companion was an attractive, slender girl with dark skin and large, almond-shaped eyes.

"Please do!" Bob said with obvious delight.

"I'm Renée," the blonde said, looking at David and smiling. "And this is Nikki."

"Hi," David said, "it's a pleasure to meet you."

Three hours later, after Bob had gone home to his wife and kids, and Nikki had gone back to the dorm, David was left alone in the bar with Renée. Even though they were alone in the booth, they were still sitting next to each other on one bench. Renée smelled delicious, like ripe fruit.

"So you're studying literature, huh, Renée?" he said, wondering where all this was leading. Was he really going to take this young girl to bed?

"Yeah, working on the Romantics right now." She rubbed her thigh against his.

David looked at her. She was undeniably pretty, and she was pleasant enough; the only trouble was, she wasn't Liz.

"Another beer?" he asked, accommodating her by pouring the last glassful from the pitcher before she could reply.

"Thank you, David." Renée accepted the glass and set it in front of her. "Do you live on campus?"

"Oh, no, I've got an apartment over on Fourth. I'm not a student."

Renée laughed. "I know, but I thought you might be faculty."

"I sure don't have all my faculties about me now," David replied. But her answer saddened him. By this late date, he really should have done more with his life than this. Maybe that was the real reason why Liz threw him out. "I think I better go."

Renée looked a little crestfallen, but she didn't try to talk him out of leaving. She was too proud for that.

"Maybe I'll see you around," David said as he got up. "Got a lot to think about, and this juke box is getting to be a pain."

"Sure."

David wondered if he'd lost his mind as he drove his jeep around by himself. "Shouldn't have passed up a young babe like that," he said into the night wind. "Didn't even get her phone number, for Christ's sake."

While he was driving, he thought about renting a camper, so that he could set up shop as close to Liz's as possible. Flanagan couldn't keep him out forever, and he wanted to be near enough to help Liz if she needed him. Trouble was, the cost would be prohibitive.

"Gotta be something I can do," he said, stopping at a 7-Eleven for a six-pack. "I'll figure it out in the morning, when I'm sober."

He pulled into the store's parking lot and parked the jeep. As he got out, he almost bumped into Bernie Mc-

Carthy, a guy he'd hung around with years ago. Bernie
was a plumber and pipe fitter nowadays. They didn't see
much of each other, but they'd been on a couple of construction jobs. Bernie had even offered to bring David into
his business, but David had declined. He was only committed to dinosaurs, it seemed.

"What's happening, dude?" Bernie inquired.

"Not much, Bern. How you been?"

"About the same. Oh, what's this I hear about big do-
ings out at your old girlfriend's place?"

"They're . . . conducting a government study." Why
was he lying to Bernie? Did he want Margolis to get away
with it? No, it was just too much to explain right now,
especially in the condition he was in.

"Government study, huh? So that's why there's a helicopter out there."

"A helicopter?"

"Yeah, catch you later."

David was left standing on the pavement in front of the
7-Eleven with a vacant expression on his face as Bernie
got into his van and drove off.

"Let me just think about this for a minute," he said,
trying to make his brew-fogged brain work. He got back
into the jeep, cranked it up as if in a trance, and drove
toward Liz's place.

"You asshole," he excoriated himself. "You shouldna
got drunk with Bob." Liz had always told him that alcohol
would be his undoing. She was right, of course, and it
pissed him off that she had won the argument—not so much
because he had lost a round with her, but because he had
lost an awful lot more than that due to his drinking. And
he'd refused to see her shrink, out of sheer contrariness.
He'd felt coerced, and his defiant nature had rejected the
notion. Liz hadn't taken that very well. His tires screeched
around a curve, and he realized that he was doing sixty
miles an hour in a forty-five zone.

"Whoa!" David slowed down, remembering the last

time he'd been stopped for DWI. It was no fun to lose your license, as his dad had always told him. The old man had suffered from a drinking problem too, though he hadn't suffered from it as much as David's mom. She had borne with the old man until he dropped dead at forty-five, an age that David continually reminded himself he would reach in not so many more years. He could not afford to keep drinking like an undergraduate.

It seemed as if he'd just pulled out of the parking lot when he came up on Liz's place. It looked like a military compound, with a hurricane fence around the property, and temporary buildings going up; people in fatigues were all over the place. There was indeed a helicopter sitting in a white circle on flattened grass behind Liz's property, powerful lights showing it up like a giant mosquito against the dark prairie. So much for keeping things secret.

He pulled into the front yard and yanked the emergency brake up. No sooner had he jumped out of the jeep than three guys in suits surrounded him. He saw TV cameras, and bright lights shone into his eyes. Everybody seemed to be talking at once, and he couldn't tell who was media and who was government, until somebody grabbed his arm.

"I'm here to see Charles Margolis," he said.

"Do you have authorization?" a hawk-faced man asked.

"No, but I think you better take me to him. I know something about dinosaurs, and chances are nobody else around here does."

The agent looked at the man standing next to him. The media people seemed bemused.

"Dinosaurs?" a woman said. Her colleagues laughed. "How about pink elephants?"

The hawk-faced guy frowned and shook his head. He turned back to David, who could see that it hadn't worked.

"Who is that?" a voice called from behind Liz's screen door. It was Burles, David saw as the agent opened the screen. "You," he said, charging across the driveway toward David.

David thought the guy was going to attack him, and an adrenaline thrill went through him, dulled a little by alcohol and lack of sleep. But Burles stopped short of hitting him.

"We've been looking all over for you," he said. "Don't you ever go home?"

"Not if I can help it," David admitted. He could tell that Burles thought he was being a wise guy, but he wasn't. "I thought I wasn't supposed to come around here anymore."

"The secretary wants to see you." Burles turned and started walking toward Liz's house, and the sea of agents and news people parted. David walked behind Burles, marveling at how his status could change so rapidly. He felt very excited as they went inside, but the alcohol served to keep him calm.

He was ushered into the kitchen. The house was full of people now—three or four times as many as there had been earlier. Military uniforms were prevalent, representing the army, navy, marines, and air force. They seemed to be high-ranking officers, to a man.

"Wait here," Burles said. He went out the back door.

David leaned against the kitchen counter, listening to the businesslike voices of men and women coming from inside and outside the house. Brilliant lights cast sharply defined shadows against the windows; he felt as though he were on a movie set.

The back door opened, and Jaffrey Flanagan entered. "Mr. Albee," he said.

"Secretary Flanagan." David looked at this tall, handsome, imposing man with gray hair and steel blue eyes. He was sure this guy was going to be more trouble than Margolis. "You want me here, or not?"

"I want you here." Flanagan smiled and extended his hand.

David took it after a moment, and found Flanagan's grip was firm. David's heart thumped in expectation. "They've hatched, haven't they?"

"One of them, and a second is about to."

"So what do you need me for?" David asked, trying to control the urge to charge past Flanagan and see a living dinosaur for himself.

"We want you to identify the, uh, baby."

"Hatchling."

"What?"

"Baby dinosaurs are called hatchlings."

"I see."

David waited. Flanagan still wanted him to know who was in charge, so there was no mad rush to the door. Apparently he had replaced Margolis as head man around here, and things were being run differently. These two were reportedly rivals in the corridors of White House power, so control might change hands again. Better get what he could out of it while it lasted. At last David said, "What are we standing here for?"

The Secretary of Morality shook his head. He turned wearily and led the way through the back door. A large tent had been added to Liz's backyard, and some guards— the first enlisted men David had seen on the grounds—were feeding the sick domestic and farm animals.

They entered the shed. Liz and a navy nurse were inside. The incubator seemed untouched, but there was a portable CAT scan pushed against a wall, and a small isolation unit—the kind used in maternity wards—though here it was separated into five sections. The usual animal smells had been subtly changed by a new odor. The odor of dinosaur.

"I tried to reach Bob Pierce," Liz said, "but his wife said he wasn't home."

"That's true. He was drinking with me."

A smirk of self-righteous distaste flitted over Flanagan's face, but he said nothing.

"So where's the happy hatchling?" David asked.

Liz, who looked very tired, didn't say anything. Instead, she led him to the isolation unit. David peered
through the glass covering one side of the unit, actually
trembling in anticipation.

He didn't see what he expected to see.

7

     Its twelve-inch-long theropod body was saurian, except for the tiny, clawed five-digit forelimbs. It appeared to possess opposable thumbs. The creature actually had hands. One other remarkable feature surprised him, too. That was the head—much too large a cranium. At first David thought it might have been a pachycephalosaurus, the so-called "bone-headed dinosaur," but it wasn't. The size of its head was not due to protective ridges, it was just a *very* big cranium, offset by the unexpectedly small jaws. Its thin eyelids were shut, but they flickered with life as if the creature were having a bad dream, and its belly distended and contracted as it breathed. Its tail twitched with a similar impulse.

     An eyedropper and a bottle of pink nutrient stood next to the hatchling. And two black gloves fit in holes in the unit's side, so that an attendant could feed the creature without exposing it to harmful bacteria.

     "Do you know what it is?" Liz asked, her voice hoarse. "I sure as hell don't."

     "It doesn't look like a dromaeosaur," David said. "That's for sure."

     He began to notice other details. Its jaw was prognathous, but did not extend very far. It was more like an ape's than a reptile's, in that respect. And yet the creature resembled a theropod dinosaur not only in its hip structure and powerful, birdlike hind legs, but also in its rictus, which revealed already quite well-developed needlelike teeth. Its hide was squamous, like a reptile's, with bright blue and yellow beads, but there were also porous patches that might soon sprout hair follicles or pin feathers. Its odor was not unpleasant, just strange.

"Well?" Jaffrey Flanagan said.

David backed away from the astonishing sight. "It's a dinosaur, all right," he said, "but of a previously undiscovered type, as far as I can see. That's about all I can tell you."

"Previously undiscovered. . ." Jaffrey Flanagan thought that over. "You're saying that you don't really know what it is?"

"Basically. There are some features on this hatchling that I've never seen on a dinosaur before. Literally thousands of different types of dinosaurs have been discovered, so this is highly unusual."

"But you're certain it *is* a dinosaur."

"Absolutely."

Liz squatted by the isolation unit, fitted her hands into the gloves, and drew some nutrient out of the bottle, using the dropper. She squeezed a few drops into the hatchling's gaping mouth. Its forked tongue snaked out hungrily as it swallowed the stuff.

"What's in that?" David asked.

"Mostly protein," Liz said.

"Well, this guy is definitely carnivorous," David said. "It should be good for him."

"Another one's coming out!" It was the nurse, standing by the incubator.

Everybody surged toward the incubator to see the second egg hatch. David laughed involuntarily as he watched the crack widen and lengthen. The egg rocked back and forth as a second crack appeared, branching from the first. Fluid oozed from the rapidly enlarging opening, and a third crack appeared, forming a rough triangle.

The egg rocked again, and the triangle popped out.

"Wow!" David said, catching a glimpse of the hatchling's glistening head.

The tiny creature pecked and writhed until the egg lay

in ruins around it. This one appeared a bit smaller than the first as it attempted to walk on its shaky hind legs, tail stuck out straight behind it for balance. Liz and the nurse clapped their hands in delight.

"All right!" David shouted.

The dinosaur hatchling, hearing him through the glass, looked up at him. Its big, dark eyes seemed purplish red in the ultraviolet, and preternaturally intelligent.

"Let's get the little guy out of there," David said, so worked up that he thought he was going to drop. "He needs a lot of attention. Dinosaurs stayed with their mothers until they were pretty big, so give him a lot of T.L.C."

"Yes, marse," Liz said, saluting him.

"Seriously, his head is so large that his neck can barely hold it up. He's going to need a lot of help."

Liz faced him, arms akimbo. "David, we've already cared for one hatchling. Stop ordering us around."

"Sorry." This was an old bone of contention between him and Liz. She'd always claimed that he ordered her around too much. David had never really believed it, but he had to admit to himself that there was something to the charge this time. "I guess I'm just too excited."

"Yeah." She smiled wanly. "It's okay, though, David. This is really something to be excited about."

"Peace, Liz?" He held up two fingers.

"Peace."

"I've got everything sterilized, Dr. Tomlinson," the nurse said.

"Great. Excuse me, David."

David turned and watched the frail creature stumbling about inside the incubator. The two hatchlings were very weak; in fact, this one looked as if it might collapse at any moment.

Liz came back snapping a pair of rubber gloves onto her wrists. The nurse opened the top of the incubator, and Liz reached in to pick up the hatchling. The nurse shut the incubator as Liz held the infant dinosaur. A moment later the nurse opened the side compartment of the isolation unit, and Liz placed the hatchling inside, next to its sibling.

"Thanks, Jen," Liz said.

"This one does seem weaker than the first one," said Nurse Jen.

"Yeah." David detected a note of worry in that single syllable.

They kept a vigil on both the isolation unit and the incubator throughout the night. David wanted a beer, but he settled for coffee. About three o'clock in the morning, he began to think that drinking more coffee and less beer might have saved his relationship with Liz. Maybe he could still do it. She seemed pretty friendly, now that they were working together. Their differences didn't seem like much when measured against their potential troubles with Margolis, Jaffrey Flanagan, and his religious right flunkies. If those two were at odds all the time, maybe it would be all right, but David doubted it.

"It looks as if numbers three and four are on the way," the nurse said.

David went over to look through the glass. One of the three remaining eggs was splitting open nicely on one side, but he didn't notice either of the others cracking. Then he saw that one of them was shaking with the efforts of its occupant.

It took a few minutes for them to hatch. Surprisingly, the shaking egg burst open before the cracking one. A chunk of shell flew out as if it had been shot from a sling. The hatchling fought its way out in short order. Its sibling was free less than a minute later. These two were popped in the isolation chamber straightaway, and both of them seemed healthy enough.

"The final egg is more problematic," Liz said. "The CAT scan showed a smaller fetus than the others. It's possible that it will come to term late, but I have my doubts. Four hatching within an hour of each other might not be good news for this last guy."

"What do you mean?" Flanagan asked.

"I mean he might not make it," Liz said. "Runt of the litter, you know."

"And if he dies," Flanagan said, "it is God's will."

"You think God put those eggs in the ground sixty-five million years ago, Mr. Secretary?" David asked.

Jaffrey Flanagan looked David straight in the eye. "If the Lord wills it, it is done."

David nodded. He decided to count his blessings. At least Flanagan hadn't denied that the box could be more than four thousand years old. Maybe there was some hope for him yet. "Hard to argue with that."

The four baby dinosaurs were doing well, it seemed, but there was a certain amount of worry concerning the fifth egg. If it didn't hatch soon, the odds were against the hatchling's survival. For all anyone knew, the lives of the other four might be on shaky ground, too. Liz was constantly feeding them with the eyedropper. As soon as one opened its eyes, she was there with nourishment. They sure weren't going to starve to death.

"I could do that, you know," David said. "You look like you need a rest, Liz."

She looked up at him, her face underlit by the glow of the infrared. "I am getting a little tired."

"A little," the nurse said. "I'm beginning to think I'll have to hogtie you to get you to lie down, Doctor."

"Please call me Liz, will you, Jen?"

"Thanks." Nurse Jen smiled warmly.

David liked this woman. She was earthy and friendly, not much like the rest of these officious people hanging around Liz's—though he supposed that they were all just doing their jobs, as they saw it.

"Secretary Flanagan," David said, "what do you intend to do with these dinosaur hatchlings?"

"That remains to be seen. These, uh, hatchlings are obviously of some importance."

"Obviously."

"Just how their appearance at this time can best serve

our country must be determined by God. We can only wait and see what He decides to do.''

David didn't like the sound of that. Dinosaurs serving the country was a pretty odd concept. Besides, by the time God got around to giving Jaffrey Flanagan a sign, all the hatchlings could be dead. ''Don't you think this should be turned over to the scientific community?''

''It seems to me that the problem is in good hands.'' Flanagan smiled at Liz and the nurse.

''Yeah, well, my hands and I are gonna go take a nap.'' Liz wasn't buying Jaffrey Flanagan's phony charm, and she didn't care if he knew it. She tossed her rubber gloves on a tray and ducked as she went through the low door of the shed.

''There's a lot of noise, Liz,'' David called after her. ''I hope you've got some earplugs.''

''I'm used to it.''

David watched her walk up the back door steps and go into the house. Dogs whined and chickens clucked. She was right, there had always been a lot of noise around this place. But there were people here now, and Liz wasn't used to that. Not anymore. He hoped that she'd get through this all right.

David turned his attention back to the interior of the shed. Jaffrey Flanagan was peering into the isolation unit. It was difficult to gauge what the Millennialist leader was thinking. David was fairly certain that Flanagan perceived the hatchlings as a threat. But was he so threatened that he intended to keep this momentous event from the world? Or did he mean to do even worse? The latter didn't seem likely, since he could have destroyed the eggs easily several times over by now, and hadn't. No, Jaffrey Flanagan was fascinated by the little theropods who slept under glass and stainless steel not two feet under his nose. David was pretty sure of that.

''Amazing, isn't it?'' David said as he came up next to Flanagan.

Flanagan didn't even glance at him, but continued to stare at the strange creatures. "It is that."

"I think you're right that God can do anything He wants," David said. "And He rules a universe so vast and ancient that it's a mystery to us."

"Unquestionably."

"But the more we learn about it, the closer we come to dispelling some of that mystery."

"It seems to me that you're mistaken there," Flanagan said. "When Einstein was alive, we thought a unified field theory would explain it all. But the more that has been discovered about quantum mechanics, the less we know, half a century down the road."

This wasn't the kind of simplistic nonsense David had expected from the famous televangelist. "We might be on the verge of a new breakthrough that will tell us a lot more," he said. "Sometimes you feel like you're lost even when you're on the right road."

Jaffrey Flanagan straightened up and looked at David with his piercing eyes. "Believe me, I once thought that science held all the answers, too . . . but it doesn't."

"Does religion?"

"If you let it."

"And if you don't let it? Should you be forced to?"

"Medicine doesn't taste good, but we still need it."

"That's fine for children, but what about the concept of free will? Aren't adults entitled to make their own choices?"

"Not if those choices are immoral."

"And who decides what's immoral?"

"The good Lord decides."

"Makes things simple." David shook his head.

"The truth *is* simple."

"I wish I could believe that, but I can't."

"Perhaps you will someday." Flanagan smiled, showing two rows of straight, white teeth. "I guarantee that you'll be happier for it."

David thought that over. It was enticing, but not for

him. "Look, you have your way of looking at things, and I have mine. Maybe we'll be better off if we keep these things to ourselves."

"Mr. Albee, you are an unhappy man, if I may say so."

"Yeah, but that doesn't mean I'm wrong." David stooped to get a look at the brightly beaded, miniature dinosaurs. "I was right about this, after all."

"In what way?"

"I never had any doubts about the age of the earth. The evidence is too compelling. And I don't buy the notion that fossils were left here just to test our faith. There's no reason why a Christian can't believe that dinosaurs existed, and that evolution created Homo sapiens in its slow and tortuous way."

"Secretary Flanagan," Nurse Jen said, distracting them from their argument, "I think the last egg is hatching."

8

The fifth hatchling somehow struggled enough to get out of its egg, but its spindly body did not look healthy. It was so frail that David thought it would die in Jen's hands before she could get it into the isolation unit.

"Do you think this one should be with the others?" the nurse asked. "It's going to need special care."

"They're nesting animals," David said. "I think it's best if we keep them together."

"Okay, it's your funeral."

David wasn't sure if he liked Jen's joke, but he let it pass. Hung over and physically exhausted, he feared that this entire business was going to be disastrous for all of them. *Just because you're paranoid doesn't mean they're not out to get you.*

"All right, Mr. Albee," Jaffrey Flanagan said. "You've seen them hatch. Now give the ladies room to work."

David looked at the Secretary with a new appreciation of the man's cleverness. Had Flanagan let him stay to watch the eggs hatch because he had softened, or was he trying to ingratiate himself with David for some reason? Perhaps Flanagan thought it was possible to buy him off by allowing him to witness the birth of the hatchlings. Well, David did feel somewhat grateful. He had wondered when he would be told to leave again, and had hoped that it wouldn't be before the dinosaurs were born. Flanagan had played that hope like a stringed lute.

"All right," David said, "I'll go. And I want to thank you for letting me see this. But I must tell you right now that I'm not going to let you bury this story so that your political and religious beliefs aren't threatened. The truth is here, and you know what it is, so don't try to stop it."

Jaffrey Flanagan nodded in a manner that was not unfriendly. "We'll talk again, Mr. Albee."

"That'll be my pleasure, sir." David was surprised to hear himself say that, and even more surprised to know that he meant it. Flanagan's presence and intellect were stimulating, and he possessed tons of charisma. But David wouldn't be taken in; he had a mission just as surely as did Jaffrey Flanagan, Secretary of Morality. He went out of the shed and into the house. He almost walked into the bedroom without knocking, and then realized what an intrusion that would be after all this time. He was taken with a swelling ache in his chest as he looked at the white door. He knocked.

"What?" Liz's voice was sleepy.

"It's just me, Liz."

"Oh, David. Come on in."

He opened the door and walked into the bedroom he knew so well. The queen-size bed was a pale rectangle in the darkness, and Liz seemed tiny lying on it. David reached out and squeezed her hand. "I'll see you later, hon."

Liz's shining eyes were full of something he couldn't readily identify. Was it love? Yearning? Fear? He couldn't be sure, but he knew that he must help her get through this. There would be no holding back, as there had always been in the past. She really needed him this time.

"Thanks, David," she said, and he knew that she was barely able to control her emotions. "Thanks for being here."

"I'll be around." With that, he backed away and left her alone, shutting the door gently behind him. A couple of minutes later he was sitting in the driver's seat of his jeep, sliding the key into the ignition. He was astonished to discover that he was perfectly sober. He turned the jeep's motor over and drove away from Liz's, the stars glimmering like jewels in the blackness above his head.

When he got home, David didn't even have time to bemoan the sorry state of his apartment. The place was a mess, and he hadn't done the laundry in two weeks. Dirty dishes were piled up in the sink, because he hadn't had time to do them before he went on the dig.

"The dig . . ." He collapsed on the bed fully clothed. The box spring and bed frame groaned under him. He'd been drinking too much beer lately, and had been putting on weight. Everything was depressing him around the apartment. Maybe the best thing to do was just get away in the morning and go back to the dig. Or in the afternoon . . . whenever he woke up.

"Shit." The trouble was, even though he was dog-tired, he couldn't get to sleep. His heart was pounding and his head was throbbing. He was so excited that he couldn't even think of sleeping. Maybe the thing to do was go out to the dig now, and sleep under the stars.

He managed to haul his exhausted body out of bed, throw a few things into a sack, grab his sleeping bag, and head back out to the jeep. He was on the road again a few minutes later.

The dig was undisturbed, though both tents were gone. Hiram and Cilla had gone back to school. Charlie and Ferd had probably taken jobs on a road construction crew. There was nobody out here tonight but David Albee and the crickets.

"Not quite as good as Buddy Holly and the Crickets, but I guess it'll have to do." He spread the sleeping bag out on the ground and lay on top of it. Making a pillow with interlaced fingers, he looked up at the sky.

"Where did it come from?" he asked the stars. That box was built in space, by beings from another world. Where were they now? Were they long gone, sixty-five million years after they had left those eggs here? Or were they still out there, planning to swing around and pick up the box sooner or later? What was it Fine—or Sosnowski—had said about the energy discharge when the box had been opened? A pulse.

"Or maybe a signal."

David closed his eyes and dreamed of a signal escaping from the box and traveling through space, revealing to an ancient and wise alien race that intelligent beings had found the box and opened it. And what would the creatures on our world do with this discovery?

That remained to be seen. Jaffrey Flanagan had seen something that he didn't expect, that didn't fit into his conception of the way the universe works. It could only change him, for better or worse.

David sighed. If Flanagan did his worst—if he covered up the discovery, destroyed the eggs, imprisoned everyone who knew about them—it wouldn't matter. Something had happened that dwarfed politics and religion. Or maybe this *was* religion, if you defined religion as a yearning for something beyond this world, something far greater than this life of struggle and squalor. Maybe this was *really* religion.

The stars seemed to brighten and move toward him as he dozed.

"Wake up."

David was far away from Earth when he felt himself being nudged on one shoulder. He resentfully opened his eyes to the early morning glare, and saw the familiar shape of Bob Pierce standing over him.

"Bob, I saw them." David sat bolt upright.

"You did?" Bob's eyes were shining, moist as if he would weep.

"I saw them hatch." But it seemed like a dream now. "One was already born when I got there, but I saw all the others being born."

"I know, David. I talked to Liz this morning. She said she tried to reach me, but I had my answering machine turned off. Probably they would have sent the marines if you hadn't turned up at Liz's. I missed everything, I guess, snoring away in a drunken stupor. But I'm glad the hatchlings made it, even if I didn't get to see them.''

"It was amazing." David rubbed his eyes. "How'd you know I was out here?"

"You weren't at home, and Liz called to say you left her place at four o'clock this morning." Bob squatted next to David. "Got any coffee, David?"

"No, I didn't bring anything, really." David yawned and stretched. "I could use a hair of the dog right now, though. I feel like shit."

"Nonsense, my boy. It's a beautiful morning, and something marvelous has been added to our beleaguered old world since yesterday. Living dinosaurs."

"Well, that's true, Bob, but they aren't quite what I expected."

"No, I don't suppose they would be quite what we expected, would they?" Bob asked. "Our perception of the dinosaur has changed a lot in the past twenty years or so, anyway, just from the fossil evidence. I guess the real thing is a radical departure from our reconstructions, huh?"

"Bob, you don't know the half of it."

"So tell me. I'm all ears."

"Let's go to McCullers' and see if we can get that cup of coffee. This is gonna take a while."

Twenty minutes later the tiny bell rang as they stepped through the front door of the rock shop. Emma was seated on a stool at the counter, and Jack was sweeping up the back room.

"Got any coffee brewing?" Bob asked.

"Well, well," Emma said, "look what the cat dragged in."

"Howdy, Bob, David," Jack called to them. "Be right with you."

"Haven't seen you in a 'coon's age, Professor," Emma said.

"Can't go on digs anymore, Emma. Doctor's orders."

Jack brought two folding chairs out from the back room. "Coffee's coming right up," he said, hurrying to fetch it.

Emma leaned her stool back so that her shoulders were resting against the wall. She was a leather-faced, large-boned woman about fifty years old. "Sun get to you, Bob?"

"Yeah, several cancers. I still have to get a little skin sliced off from time to time."

"And of course, the government is still not sure the damage to the ozone layer is significant," said Jack, returning with two steaming Styrofoam cups.

"Of course not." David accepted a cup gratefully. "It's probably typical for a country sliding into decline to be heavily into denial."

"Nineteen years ago, *this* country made a decision to hire an actor to cheer us up rather than face up to our problems." Bob took the second cup and sipped it without waiting for it to cool. He winced, but took another sip. "And as we sink deeper into the hole, things have been taken over by those whose job it is to decide how many angels can dance on the head of a pin."

"Jaffrey Flanagan." David took a slug of coffee, and felt more awake instantly.

"Is he really here?" Jack asked, pulling a chair around to sit with them. "I mean, we've heard rumors."

"He's here, out at Liz's with a whole army. Chuckie Margolis was at Liz's yesterday, too."

"Yeah, everybody's talking about it, but we didn't know for sure if Flanagan was out there."

"He is," Bob said, "and he's trying to cover up the scientific find of the age."

"Then it's real," Emma said. She brought the stool forward and leaned over the counter.

"Five little hatchlings," David said, "theropods, but more than that, I can't say."

"Well, I'll be damned," said Jack.

"I got the impression last night that Flanagan can be

reasoned with. He knows how important this is, and he did call us back—even if you slept through it, Bob."

"He's working his political wiles on you, David," Bob said. "Don't believe it for a second."

"Well, he didn't promise anything, but he did acknowledge that he needed our help. That's something, isn't it?"

"Yeah, that's something."

"Poor little Liz," Jack said, "all by herself with that son of a bitch strutting around like he owned the place."

"She doesn't take any shit off Margolis or Flanagan," said David. "Don't worry."

"Good for her!" Emma said.

But David was worried. As he finished his coffee, he thought about the strain this must be putting on Liz. She couldn't go off and get drunk even if she wanted to, as he and Bob had done last night. She had to stay there and look after things. That had never bothered her in the past, and he had even accused her of being anal retentive on occasion. Of course, the truth probably was that he was too irresponsible. Anal expulsive? Maybe he should have gone to see Liz's shrink. What harm could it have done? If it had made her happy, things might have worked out.

"You okay, David?" Emma asked. Concern creased her weathered brow.

"Huh? Yeah, Emma, I'm just brooding a little, I guess."

"Well, I guess you've got a right to brood. Must be damn depressing to see all those C.M.s running roughshod over Liz's place."

"C.M.s?" David asked.

"Christian Millennialists," Bob said. "Got any more coffee, Jack?"

Jack went off to refill their cups. When he came back, he said, "Sure would like to see one of them little devils."

"Me, too," Emma said.

They all smiled, but David thought that it was a shame that Jack and Emma probably never would see them. The question that troubled him was whether the rest of the world would ever know what had happened here in rural eastern Montana these past few days. He was trying to be optimistic, but it wasn't easy, especially with Bob around. But Bob was no fool, and the more things developed, the more it looked like Bob might be right.

"How about some more coffee?" Jack asked.

"Yeah, thanks," David said. "That'd be great."

9

"They seem to be growing very quickly," Nurse Jen said. "I don't know much about lizards, but it seems almost unnatural."

"Whoever put those eggs in that box," Liz said, "also put a directive in the genetic makeup to accelerate growth." She was tempted to mention that the hatchlings weren't lizards, but she didn't bother. Jen knew that they were warm-blooded, and if she thought of them as lizards, it was all right. Together Liz and Jen had named all the baby dinosaurs but one: Egbert, Marie Antoinette, Franny, Zooey—only the oldest and largest remained nameless. They just hadn't come up with the right moniker for him yet. The others had been easy. Franny and Zooey because they had been born close together; Marie Antoinette for her habit of letting the others eat while she watched aloofly; Egbert, because he had been so reluctant to leave the egg. They'd tried different names for the firstborn: Adam, Isaac, Ozymandias, Ace, Butch. None seemed appropriate.

The two women leaned against a fence enclosing the infant dinosaurs, who now ranged from forty-seven to fifty-eight inches in length. They were three days old. The strange little creatures darted about in the mud, all except for the last born, who was still quite weak. Egbert, as he had been named by Liz and Jen, remained in the incubator. They didn't hold out much hope for him. Egbert had barely grown since he'd hatched. He just seemed to get worse no matter what they forced down his throat. This

63

morning he had taken no interest in food at all. Even Marie Antoinette had grown tired of waiting for him to eat, and had taken some food.

"I've seen this happen to baby birds," Liz said. "There usually isn't much you can do."

Jen nodded. "It's true with humans, too. If they don't have the will to live, they usually don't. The poor little thing is too weak to eat. We can force-feed him, but even if we do, I don't think he's going to make it."

"Well, at least we have four healthy dinosaur babies," Liz said. "Who else can make that claim?"

Jen smiled and reached over the fence toward a hatchling. "I think that one's Marie Antoinette, isn't it?"

Before Liz could answer, the little dinosaur leaped toward the extended hand and bit the flesh between Jen's thumb and forefinger. Jen yanked her hand back and held it to her breast. Blood seeped from between her fingers.

"Jen!" Liz cried. "Are you all right?"

"Maybe we should increase the number of feedings," Jen said, trying to laugh as Liz led her back toward the house.

"That looks nasty. I've got a first aid kit in the bathroom," Liz said. "I'll fix it for you."

Jen laughed in spite of the wound. "Liz, I'm a nurse, for crying out loud."

Liz smiled at Jen's comment. But as she steered her friend past half a dozen gawking men and women in uniforms, she glanced back at the pen where the hatchlings were kept. Marie Antoinette watched them curiously, and so did the other three dinosaurs.

"I wish you could dig with me, Bob," David said.

Bob was sitting in his old silver Nissan Sentra, about to drive back into Billings. "Me, too, but duty and melanoma forbid it."

"Try to keep in touch with Liz, will you, Bob?"

"Sure, and I know where to find you if I need you."

"Somewhere in these parts, Perfesser."

"And don't make the same mistake twice. Next time you make the discovery of the century, don't call some old fool who sold out to the establishment thirty years ago."

"You never sold out, Bob. But you still had faith in the way things run, enough to try to play by the rules. So did I. Don't blame yourself."

"You mean you're not a callow student anymore?"

"Uh uh. Middle age approaches fast. I've learned from the school of hard knocks. See you, Bob."

"Take care." Bob cranked up the engine and drove off toward Billings.

David watched until the Sentra was out of sight, and then walked back to the dig. He'd wasted enough time worrying about Jaffrey Flanagan and the hatchlings. It was time to get back to work.

He walked past the trench where the box had been unearthed. A government team had made an alginate cast of the excavation, and had removed samples of the shale for study. A few days ago, David was amused to think, he would have despised the Christian Millennialist for trying to expose this phenomenal event as a fake. But now he was willing to admit that they were only doing their job, just as he was.

"Just because you don't have a degree and nobody's offering a grant," he said aloud, "doesn't mean you aren't a paleontologist, Davy boy."

There was a spot a couple hundred yards to the west that looked promising. He'd been meaning to take a look at it before the shit hit the fan. This seemed a good time to get back to that eroded hummock, and see if there was anything there.

He got a spade out of the truck and walked the distance. After he got rid of the surface sand anchored by prairie grass, he would use the pick on the shale below. As he planted the spade's blade in the crumbling earth, he wondered if there were any more metal boxes in the vicinity.

"Forget it," he said. "That alien glamour stuff's just a lot of trouble."

After a half hour's digging, David got thirsty. He dropped the spade in the prairie grass and turned to go back to the jeep, where he had some drinks stored in an ice chest. A car was kicking up dust in the distance, coming toward him. David didn't much care who it was; let the fundamentalists come and shoo him away. He'd find another spot.

But the green van that pulled up next to his old army jeep was driven by none other than Ferd. Charlie sat next to him in the passenger's seat. They were both grinning broadly as they jumped out of the van.

David felt his eyes moisten, but that wouldn't do. "You bozos lose your way to the construction site?"

"Nope," Ferd said. "No work available for unskilled laborers, so we thought we'd come out and look for more boxes."

David knew that there was plenty of work available in the area, but he didn't say so. Ferd and Charlie had heard about what was happening, probably through Cilla and Hiram. It might have been third-hand information, but they must have had some idea of what was going on.

"We find another one," Charlie said, "let's send it to *Rolling Stone.*"

"Okay," David said, laughing. "Look, I don't have enough picks and shovels to go around."

"It's okay, Dave. We brought our own." Ferd climbed in and started unloading them from the back of the van. "Never leave home without 'em, I always say."

"Those commercials you saw when you were a kid seem to be imprinted on your tiny brain," Charlie said.

"Fuck you," Ferd muttered amiably as he unloaded their gear.

They carried the tools to where David had been digging and pitched in, not talking much once they got into the rhythm of their work. Their disappointment was alleviated by their labor, and their sweat flowed as if to atone for what had been done to the world by Jaffrey Flanagan and his ilk.

They worked till noon, at which time Ferd threw down his pick and said, "Time for a beer, gents. What do you say?"

"Cool," Charlie said.

"Just water for me," David said.

"Hey, you know the rules around here, pard," said Charlie. "It's brew or nothin'."

"I've been drinking too much lately." David set his spade down and walked along with them. "Been thinking about a lot of things."

"I'll bet one of those thing begins with a capital L," Ferd said.

"Yeah, I didn't expect to be seeing so much of Liz so soon. You know, I thought I might run into her once in a while, but not spend a whole day and half a night with her."

"You could have moved away," Charlie said. "Gone back to Helena."

"No, I might have to do that if my stepfather's condition gets worse, but right now my mother can handle it. This has been my home since I was eighteen, and I don't know if I'd ever want to move."

"Dinosaurs," Ferd said. "They're the real reason you don't pack up and get out of here, right?"

"Very perceptive of you, Ferd."

They were at the van now, and Charlie hauled out the ice chest and set it in the shade by the rear bumper. "There's a chocolate milk in there for you, Dave."

David smiled. "You guys think of everything."

"We've seen you on the wagon before." Ferd smiled as he removed the top of the ice chest and pulled out two cans of beer, handing one to Charlie. He reached in and withdrew a brown carton and handed it to David.

"I hope it lasts longer this time," said David.

"We could all stand to cut down on this shit," Charlie said, popping the top of his beer. "Poison."

David watched them both slurp up the suds for a minute, and then tore open the seam of the chocolate milk.

He sat on the ground with his two friends and drank silently.

Liz put Mozart's twenty-first piano concerto on the CD player, and went back into the kitchen to wash dishes. Things had become a little more tolerable since the helicopter left, taking the Secretary of Morality with it. A lot of the military personnel were gone now, too, most of the generals, colonels, and majors. Only a group of ten or twelve marines was left. Captain Torrance was in charge, and he didn't bother her much. It was a nice, sunny day, and a robin sang somewhere nearby. She just hoped that it didn't get too close to the dinosaur pen. Those growing babies were hungry all the time.

She just hoped that David was all right. He'd been drinking the night the hatchlings were born, but he had been wonderful in spite of his inebriated condition. He had stood by her as if there were no other way to look at things but hers. Still, she didn't regret breaking off with him. Things had been going badly, and she had felt trapped by his frequent states of depression. She never knew what he was going to be like from day to day, his moods changed so rapidly. And he refused to seek counseling. How many times had she heard him say that he didn't want "some shaman shaking a stick" at him? It was frustrating to try to talk to somebody who could be so evasive and clever with words. Of course, David might very well have said the same thing about her. He could also accuse her of not being truly committed to any human being. Well, at least she had the animals.

Shouts coming from the yard distracted her. She set the salad bowl she was working on in the steaming water and dried her hands on a dish towel. Then she hurried out the back to see what the growing fuss was about, a heavy feeling in her chest.

Everybody Flanagan had left behind was gathered around the pen. A marine had a big net in which one of the dinosaurs struggled. It looked like Franny to Liz, but its writhings made it hard for her to be sure.

"It's okay, I've got it." The marine wore thick gloves to protect him from bites. He deftly flipped the net over, and Franny landed on her tail inside the pen, blinked, and quickly got up to join her siblings.

The largest of them, the one that Liz and Jen hadn't got around to naming yet, was not in the pen.

"Where's the big boy?" she demanded.

The marine looked puzzled. "I don't know."

"You don't know? Well, he's not in the pen."

"I only saw this one jump out of the pen, Doctor. The others helped."

The others helped. "What did you say?"

"The others helped him get out."

"Her."

"What?"

"Her. This one's a female."

"Sorry."

But the gender of Marie Antoinette was insignificant beside what had happened. "Are you sure that the others actually helped her get out?"

"Yes, ma'am—uh, Doctor. I'm sure."

"How?"

"They used their hands. Boosted him—her—right over the fence."

Liz had known that the dinosaurs were intelligent, but this was more than she had been prepared for. If this boy's story was to be believed, the dinosaurs were capable of working together toward a common goal. Like getting each other out of captivity. But that still didn't explain where the big one had gotten to.

"Are you sure they were all in the pen when Franny went over the fence?" she asked.

"Yes, ma'am."

"I saw it too, ma'am," another marine said. "They were all there."

Liz chewed her lower lip as she thought over the implications of what she had just learned. Had the dinosaurs created a diversion so that their oldest sibling could escape? Obviously Franny couldn't get away with everyone watching her, but she had made an attempt, nevertheless. What if she really *hadn't been trying* to get away? What if she had been creating a diversion to help the big boy to escape?

"We better put some chicken wire over the top of the pen," Liz said, "And start looking for big brother. He couldn't have gone very far with all these fences you people have put up around my property."

"Yes, ma'am." The marine looked as if he was going to salute her. "We'll find him right away."

10 ━━━━━━━━━━━━━━━━

"Maybe the best place to look would be down by the pasture," David said. He stood with his friends on a slope descending to the grazing land he spoke of.

"Nah," Ferd said. "Up on the rise."

"What do you think, Charlie?" David asked.

"I think I agree with old Ferd for once."

"Let's split up, then. I'll go down to the pasture, and you guys go up on the hill."

"You take the high road and Oil take the low road," Ferd sang, none too tunefully.

David turned and headed downhill. The rancher who owned this property had given them permission to search for fossils here, so they could pretty much go where they wanted to go. It seemed to him that the low-lying areas would be more likely to have fossils, which would have washed them back when there was abundant water in the area. Of course, he might have to dig deep to find anything. It was easier to find them at higher ground . . . if there were any there.

As he tramped through the prairie grass, he approached a stand of dogwoods. A brook trickled between the trees, and he stopped just to the right of the trees to kneel and rinse his face in the clear water. The smell of late summer was in the air, and yet the place seemed cool and inviting. He lingered a moment.

He looked up to see a jersey breaking away from the herd, advancing cautiously toward him. It was curious

71

about him, he supposed. Or maybe it was his bovine coun-
terpart, leaving her friends behind for the sake of a little
solitude, herd animal though she was. He chuckled, and
the sound made the cow a little skittish. She backed away
toward the trees.

David made himself become very still. He fought the
impulse to call out to her or extend his hand. Movement
or sound might frighten her. Gradually she stopped moving away from him, until she ended up just a few yards
from the trees. His knees had begun to hurt from kneeling
on the ground, but he didn't stand up.

A flash of yellow and blue shot out of the woods, needle
fangs exposed in a gaping, red maw. It moved so quickly
that the cow had no time to get out of its way. The young
dinosaur leaped onto the cow's back and sank its talons
into her hide.

The cow bleated, thrusting her muzzle outward. She
started to run clumsily, back toward David. He stood up,
not sure of what to do. Red darkened the white spots on
her hide, and she staggered for a moment. Then she
started to run, as if the forward motion might somehow
dislodge the painful thing that had attached itself to her
back.

It didn't help. The claws dug deeper and the fangs
slashed away at the vulnerable flesh under the torn hide.
The cow began to reel, and she turned in circles, her head
lolling. Her hooves splashed through the brook, and she
collapsed on her side not twenty feet from David.

The dinosaur gutted the still-living cow as she shuddered and became still. It ate greedily, blood flying in all
directions as it thrust its muzzle into the mutilated animal's entrails and pulled out dripping chunks. It used its
hands, too. The nasty claws on their tips scored the cow's
belly and opened it even wider. The young dinosaur pulled
meat out and stuffed it into its mouth in an all too human
way.

David wanted to run, but he couldn't. He was fascinated

by seeing an actual carnivorous dinosaur feeding on its prey. Its motions were quick, birdlike, and precise. Would it have hesitated to attack *him* had the cow not wandered away from the herd?

Sated, the dinosaur stepped down from its perch on the cow's haunch and, legs moving like pistons in an engine, walked to the brook. There it drank and cleaned itself off in the pinkish water, using its hands to wash its face.

David hadn't moved since the cow's initial approach. He was certain that the dinosaur saw him, but it didn't seem interested in attacking him. He had to befriend it, and take it back. But what if it got hungry? How could it have grown so large in such a short time? It was almost six feet long from tail tip to snout. It was so big now, he might not be able to fend it off even with the spade he was holding. And even if he did slam it with the spade, he was taking a chance on killing one of the only living dinosaurs on earth.

The dinosaur faced him. Or rather, it turned its body toward him, and cocked its head to one side. It peered at him from its left eye.

David thought his bowels were going to let loose, but somehow he stood without flinching. He told himself that he was a human being, the most vicious killer of all, and that he had a brain in his head and a weapon in his hand. But he was still scared nearly to death.

The dinosaur began to move toward him, its head jerking back and forth like a chicken with each step. It didn't seem to be in a hurry, and it didn't appear to be hostile. Still, David clutched the spade handle tightly, just in case.

The dinosaur moved within five feet of him and stopped, cocking its head once again and watching David calmly. David could see its distended belly move in and out with its breathing.

The liquid sound of the brook seemed to David the very

blood in his veins. It could flow as easily as water into the ground. He would be dead then, and all his troubles would be over. He didn't want to die, though. He wanted to live, to see Liz again, and to see how this was all going to come out. These two things were more important to him than anything else on Earth.

"Hello," he said.

The dinosaur's head jerked a little at the sound of his voice. Perhaps it had not been certain he was a living thing, so still had David been. Now there could be no doubt.

"I'm your godfather," David said. "Remember me?"

Was that a gleam of recognition in its sable eye? David could almost believe it. But how could it have such a memory? Could it have imprinted like a newborn duckling? If so, it would have been Liz or Nurse Jen, not him, that the creature was fixated on. And yet he was one of the first living things it had seen. Maybe that meant something.

The dinosaur said *cheep*.

"At twice the price," David said, remembering something his father had always recited when he was told something was inexpensive.

"You're like a different dinosaur now than you were before your lunch," he said, glancing at the partially devoured carcass a few yards away. "Jekyll and Hyde."

The dinosaur *cheeped* again.

"Look," David said to it, "the rancher who owns this land—not to mention this cow—is not going to be very happy with what you've done here, so maybe we better go someplace else."

The dinosaur didn't budge.

"He'll think it was a dog or something. He'd never believe it was you . . . unless he saw you."

David motioned toward the hillside with his head. That had no effect, so he started walking slowly back toward the slope. He glanced over his shoulder and saw the dinosaur still watching him. After a few more paces, David looked again.

It was following him.

"Got quite a surprise for Ferd and Charlie," David said, turning every once in a while to make sure the dinosaur was still with him. "They thought they'd never get to see you, Jekyll. I hope you're Jekyll right now, anyway, and not Hyde."

Cheep.

David led the dinosaur up the wash, picking up his step a little when he heard the sound of a pick hitting shale. The dinosaur paced him, staying about ten to twelve yards to the rear.

As David topped the rise, he caught sight of Ferd's soaked sweatshirt. Ferd lifted the pick high over his head and brought it down. Charlie leaned on a spade, watching him.

David fought the impulse to shout their names, afraid that he might frighten the dinosaur. It wouldn't do to have them turn around to see him standing by himself at the top of the hill, claiming that a dinosaur had been with him just a few seconds ago while Jekyll scurried away.

"Come on, Jekyll," he said, seeing that the dinosaur was still out of Ferd and Charlie's sight. "Just a few more feet of bouncing along there, and you'll make two new friends."

But Jekyll hesitated, though it seemed to be listening to the sounds of the pick ringing in the still summer air. David couldn't tell if it was going to run or continue on behind him. If it ran, there wasn't much he could do. He decided to keep on walking, in the hope that its curiosity would get the better of its fear.

He walked a little slower than before, just to give Jekyll more time to make up its mind. But then he thought better of it, and picked up the pace. He didn't look back until Charlie glanced his way.

"Oh, mighty Hiawatha," Charlie said in imitation of Bugs Bunny's voice. And then his eyes darted to a point beyond David and opened wide.

David raised his hands, palms down, and lowered them urgently, indicating that Charlie was not to shout or act excited. Ferd looked up at Charlie and saw that something was wrong.

"What's going on?" Ferd asked. His voice carried clearly, but the sound wasn't loud enough to frighten the dinosaur—at least David hoped it wasn't loud enough.

Charlie shushed Ferd. Now everything would probably be all right as long as Ferd didn't get defiant at being shushed. He didn't. Instead, he looked toward David, and after a few seconds his shining face registered as much surprise as Charlie's.

David kept on walking, until he was close enough to speak in low tones and be heard. Then he stopped and waited to see what would happen.

"Hi, guys," he said. "I brought a friend."

Ferd and Charlie gaped. Charlie whispered, "Is that what I think it is?"

"Probably." David looked back to see Jekyll maintaining a safe distance, cocking its head as it stood back a little way down the hillside. "I call him Jekyll."

"Nice name," said Ferd. "But how about Mr. Hyde?"

"He killed a cow down in the pasture. Not a pretty sight."

"What's to stop him from jumping one of us?" Ferd asked, looking very nervous.

"He's full right now."

"And what if he gets hungry."

"Let's go down to McCullers' and see if they've got any hamburger," Charlie suggested.

"Good idea," David said. "In the meantime, there's some cheese and tuna fish in the ice chest."

"Right, and maybe we better just head back toward camp before he gets an appetite," said Charlie.

"You go first," Ferd said, doubtless noticing that they had to pass Jekyll to return to their campsite.

"Pussy," Charlie said. He took a hard, squinting look at Jekyll. "Dave, you go first."

"Okay, but wait a little while before you start after us." David turned and looked at Jekyll, wondering if he should go straight toward the dinosaur or make a detour. He decided that a detour would be wiser. He started to walk off to the south as if he were headed down the far slope. As soon as he had given the dinosaur a respectful berth, he made his way back toward the path to camp. He hoped that Jekyll would follow him, and that it wouldn't be disturbed by Ferd and Charlie following them. Fortunately, they restrained themselves and didn't start until David was nearly halfway back to camp. The distance appeared to be sufficiently reassuring to keep Jekyll in line.

Soon the four of them were gathered around the ice chest, Jekyll still keeping its distance. David opened the chest and removed a package of cheese. Unwrapping it, he watched Jekyll snap at a fly unsuccessfully.

"I think he's getting hungry again," Ferd said.

"He's got the metabolism of a shrew," said Charlie.

"Well, he's a growing boy." David had been thinking of Jekyll as an "it," but he was pretty sure they were right. Jekyll was a male. Three males and two female hatchlings had been born just four days ago, and David was sure this was the eldest. It was certainly the largest.

"How could he grow so fast, though?" Charlie asked. "Didn't you say that they were only six or eight inches long when they hatched and that they weighed in at just a few ounces apiece? This guy is at least ten times that length, and he must be several times that in volume."

"I can't account for it," David said, breaking off a chunk of Monterey Jack cheese. "The beings who left the eggs must have stepped up their growth genetically, just like they increased their intelligence and gave them pre-hensile hands instead of claws.''

"But why make them grow so fast?'' Ferd asked.

"I don't know. Maybe it was just an experiment.'' David tossed the cheese to Jekyll. It flew a bit wide of the mark, but Jekyll darted off to his right and caught it in his jaws, gulping it down greedily.

"Jeez,'' said Ferd, "he sure is quick.''

"You should have seen him go after that cow, you think that's quick.'' David lobbed another chunk of cheese at Jekyll.

"That thing is really cool-looking,'' Charlie said ad-miringly. "It might be a weird dinosaur that's been tam-pered with genetically, but it's still a fucking dinosaur.''

"Yeah, it sure is,'' David said, tossing another bit of cheese, "unless we want to invent a whole new classifi-cation.''

"Like what?'' Ferd asked.

"Saurus sapiens, or something.'' David pitched the last of the cheese, and Jekyll fielded it as adroitly as he had the rest of the package.

"Think we ought to open the tuna?'' said Ferd.

"So soon? He can't be hungry yet.'' Charlie was watch-ing Jekyll closely as the dinosaur finished eating and began to groom himself.

"I hope you're right, but like David said, he's got a high metabolic rate.''

"So have you, Ferd, but you don't eat *all* the time, do you?''

"Only when nobody's watching. You know how self-conscious we chubbettes are.''

"Yeah, right.'' Charlie's teasing was halfhearted. He was just too fascinated by Jekyll to concentrate on tor-menting Ferd today.

"You know,'' David said, "I think Jekyll's moving a little closer.''

They all looked at the young dinosaur. He had some-how contrived to move toward them without anyone noticing until now. It might not have been a conscious movement, but as Jekyll trusted them more, he shied away less.

"Well, we've fed him," Ferd said. "Now what?"

"Good question," David said. "Now what, indeed."

11

They laid in a supply of bacon, eggs, chicken, beef, hamburger, and pork chops. Using their tools, they built a cage for Jekyll. It was made of some old lumber they found behind McCullers' on a meat run, and some chicken wire. They lured him inside with a rib eye steak. Jekyll didn't mind being penned up as long as the meat kept coming.

"If we could refrigerate the remains of that cow, I'd do it," David said, "provided I knew the rancher could never find it. I'll bet he's fit to be tied."

"Yeah, he'd probably shoot us if he knew we were harboring the culprit," Ferd said.

"You're a *bad* boy, Jekyll," Charlie said as he tossed a blob of burger into the cage. "I think that's why I like you."

"You sound like Lou Costello," David said.

"He and I are both from the bad old East Coast," Charlie replied. "Maybe that's why everybody around here sounds so funny."

"Bet you didn't have any dinosaurs in New York."

"Are you kidding? The place is crawling with them. Just take a subway sometime, and you'll see what I'm talking about, Davie."

David had never been to New York; in fact, he'd never been east of Chicago, and never west of San Francisco. He had been to Canada and Mexico, but he'd never had enough money to go to Europe or Asia. It seemed odd to him that Jekyll's care and feeding had fallen to a man who knew so little about the world. It was as if the mountain had come to Mohammed. He knew that such thoughts were solipsistic in the extreme; he really had very little to do with what was happening. Any fossil hunter might be here in his place. But he was the one, as it had turned out, and the dinosaur was his responsibility.

"Funny how he came back here," Charlie said.

"Yeah," said David. "You'd think he'd stick around Liz's place. That's what Horner's discovery of the maiasaurus nests proved, that dinosaurs stayed near their birthplace. This guy seems to have been attracted to the place where his egg was stored."

"Unless this was a place where his folks had been breeding for a long time," Ferd said, "like *The Beast from Twenty Thousand Fathoms.*"

"No, I don't think it works that way," David said, even though he knew Ferd was joking.

"Where's yer sense of humah?" demanded Charlie in one of his Looney Tunes voices.

"Back there somewhere at Liz's place, I guess."

Neither Ferd nor Charlie knew what to say to that, so they didn't say anything. They fed some more hamburger to Jekyll, and wondered how much longer they had before somebody came after him.

Liz watched the helicopter come down, shielding her eyes from the wild dust storm it produced, even from a hundred feet away. It came to rest in the white circle, which appeared to be made of the same powder that marked yard lines on a football field.

A terrific noise of machine wind died down, and the rotors churned more slowly as the engines were cut. Jaffrey Flanagan stepped out, stooping to avoid the still-spinning blades. He walked straight over to Liz.

"Don't worry," he said, "agents have already been dispatched to organize search parties. That little fellow couldn't have gone too far. We'll find him."

"Tell them to be careful," Liz said. "He's not such a little fellow anymore."

"So I understand." He opened the door for her in courtly fashion. They went in through the reception room, through the corridor, and into the kitchen.

"The aliens—let's face it, who else could have done it?—who left the eggs have accelerated the dinosaur's growth, for some reason. This means that they're hungry almost all the time."

"Well, that's not unusual for dumb animals when they're very young, is it?"

"No, but we're not talking about a normal rate of growth here."

"What are we talking about?"

Liz wasn't sure it was wise to talk about this with Flanagan. But the men and women out looking for the dinosaur should know there was an element of danger. "I'd say that these young dinosaurs have a burning need for protein, and they're not choosy about where they get it."

"Oh, I see."

Liz couldn't read his expression very well. It seemed to her that Flanagan might very well use this important information unscrupulously, to proclaim the dinosaurs godless brutes. Maybe she was just paranoid. So far he hadn't done anything like that. In fact, he had just referred to them as "dumb animals," which indicated that he underestimated them. Maybe that was his plan, to put a spin on them that made them seem like harmless freaks.

"Tea?" Liz asked, gesturing for Flanagan to sit down at the kitchen table.

"Yes, thank you. But I'll fix it. I always do at home. It took Sylvia—that's my wife—some time to get used to that when we were first married."

By this time, a box of tea had been supplied for Jaffrey Flanagan: Darjeeling, Earl Grey, orange pekoe, and half a dozen other flavors for his delectation. It seemed to be his only luxury, Liz had to admit. He didn't even look at women lustfully, at least not while on the job. Too bad;

she hated to see the stereotypes about televangelists proved not to be true. She'd seen him and his mousy, strawberry blonde wife on TV many times, and though her gorge rose, she was envious in a way. At least Sylvia Flanagan had a husband. Woops, better turn in her feminist credentials if she kept thinking like that. Was the Secretary of Morality equally saddened to see that stereotypes about much-maligned secular humanists weren't true? No, because he had been associated with secular humanists at some time in his earlier life. Perhaps an early fling with liberalism at college?

"Were your folks fundamentalists?" she surprised herself by asking him.

Jaffrey Flanagan paused as he brought the box of tea bags down from the cupboard. He looked at Liz thoughtfully and spoke in a measured tone. "No, they weren't very religious at all."

"Really." So that was it. He had rebelled against his godless parents.

"While I was in college in the early seventies, something happened. One day in anthropology class another student handed me a pamphlet. It showed monkeys on one page, and a picture of God—as an old man with a long, white beard—on another. The text asked if we were descended from apes or created by God."

"Jesus freaks." Liz turned on the gas under the kettle and listened.

"That's right. That's what we used to call them in those days. Kids burned out on acid had turned to Jesus. I hadn't thought much about them before that. But then I began to talk to some of them. I didn't want to think that we were descended from animals, and I had to admit that to myself."

Dumb animals. Liz watched the blue flames vibrate underneath the kettle, trying to understand this powerful man. She let him go on talking, hoping that he would reveal something that would help her and the dinosaurs . . . and David.

"I began to talk to Christians. Mass baptisms were going on everywhere, and they were easy to find. Jews for Christ, Buddhists for Christ, you know. I began to understand that these people had all experienced the same thing—a vision, if you will. A vision of heaven and hell. I envied them."

Was he saying that he had no vision? Was that what troubled him so? It seemed to Liz that he had spent his adult life trying to enforce a vision on others, but it wasn't really his. Was this only a way for him to compensate for his own lack of vision?

"But I was consumed with a sense of mission," Jaffrey Flanagan said. "I had to save myself. And the only way to do that seemed to be to help others save *them*selves."

Liz wasn't quite sure she saw the logic in that, but she kept that thought to herself. If she could find a way to communicate with this man, there might yet be hope.

"We live in a world that's festering in corruption. I used to kid myself into thinking that this was just human nature, or entropy, or misunderstanding. I came to realize that it's none of those thing. It's something far more profound. It's evil, wickedness, sin. The devil."

"More profound than the second law of thermodynamics?" Liz said, trying against her better judgment to dissuade him from preaching his gospel to her. "Hard to believe. Entropy's a pretty heavy concept. The universe losing heat at a random rate, breaking down. Whew."

Surprisingly, Jaffrey Flanagan smiled at her. "You're joking, of course. But there's a grain of truth in what you say, and it's been said before. Science is a religion to many."

"Yeah, some people worship it a little too much," she said, "but you don't think it's intrinsically evil, do you?"

"If it overmasters man's love for God, then it is evil."

She couldn't quite believe that he was serious. But he was. She could see that he meant every word of it. It was disturbing, to think that this man, obviously intelligent and well educated, could dismiss the world of reason so completely. "Can't God and science coexist? Isn't science sort of like God's work, if you believe that all of us are His children, I mean?"

"Pride and arrogance. These are the sins that science is guilty of."

"What about murder? Hiroshima and Nagasaki. Surely the atomic bomb is more sinful than pride and arrogance."

"That was war. It had to be done."

That stopped her short. Did this man come from the same *planet* as her? Could he really believe that digging dinosaur bones was worse than wiping out hundreds of thousands of people, giving the survivors fatal radiation sickness, and creating the Cold War? This was an insane conversation.

"Doesn't the Bible say . . ." She spoke very carefully and slowly. ". . . 'Thou shalt not kill'?"

As if awakening from slumber, the teapot whistled. Jaffrey Flanagan looked at it as if he didn't quite know what it was, and then snatched it off the burner and poured steaming water into a teacup before it could become even more shrill.

"The Bible also says, 'I am the Lord thy God, and thou shalt worship no false gods before me.' False gods do not always possess names such as Moloch and Baal, Dr. Tomlinson."

He dropped a tea bag into the cup and watched orange billows emerge from it and spread through the hot water.

"Science may not always do what we want, but it is basically in the service of humanity," Liz said.

"It should be in the service of the good Lord first, and then in the service of humanity."

"Surely you know that science would be held back by that attitude, as it was in the Dark Ages."

"The Dark Ages? At least men knew who to turn to in their hour of need in the so-called Dark Ages."

Liz began to realize that there was simply no talking to Jaffrey Flanagan without having the baggage of religious fanaticism weigh down the conversation. Flanagan couldn't be taken far from his basic song and dance about God. Human endeavor was unimportant in his estimation, unless it was religious in nature. He had publicly declared many times that the earth was only four thousand years old, and yet he knew that it wasn't true.

"What about these dinosaurs, Mr. Secretary?" Liz said. "Don't you feel that their existence proves certain things you believe might be incorrect?"

Flanagan grimaced as he took a sip of hot tea. He set the cup down on his saucer and stood. He went to the window and looked out at the pen where the hatchlings were kept. "The good Lord might have put them here to test us."

"I thought you might say that."

Jaffrey Flanagan smiled. But before he could say anything else, the back door was flung open. Nurse Jen, still wearing a bandage on her hand, entered. Her expression was grim and purposeful. When she saw Flanagan, she hesitated.

"What is it, Nurse?" Flanagan asked.

"Mr. Secretary, I came in here to tell the doctor something. I didn't know you were here."

"Is it private?"

"No, I guess not." Jen looked at Liz.

"What is it, Jen?" Liz asked gently.

"It's Egbert."

Liz was pretty sure she knew what Jen was going to say. "What's happened to him?"

"He's dead."

12

"We're going to have to make a decision," David said. "Do we turn Jekyll in, or do we try to keep him with us?"

Jekyll, who was now well over four feet tall and nearly nine feet long, had just consumed a raw porterhouse steak, a dozen eggs, and a pound of Canadian bacon. This kept him reasonably calm while they let him out of the cage they'd hammered together to hold him when he wasn't dining. Head cocked quizzically, he watched them nail beams together, increasing the size of the cage to anticipate Jekyll's rapid growth rate.

"I'd like to keep him with us," Ferd said, "but I don't think we can afford him."

"Ferd, we can hardly afford you," Charlie said. "I mean, you've got a hell of an appetite."

"Thank you very much," Ferd said. "Next you'll be making fat jokes."

"I already *am* making fat jokes."

"All right, so we can't afford to feed him," David said. "But can we afford to turn him in, so that Jaffrey Flanagan can keep him under wraps?"

"Well, what else can we do with him?" Charlie demanded. "We can't just let him run wild. Some rancher will shoot him, or the reports of his feedings will get back to Flanagan, and they'll come and take him back. I don't see what choice we have."

"Unless we could get the media out here."

"All the networks are owned by people in Jaffrey Flanagan's pocket."

"Not all of them," David said. "There are still some independents, and there's still some spirit left in the print medium here and there."

"That's fine for the ten or fifteen people who can still read," Charlie said. "But it's not gonna save Jekyll's ass."

"Well, we can't just give up. If I were a religious man, I'd say that it was miraculous the way Jekyll came back to us. I'm not religious, so I'll just say that it was a hell of a coincidence. We'll never get another chance like this again. Jaffrey Flanagan will see to that."

"Yeah, but we can't take Flanagan on, David," Charlie said. "He's got resources in places where most people don't even have places."

"Whatever that means," David said.

"Company's coming." Ferd was looking at the dirt road in the distance. A white vehicle was kicking up dust in the morning sunlight.

"They can't see the cage from the road." David said. They had taken precautions, setting the cage in a depression behind some juniper bushes. "Maybe we better start putting branches over it, in case a helicopter is sent out this way."

"Yeah," Charlie agreed, in spite of what he had said a few minutes ago about the hopelessness of it all. "Better move back out of sight ourselves, though. We don't want to make anybody wonder what we're doing up here."

The white vehicle came to a stop below them before they could move away. As the dust settled, David recognized it as the nearly forty-year-old ambulance that Liz used to transport larger animals to her place. The driver's side door opened, and she got out.

"Liz!" David shouted.

She waved at him and started walking up the hill, slipping once or twice as the going grew steep. By a process of running and sliding, David met her halfway and took her by the hand. She didn't resist him.

"Got the day off," she said.

"I see." David led her up to where Ferd and Charlie were standing. They both grinned at her.

"I couldn't stand being around the place any longer. One of the hatchlings died."

"Oh." The news wasn't so much surprising as it was depressing. They had reached the crest of the hill. David was sure that Ferd and Charlie must have heard what Liz said.

"And another one actually got loose from the compound. He's still at large. If this keeps up, Jaffrey Flanagan won't have anything to cover up."

"Maybe not." David ushered her down the other side of the hill, into the depression.

Liz was still talking about how bad things were when she caught sight of Jekyll, who was attempting to open the ice chest with his clawed fingers.

"Hey!" David shouted at him. "Stay away from that!"

Jekyll had the lid off the chest now, but he dropped it at the stern sound of David's voice. He swiveled his body up on his rooster legs and cocked his head to look at Liz.

"He eats all the time," David said.

"Tell me about it," said Liz.

"We named him Jekyll."

"That's funny, David. He was the only one of the dinosaur babies I didn't name."

"That is funny, isn't it?"

"Yeah." She smiled at him, and he felt glad to be alive. "I guess it's synchronicity."

"Or something."

Ferd came up and stood beside them. "It's probably time to finish hammering this cage back together and coax junior inside it. Otherwise we could all be missing a few fingers before dinnertime."

"Right you are, me bucko." Charlie hefted a hammer and started driving nails. "Me and Ferd can probably finish up here alone, Dave."

David took that as his cue to go for a walk with Liz.

"Care to stroll a bit?" he asked, raising his elbow so that she could take his arm.

"Delighted," Liz said.

They walked together a little way, back toward the ambulance. David showed Liz where to park it on the far side of the hill, near the jeep and Ferd's van. It was rough going for the ambulance, but it was an inconspicuous place for them to park. The vehicles were practically invisible from the road.

"I guess it won't be long before Flanagan's goons catch up with us, will it?" David said.

"He's got a lot of people out searching already," Liz said.

"Do you think they'll try to kill Jekyll?"

"David, right now I'm worried about what they'll do to you if they find out you've been hiding him."

"Hiding him?" He tried to look shocked at the suggestion. "I'm just detaining Jekyll until Flanagan's flunkies finally get here."

"Right."

"Well, that's what we'll tell them."

"I don't think they'll buy it, but you've done better than they have."

"It wouldn't be hard to do better than that bunch of jerks," said David. "But it was purely accidental. I just happened to be talking to a cow when Jekyll got hungry. Next thing I knew, we were alone with a dead cow. Too bad it couldn't have been the Secretary of Morality instead of poor old bossy."

"Jaffrey Flanagan astonishes me," Liz said.

David stumbled a little on a stone. "You're not converting, are you?"

"Not yet. But it's hard for me to understand how such an intelligent man could believe fundamentalist fairy tales."

"Makes life easier if you have a pie-in-the-sky guy who takes care of everything. No decisions, no problems. Just do what Jesus says."

"It's more than that. He feels this urge to give people something, even if he has to force it on them."

"He's a nut."

"Maybe, but there's a deep longing in him for something better. I think he feels that he has no vision, no soul. Inside that man is an emptiness so deep that he's trying to fill it up with other people's souls."

"Weird," said David.

"Maybe I'm wrong about him, David, but I don't think so." Liz stopped and crossed her arms over her chest. "He's got just about everybody fooled, but the truth is, he's got nothing inside him."

"That's kind of a disturbing thought. I mean, we all have our times when we feel hollow. Just ask T. S. Eliot. That's why I drinks a bit, *memsahib*."

"Right."

They both laughed.

"Maybe I should say that's why I used to drink," David said. "What I mean to say is that you're looking at a man who is officially on the wagon."

"Really, David? And how long has this been going on? I seem to remember you looking pretty drunk at the hatching the other night."

"Well, it's only two days now, but don't you dare tell anybody."

"Mum's the word."

They walked on a little farther, and then David stopped and faced Liz. "I've missed you terribly," he said.

Liz seemed a bit taken aback. But she said, "I've missed you, too."

"We don't have a very good chance of coming out of this thing ahead of the game," David said. "But I've learned something from what's happened."

"What's that, David?" Liz looked deep into his eyes, and it made his heart ache.

"I've always felt disappointed because things haven't worked out. My old man died when I was a kid, my mother and stepfather and I don't get along, you tossed me out, and I never finished grad school. Now I understand that I've been lucky. I had a wonderful woman who loved me, and I had good friends who stuck by me, and I'm doing what I want in spite of my financial difficulties. I've just come to understand that happiness isn't a perpetual state. Good things come along, and we soon take them for granted. We have to snatch those good things and cherish them. Otherwise we grow bitter, or become insane. I had you, hon, and I threw you away."

"David . . . I asked you to leave. You didn't *throw* me away. You wanted the relationship to continue."

"I know, but it was only because you had to get rid of me, Liz. I understand that now."

David turned away, looking across the plain that started below the hills and stretched as far as the eye could see. When he turned back, he saw that Liz's face was wet with tears.

"David," she sobbed.

He took her in his arms, and felt the tears coming to his own eyes. "I love you, babe," he said.

"I know." Liz sniffed.

They held on tight for a few seconds, and then pulled far enough away to look into each other's eyes.

"So now what do we do?" Liz asked.

"Wait for the bad guys to show up, I guess."

David put his arm around Liz's shoulders, and they walked back to join Charlie and Ferd. The guys were trying to coax Jekyll into the enlarged cage, but they weren't having much luck. Ferd was waving a chunk of roast beef in front of the entrance to the cave, but Jekyll stood at a distance, snapping at a passing fly.

"He's figured it out, boys," Liz said.

"Nah, he'll come after it when he gets hungry enough, Liz," said Charlie.

"Don't be too sure," David said. "He's pretty damn smart. Might go after one of us, instead."

"The proud papa speaks," Ferd said.

But they found out that no amount of temptation and cajolery could get Jekyll to come back toward the cage.

"He's even bigger than I thought he'd be by now," Liz said.

"Yeah, his genetic coding is pretty advanced," David said. "I'd like to meet the guys who designed Jekyll."

"It's not likely that any of them are still around," Liz said. "Not after sixty-five million years."

"Why not? Jekyll's here, isn't he? Why can't the gene designers be hanging out someplace?"

"Well, they probably have better things to do, if any of them have survived this long."

"C'mon, Jekyll," Ferd said, shaking the meat, "there's a good boy."

"Forget it, Ferd," Charlie said. "Just give him the roast beef and chalk it up to experience."

"Well, okay," Ferd said, "but what if he runs away?"

"And leave his meal ticket behind? Fat chance."

Liz laughed. "You might have a point there, Charlie."

"Ah, to hell with it." Ferd tossed the beef to Jekyll, who snatched it out of the air and gulped it down greedily. "I guess he's not going anywhere."

"And neither are we," said David. "So let's try to teach this guy something before he gets too big to handle."

"Looks like he's too big already," said Liz.

"I wonder if we can teach him to count to ten," Charlie said.

"Let's try it." David found a stick and walked over toward Jekyll. He began to draw marks in the sand.

The dinosaur watched him with interest. After David had drawn ten strokes, he handed the stick to Jekyll. Jekyll promptly drew a line in the dirt.

"Look at that!" Ferd said in amazement.

Jekyll glanced toward Ferd, and then looked back at the ground.

"That's right, big guy," David said, "draw another one."

Jekyll did, right next to the first one, in emulation of David.

"Now another one."

Jekyll drew a third, almost as though he understood what David was saying to him.

"This is pretty damned amazing." Liz moved closer to see what would happen next.

"If he stops at ten," Charlie said, "then we'll *really* have something."

They watched in suspense as Jekyll drew another line in the dirt, and then another.

"He's halfway home," Ferd said.

Jekyll, intent upon his labors, paid no attention to their banter. He drew a sixth line, a seventh, and an eighth. David noticed how Jekyll looked back and forth from the original ten marks to his own set. He drew a ninth stroke in the dirt.

Nobody spoke. David felt his heart swelling in his chest. He hardly dared to breathe. Now they would see if Jekyll could pass the test.

Without hesitating, Jekyll drew the tenth stroke.

"Yeah!" Ferd said, clapping his hands. "He did it."

David hushed him. "Don't give him any clues that he's finished. Let's see if he draws any more."

They waited. Jekyll cocked his head, but he didn't do anything else. After a few seconds, he dropped the stick and turned toward the ice chest.

They all burst into spontaneous applause. Jekyll seemed a bit disconcerted at all the noise, looking from one to the other as they cheered and slapped their hands together.

"Well, I think you deserve something for that, fella," David said, prying open the lid and coming out with a pound of ground beef. "A little raw burger is the least I can do for the world's only counting dinosaur."

"Have you noticed the down on his back and fore-limbs?" Liz asked.

"Yeah, it looks like he might have feathers coming in," David said as he tossed a wad of meat of Jekyll.

"But he must be almost full-grown. They should have filled in long since."

"Maybe the bioengineers didn't think of everything," David said. "We really don't know much about the dinosaurs' internal mechanisms."

"We'll know more after today."

"What do you mean?" David hesitated with a chunk of burger in his hand.

"They're dissecting Egbert."

"What? Who's dissecting him?"

"Flanagan brought in a team of zoologists and biologists. They're going to cut him up this afternoon."

"Christ."

"I thought they'd want me there, but they didn't," Liz said. "In fact, I got the distinct impression that Secretary Flanagan was glad to get rid of me for a few hours."

"His loss is our gain," Ferd said.

"What a sweet thing to say," Liz said.

"Shucks, ma'am, twarn't nothin'."

Jekyll finished off the pound of hamburger, and began to groom himself without benefit of water, smoothing his downy limbs and picking his teeth with a sharp claw.

"He's actually learned some basic math," David said.

"Unless he's just a very good mimic," she said.

"Chauvinist. You don't think a dinosaur can learn mathematics? We'll have him doing calculus and trigonometry before long."

"Better be quick about it."

"Huh?"

David heard the sound of the helicopter's rotors before he saw where Liz was pointing. It was flying straight toward them.

"Shit!" Ferd shouted.

Jekyll, still chewing his meat, cocked his head warily. As the helicopter hovered overhead, he bolted down the far side of the hill, back toward the woods where David had first seen him.

''Stop that animal,'' a deep voice commanded over a bullhorn.

Animal, David thought, as he watched Jekyll's bright yellow and blue back diminish with astonishing speed. In a moment, the dinosaur was gone.

13

Officially, they hadn't been arrested. Nevertheless, David felt very much like a prisoner. Once again, he sat in Liz's kitchen at sunset, drinking coffee and talking to none other than the secretary of morality, Jaffrey Flanagan, himself. It was a bit ironic that Liz had led the feds straight to Jekyll, he thought. She'd been trying to get away from all this for a few hours, and instead she had gotten even more deeply involved. David had been disturbed to see that there were no media people anywhere near Liz's house when they were brought in. He had planned to say something to them about what was going on, but he never got the chance.

"Mr. Albee," Flanagan was saying for the umpteenth time, "this is a very serious business."

"Tell me about it," David said.

"If, as you say, the creature somehow found its way back to where its egg was found, why didn't you notify us?"

"I'll tell you why," David said. "Because I didn't see you and your people making any real attempt at finding out the truth about these dinosaurs."

"And what truth is that?"

"Where they come from. Who put them on Earth. What is the limit of their intelligence. That sort of thing."

"And what makes you think we're not trying to ascertain these things?"

"Oh, come *on*. You've just been hiding them here. You've shown no interest in letting the public know what's

97

going on. You don't let a news team get within a mile of this place.''

''Actually, some have set up shop just down the road,'' Flanagan said smugly.

''They might as well be in Timbuktu, for all you're letting them see.''

''David, do you think this is a sideshow? Do we really want the media distorting the truth about what's happened here?''

''It is traditional in our country to take that chance,'' David said.

''Mr. Albee, you are very naïve.''

David glared at him. ''And you, Secretary Flanagan, are very cynical.''

Flanagan colored. ''You can believe what you like about me, but I know I'm doing the Lord's work, and I'm doing it for the good of the greatest country on Earth.''

''Well, at least you're willing to grant that I can think what I like about you. That's a step in the right direction.''

''Your sarcasm is not helpful.''

''No, I guess not.'' It would do no good to further alienate Jaffrey Flanagan. ''Mr. Secretary, could I see the results of Egbert's autopsy?''

''That wouldn't be appropriate.''

''Why not?''

''That information is classified.''

''And who classified it? You, I assume, or your rival Chuck Margolis.'' David waited for Flanagan to deny it, looking deep into his steely eyes. He remembered the final lines of a satiric Tom Lehrer song about a murderess—*for lying she knew was a sin, a sin.*

''That's none of your concern.'' Leaving David and his teacup, Flanagan got up and walked out of the room.

David sat at the table, rolling his still warm coffee cup between his palms. He was a prisoner in Liz's house now. They had put out a cot for him in the living room, and he had the run of the house, but he wasn't allowed in the backyard at all. Oddly, he had never really been told this, but guards had prevented him from leaving or going out to see the dinosaurs. When he asked whose orders they were following, they just stared blankly at him.

He went to the screen door. A marine guard stood on the back stoop. The leatherneck turned and glanced indifferently at David.

"Dit-dit-dit-dit, lookin' out my back door," David sang. The marine, who couldn't have been more than nineteen years old, obviously did not recognize the melody.

"Never could carry a tune," David apologized.

He went back through the kitchen and into the living room, where he sat on his cot. He wished that he hadn't given up smoking. At least that would give him something to do. He thought about reading, but he didn't feel like turning on the lamp in the deepening shadows. He sat alone for a while, not doing much of anything, until Liz entered the room.

"Hey," she said, "what are you doing hanging out here in the dark?"

"Feeling sorry for myself."

"Don't," she warned. "That way lies madness."

"Yeah, but with me it's congenital."

Liz sat down on the bed beside him. She said softly, "Thinking about your dad?"

"No, not consciously, but he's always with me. Liz, I don't want to be a drunken failure."

"You're not," Liz said. "You came out pretty well, considering the bad breaks you started off with."

"I've got to *do* something." He looked into her eyes. "I mean, what can I do to save those guys?"

"David, you've done everything you can. Now it's up to God or Fate, or whatever you happen to believe in."

"My problem is, I don't much believe in any of those things," David said.

"Believe that I love you."

David looked at her, at her beautiful eyes, her soft hair, the strong line of her jaw, her slender body sitting so close to him that he could feel her warmth. "Thanks for telling me that," he said. "I need you."

Liz patted the cot. "Doesn't seem very comfortable."

"It'll have to do," David said.

"No, it won't." She took his hand and led him to her bedroom. There was a lock on the door, which Liz opened after selecting a key from her key chain. "Too many people I don't know running around here," she said. "I put this lock on day before yesterday."

David felt, rather than heard, the presence of someone in the corridor, watching them. He turned to see who it was.

"Where are you going?" Burles asked, scowling at them as only the righteous can scowl at two sinners.

"We're going into my bedroom," Liz said. "And then we're going to make love."

David got a satisfying glimpse of Burles's jaw dropping just as Liz opened the door. He went in first. Liz locked the door behind them.

"That does look inviting," David said, looking at the bed. "Not as inviting as you, though."

Liz shut him up by throwing her arms around his neck and kissing him deeply. Her lips were so soft that he almost gasped. It had been a long time. They kissed for a little while, slowly, languidly, deliberately. As they kissed, they touched each other, almost timidly. They slowly sat on the edge of the bed, still kissing and stroking each other gently.

Somebody knocked on the bedroom door. It had been so quiet up to then that David was startled by the staccato sound.

Liz turned dreamily toward the disturbance. "Go away," she said.

"I'm sorry, Miss Tomlinson," said Jaffrey Flanagan's voice. "I can't allow this sort of thing to go on while I'm in the house."

Liz stiffened. She went to the door, surprising David. He thought she would defy Flanagan. His spirit sagged as she opened the door to the Secretary of Morality's doom-laden gaze.

"*You* won't allow it?" she said. "Mr. Secretary, you have taken over my house, and are now holding David prisoner in it. You have shown no respect for the law, so far as I can see, nor for common human decency. Now you tell me I cannot bring the man I love into my bed-room?"

"You're not married."

"We're married enough. We lived together for years, and we love each other. That's gonna have to do." She started to close the door in his face.

"If you'll permit me to make a suggestion," said the Secretary of Morality. "I have an idea."

"And what might that be?" Liz was wary, but she waited to hear what he had to say.

"I'd like to marry you two."

David almost laughed at the way Jaffrey Flanagan had stated it. He wondered if the secretary secretly wanted to make it a threesome. Maybe you could call it an evangel-ical sandwich. It was absurd. And yet Flanagan stood there wearing a look of such steadfast sincerity that he was well nigh irresistible.

"Are you serious?" Liz asked.

Flanagan nodded.

Liz looked back at David. He didn't say anything, but he did raise his eyebrows a little.

"We'll have to talk it over," Liz said.

"Please do. My offer will remain open for as long as you like, Dr. Tomlinson." He smiled graciously at both of them, turned, and walked away.

Liz shut the door, turned toward David, and fell back against it as if to help keep it shut. "That man has got more sand than the Mojave Desert," she said.

"He's pretty amazing," David said. "But I wonder how much of his offer is for the greater glory of the Almighty, and how much is designed to win us over, or at least neutralize us."

Liz went to him and put her arms around him. She rested her cheek against his shoulder. "At least he didn't have us put in stocks."

"For unlawful carnal knowledge," David said in a cod British accent.

"And about time, too."

"Think he's peeping through the keyhole?" David asked.

"No, but sometimes I feel as if the room's bugged."

"He's probably had the phone tapped. Yesterday was an opportune time to have it done. And who knows," David said, gazing at a stuffed dinosaur on the dresser, "that guy might have a camera in his mouth."

"I hope they enjoy the show." Liz dragged him onto the bed and resumed kissing him.

"They won't enjoy it as much as me," David said, and then he was quiet for a long time.

Jaffrey Flanagan watched the three dinosaurs play in their Mylar cage. They wouldn't be able to get out of here so easily, he thought. It was a better environment than the first, more roughly fashioned pen. And they had plenty of light. Plastic caves had been placed on one side of the eighteen-foot-long cage, so that they could have a little privacy if they needed it, and meat was constantly supplied by the people on duty. Plumbing had been routed into the cage, too. The dinosaurs were as tall as a full-grown man now, and their tails were the same length. They weighed about three hundred pounds apiece. The escaped male was larger than the others, Flanagan reflected. That should make him easier to spot. That brutish creature would be in this cage before long.

But what was he going to do about David Albee and Lizaveta Tomlinson? He couldn't keep them caged up and out of sight of the media forever. They seemed a bit surprised by his offer to marry them, but not surprised enough to accede to his wishes immediately. Or perhaps it was his lack of insistence when he asked them not to sleep together that surprised them. They would take time, those two, but he would have them in his flock yet.

"Everything all right, sir?" Marine Captain Torrance was standing next to him.

"No, Captain, and it won't be all right until we have that animal back in this cage."

"Yes, sir." Torrance stood ramrod straight, his dark face showing no expression. He had been in charge two days earlier, when the dinosaur bounded over the wall.

"At ease, Captain Torrance," Flanagan said.

"Thank you, sir." Torrance assumed an attitude of relaxation, but he was still wary. This would not look good on his record. Of course, he had no way of knowing that the dinosaurs would work as a team, and had been given no orders other than to pen them up, and make sure that they were fed, but he was still responsible. Flanagan knew that Torrance would try very hard to make up for the gaffe. In fact, he was counting on it.

"Captain Torrance," Jaffrey Flanagan said, "everybody makes mistakes. Don't blame yourself too much for this. We've all learned something from what's happened."

"Yes, sir, Mr. Secretary."

"You'd better check with your men to make sure the honorable members of the media haven't found a way in as easily as that animal found its way out."

"Nobody's come in, sir. I can assure you of that."

"Good." Flanagan turned away from him, and brooded over the Mylar cage again. Captain Torrance took this as a dismissal and went away.

How could they grow so fast and learn so much in such a short time? Flanagan watched as the only remaining male, the one the nurse and Dr. Tomlinson called Zooey, came over to the end of the cage where he was standing. It cocked its head and watched him.

"Well, I guess I'm as curious to you as you are to me," Flanagan said. But he wished that it weren't so. These animals were so bright that they were liable to be mistakenly thought of as the equals or even the superiors of human beings; somewhere between man and the angels. He couldn't allow that to happen.

Slowly he turned away and went into the house. He couldn't go back to Washington until that fourth animal was recaptured. He felt as much a prisoner as these three in their Mylar cage . . . or as much as Lizaveta Tomlinson and David Albee, for that matter.

"What am I going to do with those two?" he said. And what was he going to do about Charles Margolis, who was doubtless rubbing his palms together in glee over what had happened?

14

"Go out and play now, Jill," said Anne Diltz. "You've been watching TV long enough."

Jill, six years old next month, looked up at her mother sadly. "But, Mom, I want to watch cartoons."

"That's too bad. It's a beautiful day, and I've got too much work to do around here to listen to that thing blaring the rest of the afternoon. Now, you turn it off and go outside and get some fresh air."

Jill looked resentful, but she turned off the television and got up, walking slowly toward the door. "Nobody wants to play with me," she said.

"Oh, honey, your friend will come over tomorrow. Her mother wouldn't let her out today because she was being punished. I bet she'd love to be able to go outside."

"Yeah!" It didn't seem so bad now, Anne noticed. Just tell Jill she had something somebody else wanted, and she was happy as a clam. "I'm gonna take my jacks."

Jill went to her room to get the jacks. The screen door slammed a moment later. And Anne chuckled to herself a little. Life was hell for a six-year-old—for about five minutes, until the next thing came along.

Humming to herself, Anne went to the laundry room attached to the garage at the back of the house. She already had one load going, and the sound of the washing machine's steady churning was somehow reassuring to her. It was such a homey sound, she thought.

Once she had the clothes in the dryer, it was time to

think about waxing the kitchen floor. There were so many things to do on her day off that she felt like just sitting down and listening to a couple of CDs.

"Maybe I should watch a few of those cartoons myself," she said aloud. Such luxuries as a satellite dish did make country living a bit more bearable. Ever since they'd moved out here from Los Angeles, she'd been trying to get used to it. They'd done it for Jill, so that she wouldn't be brought up in a crime-ridden urban environment. Still, Anne often missed the pleasures of the big city. She couldn't tell how Irv felt about it; he was the same as he had been back in L.A. But Jill seemed to take to country living. She had friends and she had miles and miles of prairie to run and play in, as long as she stayed away from the road. Besides, Anne was the only practicing psychologist within twenty miles, and she had plenty of patients. It was amazing how many neurotics there were where the foothills of the Rockies met the great plains. She seemed to add a new one every week or two. Unfortunately, one of them, Liz Tomlinson, had called to say she couldn't make it this week. Caring for the psychologically wounded wasn't an easy task, she reminded herself, chuckling again.

"Which reminds me." Time to look out and make sure Jill wasn't heading toward the road. Anne had noticed that her daughter shared with her a propensity for doing things that were forbidden. Anne had caught hell at least twice a week when she was a little girl, and Jill was carrying on in the same grand tradition.

Anne went to the window on the north side of the house, where she could see the two-lane asphalt road leading to Choteau. She was relieved that she couldn't see Jill, but she could hear her.

"You could play, too," Jill said, her voice carrying clearly through the open window.

Who was she talking to? Jill couldn't see Anne from where she was. None of her friends could get here without being driven, and Anne certainly hadn't heard a car. Irv wasn't due back until six. With a rising sense of alarm,

Anne hurried around to the back of the house. Who would be talking to a child, out here in the middle of nowhere, without making his presence known to Anne? She remembered that the state prison was only a few miles away.

Almost in a panic, Anne flung open the screen door. Her heart stopped when she saw who her little girl was talking to. It was worse than she had feared. It was a nightmare.

"You've got hands," Jill said to the yellow and blue monster towering over her. 'You can do it. Throw the ball down and pick up a jack."

The monster looked at Anne with a curious sidewise glance, and then it moved closer to Jill. Anne held her breath. Her impulse was to run down off the porch, pick Jill up, and carry her into the house. But that might make matters worse. The monster didn't seem to be interested in Jill. It was looking at the jacks, which gleamed in the sunlight. Its body descended like one of those bobbing-bird statues to get a closer look at them.

It wasn't paying any attention to her now, or to Jill. Only to the jacks. Anne stealthily made her way down the porch steps toward Jill.

"Mommy," Jill said, "I think that big bird's gonna play jacks with me."

Anne dashed over and picked Jill up. She ran back up the porch steps. She had left the back door open, so they were inside in seconds. Still holding Jill in her arms, Anne kicked the door shut and bolted it. She looked out through the window to make sure the monster wasn't trying to follow them inside.

It was still gazing at the glittering jacks.

"Mommy, why did you do that?" Jill asked. "You told me to go out!"

"That thing," Anne gasped, out of breath from fear, excitement, and exertion. "It might have hurt you, darling."

"It's a bird!" Jill said, as if that clarified everything.

"I don't think so, Jill." It certainly wasn't like any bird

Anne had ever seen, in spite of its feathers. She still couldn't quite believe it, but there it was.

The monster reached down into the dirt and picked up Jill's jacks. Its hands seemed human, with four fingers and a thumb. And its face looked like a combination of a lizard and an ape. But Jill was right—there was something bird-like about it. It wasn't just the rooster legs with the spurs on them, but something about the way the head was shaped, and the feathers sprouting from its scaly back.

The monster placed the jacks in the dirt again, very carefully, one at a time.

"He's gonna play," Jill said happily.

"Shh." Anne was fascinated in spite of her fear. The monster was doing something with the jacks, all right. But what? It was so enrapt on what it was doing that this seemed a good time to call the police.

Anne put Jill down and went to the kitchen wall phone. She dialed 911 and waited.

"Police Emergency," a woman's voice finally said.

"There's a thing in our yard," Anne said. "It frightened my daughter."

"No it didn't!" Jill shouted.

"Shush." Anne hoped that the woman on the phone wouldn't think she was shushing her.

"A thing, ma'am?" said the phone voice.

"Some kind of big animal. I don't know what it is."

"What is your address?"

Anne recited her address and phone number.

"We'll send someone out, ma'am."

"Please tell them to hurry. It could easily break down the door if it wanted to."

"Yes, ma'am. Just stay in the house and make sure the doors and windows are locked."

"Okay. Thank you."

She heard a click. There was nobody on the line any-more. She and Jill were alone, and that thing was still out there. Or was it? Anne ran to the window to see.

The monster was still arranging the jacks in the dirt. Its

hands—and they really were hands, she saw, in spite of their claws and blue scales—were busy laying down the last couple. It looked as if it had formed some pattern.

For a moment the monster seemed to ponder the jacks as they glinted in the sunlight. Then it reached down and snatched them up with its right hand, cupping the other hand to hold them. As soon as it had them all, it loped off toward the west. Anne and Jill ran to the master bedroom, from where they watched it until it climbed to the crest of a hill and went down the other side, out of sight.

Anne let out a long, long sigh. She was still holding Jill, but she was trembling. She put her daughter down and sat on the edge of the bed.

"What's the matter, Mommy?" Jill asked.

Anne shook her head. When she thought about what was troubling her now, she laughed. She laughed so hard that tears were soon streaming down her cheeks.

"What's so funny?" Jill demanded.

"It's just that—" She paused, laughing too hard to continue for a moment. "It's just that when the rescue people come, or the sheriff, or whoever it is, we'll have to tell them that we just watched a monster playing jacks."

"Getting kind of crowded in there," Liz said.

"Yes, it is." Jaffrey Flanagan was looking into the transparent cage, watching the dinosaurs as they tore into a side of beef. They would soon be too big for the cage. The smallest of them, Marie Antoinette, was more than twelve feet long from snout to tail tip. Each of the beasts was at least as tall as a human when it stood erect.

"We've decided not to tie the knot, Reverend," Liz said. "David and I will just continue to live in sin as long as we're under house arrest."

Jaffrey Flanagan turned his handsome head to look at her. "Dr. Tomlinson, if you are trying to coerce me into letting you go, it won't work."

"Look who's talking about coercion," David said,

coming from behind them. "You don't give a damn about anybody's rights."

"That's not true," Jaffrey Flanagan said.

"So you say," David replied, walking up and looking Flanagan straight in the eye. "But your disregard for the Constitution and human rights is blatant."

"And your sense of responsibility is nonexistent, Mr. Albee," said Jaffrey Flanagan. "You knew perfectly well that that creature cannot be permitted to run wild. And yet you harbored it, in spite of the importance of such a discovery."

"My friends and I discovered it, in case you've forgotten," David said. "And I have a notion that its importance is a lot clearer in my mind than in yours."

"That, young man, is a matter of opinion."

"Oh, yeah? Well, if you deprive the world of this discovery, history's opinion of you is not going to be very favorable."

"Have you set yourself up as my judge, Mr. Albee?" Jaffrey Flanagan said without a trace of wryness.

"It's not my job to judge you," David admitted. "But I'm not going to stand by and let you cover this thing up without raising a squawk."

"Oh, I see. You're a self-appointed savior, too, much as you think I see myself."

That stung David. He saw that Flanagan was quite correct in a way. He was full of righteous indignation, and he did think that there was only one right way to go about this. His way.

Jaffrey Flanagan didn't seem pleased by David's abrupt silence, though. It was as if he had only been trying to gain time, as if he were really thinking of something far more significant than this impromptu debate with David.

"I need your help, not your enmity," Jaffrey Flanagan said.

"You can't expect us to go against our own principles," Liz said, "any more that you can go against your own."

"We have to catch that animal," Flanagan said, not hearing her. "I think we can agree on that principle."

David knew that it was true. They couldn't just leave Jekyll out there on his own. Somebody would shoot him, or he wouldn't be able to find enough food and he would starve to death, or he might catch some disease that his immune system wouldn't be able to cope with. David didn't believe that these were the reasons Jaffrey Flanagan wanted Jekyll back in captivity, but they were valid. If only word could get out to the people before Jekyll was apprehended.

"You're right, of course," Liz said. "He can't remain on the loose indefinitely."

"It astonishes me that the animal has been able to elude search parties for so long," Flanagan said.

"He's not just an animal," David said, "and I'm sure your dissection proved that."

"It proved nothing of the kind."

But David knew that he was lying. "You're a good actor," he said, "but not good enough to get that one past us."

Liz laughed; Jaffrey Flanagan did not.

"All the results are not in yet," Flanagan said.

"But I'm sure we'll be the first to hear when they are," David replied.

"Classified, I'm sure," Liz said.

"You're quite right about that," said Jaffrey Flanagan, again without a trace of sarcasm.

"Yeah," David said. "Just how much harm do you think could be done to the simple peasants of middle America by the release of such knowledge, Mr. Secretary?"

"Maybe you could just let the newspapers have it," Liz suggested. "If they don't see it on TV, maybe the public won't really believe it."

"Your blandishments are very engaging," Jaffrey Flanagan said, "but they're not going to help your cause very much, I'm afraid."

Captain Torrance double-timed it toward them. He didn't even look at Liz and David. "Mr. Secretary," he said, "there's a message for you. Sounds pretty urgent."

Excusing himself, Flanagan went with the captain to one of the temporary buildings, a kind of plastic Quonset hut.

"I don't think he's happy with us," David said. "I'll tell you, though, Liz, I don't know if I could win an argument against him on my own, crazy as his thinking might be."

Liz did a Bela Lugosi voice. "Hish vill is shtronk."

"Rasputin," David said, laughing. "Svengali."

Liz laughed, too, but only for a moment. She suddenly sobered and said, "I wonder what that urgent message was all about."

"Well, if it wasn't the president calling from a Bethesda golf course, it was probably about our dear friend."

"Jekyll?"

"Who else?"

"Do you think this means they caught him?"

15

As it turned out, Jekyll was still at large. This wasn't something that Flanagan revealed to them straightaway, but as time passed and Jekyll did not appear, dead or alive, Liz and David began to suspect that he was still eluding the nation's proud military elite.

"Of course," David said, slapping some mayonnaise on a cucumber sandwich, "they might have killed him and shipped his body to some government lab for study. Maybe he and Egbert can share the same jar full of formaldehyde."

"You're such an optimist," Liz said, sighing. "But who can blame you after all that's happened?"

"Yeah. A cynic is just a busted idealist, they say." David took a bite of the sandwich, and said as he was chewing, "But I don't think they've found him yet. If he gets up into the hills, he could hold out until the weather starts to get cold."

"Then what?"

"Then he'll freeze to death. Dinosaurs weren't adapted for the big chill. That's basically what killed them off."

"I guess we better hope they find him, then." Liz looked very depressed. "Even though it's not much of a solution."

"Yeah." David put down his sandwich. "Liz, there's been one good thing in all this, at least."

She looked at him expectantly.

"At least you and I are together again."

She didn't smile. "I'm still not sure that's for the best—for either one of us."

"Oh, come on, Liz, we make a great team. We can do better than before."

She shook her head, repeating, "I'm still not sure."

David sighed, and decided that it would be wise to change the subject. "I wonder what's happened to Ferd and Charlie."

"I imagine they've been detained."

"Yeah, but where?"

Ferd didn't mind this as much as he'd thought he would. Working in a lab with Professors Fine and Sosnowski was interesting enough, though he knew he'd been placed here to keep him out of circulation. His background in physics had come in handy, though, and Fine had spoken up for him when the holy rollers had thought about sending him to a detention center. Fine was only working for the big government physicists, but they seemed to respect him. Charlie was working for Sosnowski, which Fine had also arranged. He was a good guy, Dr. Fine.

"Ferd!" It was his mentor calling; they probably needed help now that the housing was being removed from the gadget inside the egg box.

"Ferd," Dr. Fine called again from the other end of the room, "give us a hand here."

Ferd hurried to join Fine, Sosnowski, and a woman named Dr. Janet Munnero. They were examining a cutaway section of the box. It was the back, which had not been touched by the laser when the box was first opened. The raised section inside had been lasered out and removed, revealing what was inside.

"Pretty weird," Ferd said.

There were two mechanisms, one on each end of the oval area. One was crossed-shaped, and the other was a series of overlying rectangles.

"We think this is the stasis field generator," Sosnowski said, "but we don't know what this other device is for."

"Maybe it's an egg timer," Ferd offered, noticing how somber everyone was.

Nobody laughed. This problem was consuming all their attention, and they were in no mood for gags. Ferd decided not to try any more jokes; they might decide to send him to Siberia if he didn't keep his mouth shut.

"It's as likely an explanation as any we've come up with," Dr. Fine said, still not cracking a smile. "I'll be damned if I can make anything out of it."

"Of course," Janet Munnero said, "we don't have the faintest idea of how the stasis fields works, either. In fact, we can't even be sure which one of these *is* the stasis field generator."

Oh, great, Ferd thought. We're getting nowhere here. Might as well call in the marines.

"It seems to me that it's the one with all the ovoids," Dr. Fine said. "And I think the interior of the box itself is part of what makes the field work."

"You mean it bounces around off the inside of the box?" Ferd asked.

"Something like that. And its diminishing waves return to those ovoids in a sequence that is redirected and reamplified each time."

"So it never runs out of power."

"Possibly."

"That's too simple," Munnero said.

"Perhaps that's why it's so reliable," Sosnowski said. "If the field is generated and then reamplified in an undisturbed cycle, there's no telling how long it might last."

"It also accounts for the cessation of the field as soon as the box was opened," Fine said. "If, as Ferd says, waves bounced off the walls in sequence, the removal of one wall would end the sequence."

"The alloy was designed specifically to contain the field. When one wall was removed, the wave was redirected. The result was a localized power failure, and the resumed

development of sixty-five-million-year-old dinosaur em-
bryos.'' Dr. Fine removed his glasses and rubbed the sides
of his nose.

"Seems plausible to me,'' Ferd said, pleased and astonished that his comments were being taken seriously.

"Yes, and perhaps the other device is some sort of
timer, as you jokingly suggested,'' Dr. Sosnowski said.
"Or perhaps it was some sort of homing device, so that
the, uh, beings who put it here in the first place could
come back and find it.''

"There's another possibility,'' Dr. Munnero said.
"What if it's designed to destroy the box?''

"Wouldn't it have done so already?'' Ferd asked.

"Not necessarily. After sixty-five million years, it might
not go off. Explosives from World War II were still dangerous in the seventies.''

Ferd remembered stories about that, London bomb dis-
armament squads in tense, sweaty black-and-white movie
thrillers.

"It's possible, I suppose,'' Sosnowski said in his thick
Polish accent, "but I don't think it's likely. This box was
not designed for war. There wasn't anybody on Earth to
make war against when this was placed here.''

"How do we know that?'' It was Charlie, can of diet
soda in hand, who had just entered the lab. "The discovery of these eggs changes everything we know about the
history of our planet. If one race left the box of eggs here,
another could just as easily have been here, too.''

"Let's just go on the evidence we have, Charlie,'' Dr.
Fine said, holding up one hand. "We only know that this
one box was left here in the late Cretaceous. It was obviously designed and built by a superior intelligence, and
seems to have served a zoological purpose. If we go very
far past these assumptions, we get mired down in idle
speculation. We don't need a galactic war, because we've
got enough drama and mystery already.''

That, thought Ferd, was understatement if he'd ever

heard it. He turned to Charlie. "Yeah, chucklehead, don't complicate the issue any more than you have to."

Charlie sneered at him.

As Bob drove up into the mountains, he thought about the dour look his wife, Laura, had given him at breakfast. She didn't mention his skin cancer, but it was on her mind. He didn't give a damn, though. He was going camping, just like in the old days. He popped a homemade tape in the deck, Lord Buckley monologues from the fifties.

When "Governor Slugwell," a ripe parody of politics, failed to make him laugh for the first time ever, he shut off the car stereo. He didn't want to think about politics just now, even in comedy form. He drove on in silence until he came to a dirt road, which he followed until he feared for his shock absorbers.

By midafternoon, he found the spot where he used to camp quite frequently, on a flattish stretch by a stand of lodgepole pines. He hauled his gear out of the back of the station wagon and looked around. A stream meandered nearby, but Bob opened his first beer as soon as he had set up the tent. He was breathing pretty hard by the time he'd finished, and the brew helped a lot. He'd fill a canteen later.

"Better stay out of the sun, old boy." Bob looked at the Green Party sticker on the bumper of the wagon, and remembered the failed promise of the environmental movement in the early years of the decade. You had to drive pretty damn far out of town to get away from all the development nowadays. One of the reasons he had stayed in Montana was its wide open spaces, but they were disappearing fast even here. In a few more years it would be like Southern California, without the sunshine and the ocean.

"With the space goes our freedom," Bob said, taking another swig of beer. "And with our freedom goes our dream."

He downed the rest of the can. "It's time to get out the

old L.L. Bean.'' He dragged out the tent and fumbled with it until he had it set up. Then he got the lawn chair out to unfold it. He settled in with a good book in the shade—he'd promised Laura he'd be careful about his skin, though he was pretty much past the point of giving a damn—but he soon found himself dozing.

He was awakened by a man's voice. Opening his eyes, Bob saw the silhouette of a guy wearing a Stetson standing over him.

"Howdy." The guy's voice was almost comically high-pitched. As Bob focused on him, he saw that he was looking at an aged cowpoke wearing a short-sleeved shirt, jeans, and boots.

"Howdy yourself," Bob replied. "Where'd you come from?"

"Down the hill," the cowpoke said, gesturing vaguely at a beige vehicle parked behind Bob's station wagon.

Bob grunted understanding.

"Sorry to wake you," the man said. "But I got to." He pulled a badge out of his shirt pocket. "Deputy sheriff."

Oh, Christ, Bob thought, what now? "What can I do for you, sir?"

"Well, just thought I might mention there's some cattle mutilations goin' on in the area."

"No cattle up here."

"No, that's right. But other animals been found in the vicinity all tore up. Whatever it is, bear, mountain lion, could be dangerous to folks, too. It come up this way last couple days."

There was a touch of kindness in the warning. This man was seriously concerned that people might get hurt.

"I've got a .22 pistol," Bob said. "Keep four chambers loaded in case of an emergency."

"That's good. I don't know if it'd stop this animal or not, since we can't be sure what kind of critter it is, but at least a .22's something."

Bob nodded. They chatted amiably for a few minutes,

LORDS OF CREATION   119

and then the cowboy got into his beige four-wheel-drive vehicle and drove away.

Bob sat with the book still lying open on his beer gut. He thought about reading some more, but something nagged at him. *Whatever it is, bear, mountain lion . . .*

He could think of only one large, carnivorous creature in the vicinity that might elude easy identification.

"Hot dayum," Bob drawled. He waited until the dust trail of the deputy's vehicle settled down, and then got up to get the .22 out of the glove compartment.

He removed it from its holster and looked at the light pistol in his hand. "Hell, I don't want to shoot him," he said. But he did have to protect himself if the dinosaur was as dangerous as this guy claimed. Laura would never forgive him if he let himself be devoured by a prehistoric animal.

"Now, if I were a young dinosaur, where would I go to hide from the depredations of our moralistic masters?" There was plenty of cover up here in the mountains, of course. Lots of timber to get lost in, and plenty of game. Bob reasoned that it just might be smart to stay here with his trusty firearm and see if the dinosaur showed up.

16

"You're letting me go?" David asked. He had been summoned into Liz's front yard by Burles, and was now looking at his own jeep, which had the motor running, with the exhaust pipe emitting blue vapor.

"Needs a tune-up," Burles said.

"Yeah, it's a little shaky," David said, unsure if they were talking about him or the jeep, "but it still runs."

Burles nodded. "I wouldn't let it get any more run-down than it already is."

"Thanks, I needed that." David turned toward the house. "Mind if I say good-bye to Dr. Tomlinson?"

"When this is all over, you can. You'd better go now, though, Mr. Albee."

David sighed. "You're such a bitch sometimes, Burles."

He caught a satisfying glimpse of Burles's reddening face as he turned away and climbed into the jeep. "Thanks for starting it up for me, fellas," he shouted merrily at two marines. "Pain in the ass to get a cold engine going."

One of the marines, a woman, smiled back at him. He didn't see the other's reaction as he backed up, turned around, and headed toward town. "Nothing like a few days of rest and relaxation in a hotel run by fascist fundamentalists," he said into the wind.

As he drove along, the implications of what Burles had said sank in. Did Flanagan expect this to end soon? If so, did that mean they had located Jekyll? Or even captured him? They might even have killed him by now.

120

David was sickened to think of such an atrocity, but he really had to face the possibility. But no, it didn't seem likely. Not that he would put it past Jaffrey Flanagan, but he thought the great televangelist was as curious about where this was all leading as anybody else.

David drove out to McCullers' Rock Shop. Jack wasn't there, but Emma was. She offered him a cold drink, and he gratefully accepted. It was getting hot.

"You wouldn't believe the shit that's going on out at Liz's," David said.

"Got anything to do with the hatchlings?" Emma asked.

"It does have something to do with them."

"I know," Emma said. "Bob Pierce told me a little about it on his way out to the mountains."

Neither of them said anything for a minute, while David finished his beer. He decided not to say anything more about the dinosaurs, since Flanagan still had Liz under lock and key. "Did Bob say which road he was taking?"

"No, but he did say he was going to the usual place."

"Ah, comes the dawn." David remembered Bob's favorite campsite. You took a dirt road about twenty miles northwest from here, to a small plateau about halfway up the side of Mount Larkin. There was a stand of pine trees, a stream, everything a camper, happy or otherwise, could ask for.

"When was he here?" David asked.

"This morning, about nine-thirty, ten o'clock."

David slapped a buck down on the counter. "Thanks a lot, Emma."

"Little warm today," she said. "Should be nicer up in the mountains."

David smiled.

He gassed up at the nearest ARCO, and headed northwest. It would be good to see Bob, and it would be relaxing to camp out. Hot wind blasted his face as he drove, and he popped a CD in—Nubile, a new group that had

been recommended to him by Ferd. He told himself over
and over again that Liz would be all right, and it took him
ten minutes to realize that he hadn't heard a note of Nubile's music.

"You're probably wondering why we let Albee go,"
said Jaffrey Flanagan.

Liz, emerging from the bathroom, was caught by surprise. "The Lord works in mysterious ways," she said.

Flanagan let that pass. Liz tried to stare him down, as
the hiss of the filling toilet issued through the open bathroom door. She couldn't do it. Flanagan's cool blue eyes
stared into hers intently, and she finally broke contact and
walked around him to go to the kitchen.

Flanagan stayed with her, but somehow he didn't seem
to be following. Liz opened the fridge and got out a jar of
cranberry juice. Pouring herself a glass, she said. "Okay,
I'll bite. Why did you let him go?"

"Because I think he'll lead us to the animal."

"Look, it was a coincidence that David found Jekyll the
first time. You really don't think it's going to happen again,
do you?"

"Yes, I do. There is some special affinity between
them."

Liz took a sip, gulped, and said, "Satanic?"

"Perhaps."

"So now the hatchlings are from hell, right?" Liz rolled
her eyes.

"There are more things in heaven and earth—"

"Is that what you tell the President and the congressional leadership when you make them toe the line, Reverend?"

"The men you speak of so contemptuously are doing
God's work," Flanagan said.

"Sure they are, by letting you and your flunkies take
away the rights that people died for in the past. That's what
God wants, is it?"

He looked at her with a superior expression on his handsome face, an expression that suggested she was too much of an infidel to understand the complex intricacies that link church and state. Liz wanted to throw her cranberry juice at him. "The President and the congressional leadership are protecting the rights of the majority, seeing that community standards are upheld all over our country. They stand for what Lincoln called our better angels."

"Have you noticed that our country is sliding further and further into decline while you and your political bedfellows watch our better angels dance on the head of a pin?"

"Our economic difficulties are a result of the licentious waste that went before."

"Still blaming it on the liberals? They haven't been in power for nearly twenty years. Good thing for you we don't have free elections anymore."

"We most certainly do have free elections, and the people have made their wishes known."

"Sure, they vote for the candidate they see most often on TV, and his ads are paid for by megacorps, who don't give a damn about anything but profit. I never heard the people say we should have only two classes, and that only one of those classes should have any rights."

"That's a blatant distortion of the facts."

"Not from where I'm sitting, it isn't." Liz's anger welled up inside her. The way they were using David infuriated her. He'd been jerked around like a puppet on a string for the past week, and now they were going to toss him out as a lure for Jekyll.

"Your thinking has been corrupted by your association with misguided authority figures."

"Bullshit." Liz set her jaw. For some reason she thought of Bob Pierce.

"Hot dayum!" Bob shouted as David's jeep pulled in at sunset. "I thought I was gonna be eaten by a dinosaur. At least we'll be devoured together."

"What the hell are you talking about, Perfesser?" David asked, grinning.

"I'm talking about safety in numbers, David." Bob hefted his pistol. "I'm talking about getting the heebie-jeebies while I've been waiting for a carnivorous brute to show his anachronistic face."

"You mean you think Jekyll's in the neighborhood?"

"Jekyll? Is that what you call the damn thing?"

"Yeah. Put that popgun away, Bob. Got any meat or eggs with you?"

"Laura fixed me some hard-boiled eggs before I left this morning." Bob set the .22 down next to the book he'd been reading, on a little folding table, and reclined on his lawn chair once again. "Why, are you hungry?"

"No, but our fine feathered friend will be when he turns up, if he does turn up."

"Growing boy, huh?"

"You won't believe your eyes when you see him scarf down a roast."

"I can't wait." Bob opened his cooler and got out a beer for David.

"What makes you think Jekyll's come up this way?"

"Deputy sheriff said there've been cattle mutilations, and he couldn't identify the animal."

David nodded and popped the beer can's top. "Sounds like it might be our boy, all right."

"Think he might still be hungry, though, even after consuming a few cows?"

"Yeah, he's got the metabolism of a shrew." David parked his buttocks on a rock a few feet from Bob's lawn chair and took a mouthful of beer. "He's even smarter than I thought he'd be, Bob. His intelligence seems to be growing as fast as his body, and that's pretty damn fast, I want to tell you."

"Oh, I see."

David filled Bob in on everything that had happened since they'd last talked.

"Wow" was all that Bob said when David had finished.

"Yeah, it's been pretty damn strange. I don't think Flanagan's going to let this get out."

"Well, we've got to see that it does . . . somehow."

David mulled that over. He didn't quite see how they were going to do that, but he knew that they had to try. "The first thing we need to do is find Jekyll."

"Well, that occurred to me, too, David. And there's nothing I'd like more than to see a living dinosaur, but do you think the little fella's going to be that easy to catch up with?"

"He's not little anymore, Bob. And no, I don't think he's going to be easy to catch up with. But we do have certain advantages."

"Such as?"

"Well, for one thing, we're only two people. I imagine that the troops sent out to beat the bushes are unintentionally warning Jekyll and all the game in the country to get out of sight. We won't be intimidating, and Jekyll already knows one of us."

"Not in the biblical sense, I hope."

"Fun-nee! We better get a move on, if we want to find him before Flanagan's people smarten up and start looking up here in the mountains."

Bob slowly got to his feet. "Where do we start looking?"

"In the woods, I guess." David pointed to a stretch of Douglas firs sloping upward on the other side of the stream near where Bob had pitched his tent.

Bob got his hard-boiled eggs and picked up his pistol. They forded the stream and walked to the forest. A towhee sat on a branch at the edge of the forest and sang until they came too close, then flitted away. As soon as the shadows of the forest enveloped them, Bob said, "I can't decide whether this is more Freudian or Jungian."

"Take your pick." David began to thread his way between the trees. His footsteps crackled as dry underbrush snapped. "Approaching drought conditions, I'd say."

"That's what the weatherman says, too." Bob lifted a branch hanging in his way and walked on, puffing and sweating a bit. "God, I'm so fat I waddle," he said.

David laughed. "Come on, Bob, you're not that far out of shape."

"That's what you say, sonny."

They went on without speaking for a few minutes. The woods grew thicker and Bob's wheezing grew louder. Gnats pestered them, and mosquitoes buzzed.

"Must be some moisture around here," David said. "Mosquitoes never go too far away from water."

"The stream," Bob said, gasping for breath.

"That's pretty far back. Must be a brook or something in the woods around here someplace."

"That's what I'm afraid of." Bob carried the .22, but he seemed none too sure of its firepower. His shirt was stained with sweat now, and it wasn't the heat. In fact, it was a good ten degrees cooler here in the woods, where no sunlight penetrated, than it had been at Bob's campsite.

They trudged on, and the forest floor became softer. Because of the sloping ground, the going was fairly rugged, but David was used to this sort of thing. Bob wasn't, so David had to frequently wait for him to catch up.

Conversations became spare, and their footsteps were almost silent on the humus. At last the forest floor leveled out, and hiking became much easier. David heard the sound of moving water, and he made his way toward it. Bob followed.

A tiny waterfall, barely a trickle in this drought season, dripped down between two boulders and cut into the earth. A few yards away, bobbing his head as he drank, was Jekyll.

David put out his hand to stop Bob, who had not yet seen the dinosaur. Jekyll, however, sensed their presence.

His head popped up. There was a look in his eyes that David had seen before.

"Look out!" Bob shouted.

Jekyll charged.

17

David pushed Bob out of the way, and dived to the ground. He got a mouthful of dirt, and he looked up just in time to see Jekyll's birdlike yellow and blue legs churn like pistons past his face.

"Jesus!" Bob screamed.

David rolled over and scrambled to his knees. He saw Bob, whites of the eyes showing, as the hissing Jekyll bore down on him.

"Shoot!" David shouted.

Bob didn't seem to hear him, but he looked down at the pistol in his hand with an expression of desperation. Without even pointing the gun, he squeezed the trigger.

The gunshot was deafening in the still forest. Bob's hand jerked upward. Jekyll was startled by the sound and halted his charge not five feet from Bob. There was a moment when nobody moved. The forest sounds had entirely ceased. Burnt gunpowder overpowered the pine smell.

"That was just a warning," Bob said, pointing the gun at Jekyll. "Come any closer and I'll shoot."

"He doesn't know what you're saying, Bob," David said, still on his knees.

"I think he does," Bob said, taking a tentative step toward Jekyll while holding the gun up to the dinosaur's snout. Jekyll backed off a little.

"By God, you're right."

"Pick those eggs up," Bob said. He didn't take his eyes off Jekyll as he spoke.

"Where are they?" David asked frantically. But he saw

them before Bob could answer. Four hard-boiled eggs were scattered in the dried humus. David gathered them up, crawling from one to the other. He stood up.

"Jekyll!" he shouted. "Catch!"

The dinosaur cocked his head, hearing David call the familiar name. His left eye was visible, and David didn't like the look in it one bit. He lobbed an egg in the air.

With a swift jerk, Jekyll caught the egg in his jaws. David heard the eggshell crunch as Jekyll chewed it and swallowed, a fleck of egg white remaining on his scaly lip.

David tossed another egg as he moved closer. Again, Jekyll took it down whole. David tossed him another, and when that one was gone, he gave Jekyll the last one, wondering if that would be enough to sate the creature.

"Let's hope that holds him," David said.

"It'll probably hold him at least as long as this popgun of mine," Bob said.

Jekyll did seem calmer, now that he had eaten four eggs. Bob lowered the pistol, though he was still wary. "I'll be goddamned," he said, "it's a living dinosaur. A funny-looking one, but a dinosaur nonetheless."

"Yup, it sure is."

"I never thought I'd see one," Bob said. "But I could reach out and touch this one."

"I'd get a little more protein into him before I did that," David warned him.

"I guess so. What do we do to hold him until we can get some meat?"

"I don't know. I guess we'll just have to hope he sticks around here. I mean, we can't tie him up. Anything might happen to him if we did that—if we *could* do that." David looked at Jekyll respectfully. The dinosaur was now taller than a full-grown man, and probably weighed 350 pounds, maybe even 400. With his dagger teeth and powerful hind limbs, Jekyll was formidable-looking indeed.

"He figured out that it's safer up here in the mountains," David said, brushing the dirt off his jeans.

"How do you know that?"

"Well, food's a lot more plentiful down on the prairie. All that cattle grazing. Jekyll must realize there's a price attached."

"Somebody probably shot at him," Bob said, looking at his pistol. "That would account for his fear of guns."

"I don't see any wounds or signs of injury on him," David said, "but he does seem to know that your gun's dangerous."

"Maybe it's just the noise and the offensive posture," Bob suggested.

"Even that would show a certain degree of awareness that Jaffrey Flanagan would rather deny."

"Pretty damned interesting," Bob said, watching Jekyll groom himself.

"We better go back down the hill and get us some meat for this poor, hungry baby," David said.

"Right."

They started back toward Bob's campsite. As before, Jekyll followed at a discreet distance. It occurred to David that Jekyll might well stay with him while Bob went for some food. After all, Jekyll knew him pretty well by now.

"Why don't you drive down to the nearest store, Bob? I'll stay with our friend here."

"Uh huh." Bob was very quick to agree. "You keep the gun with you, though, okay?"

"Yeah."

Jekyll came closer as they walked through the woods. By the time they came out into the open, he was only a couple of yards behind them. This made Bob a little uncomfortable, but David thought it was a good sign. He trusted them, at least a little bit. The walk back seemed quicker than the walk to the stream where they had found Jekyll. Soon they were coming out of the forest, and Bob's tent was visible a few hundred yards away.

They walked over to Bob's station wagon, and Bob got in without hesitation. "I'll be back as soon as I can," he said, handing the gun through the rolled-down window and starting up the engine. "If he goes for you, let him have it."

"What, and destroy one of the only four living dinosaurs in existence? Bob, have you taken leave of your senses?"

Bob was dead serious as he looked at David. "You're more important to me than the dinosaurs, David. Be careful."

"Sure thing, Bob." David watched the station wagon go down the dirt road. He coughed a little from the dust, and then looked at his companion.

Jekyll stood by the tent, his forelimbs outstretched tentatively, as if he were asking for food. Maybe he wasn't all that hungry yet, but David knew he would be within an hour.

"Old buddy," he said, "this is gonna be a true test of our friendship."

Jekyll made a deep chirping noise in response, which made David laugh. Maybe there was something he could do to entertain the young dinosaur while they were waiting for Bob.

But it seemed that Jekyll had brought his own entertainment. He was bending down, playing with some gleaming objects in the dirt. David couldn't tell what they were, so he moved closer.

"Well I'll be," he said. "Jacks."

But Jekyll was paying no attention to him now that he had the jacks out. David wondered where Jekyll had secreted them. He certainly hadn't noticed anything in either of the clawed hands when Jekyll was eating the eggs.

"You clever devil," David said. "Where did you pick those up?" But when he thought about it, he didn't want to know. What if Jekyll had killed some kid for food, and then taken the jacks as an afterthought?

Jekyll chirped thoughtfully as he arranged the jacks in two rows, and then in a roughly circular position. Was this something more than a momentary amusement? Jekyll had, after all, carried the jacks with him and hadn't dropped them even while attempting to attack Bob. They must have had some special significance for him. But what?

Once again, Jekyll arranged them in rows, and then in a circle, and finally in a couple of other designs that were meaningless to David. Was this some form of communication? Not, it seemed, for David's benefit; Jekyll seemed to have forgotten that he was there. What then? Math?

"I'll bet that's it, huh, buddy?" David watched Jekyll go through the motions again, and after a few more times, began to notice that the patterns varied slightly each time. The rows were one jack shorter or longer each time, the circle was more ovoid, and the other designs mutated as well.

"Geometry?" Or was it some math unknown to the human race? Jekyll was not forthcoming with an answer. Or perhaps he was. Perhaps he was working on something here that would tell David more about him. If knowledge had been implanted in his genes, Jekyll might know things without learning them. It might be a kind of engineered instinct. There was some kind of logical methodology here, no doubt about it, and Jekyll couldn't have learned it in the wild. He hadn't had time to learn it at the compound that surrounded Liz's house.

David stood spellbound, watching Jekyll vary the patterns over and over again. He was worried about Liz, and Charlie, and Ferd, and about the fact that the public had been denied information about a great discovery. Still, all these worries receded as he watched this fascinating display of intelligence in a creature not yet a week old. He wasn't even concerned that Bob would take too much time getting back with the food. He had the feeling that Jekyll's intellectual exercise would occupy them both for quite some time.

"I'd like to see the Reverend Jaffrey Flanagan call you a dumb animal now," David said.

Jekyll paid no attention. Had he stopped growing? Maybe he didn't need quite so much food anymore. Jekyll was now the size of a full-grown dromaeosaurid, slightly larger than a human being, not counting the tail, which served as a counterweight to balance his torso on his massive hind legs. His feathers were growing thicker, but they were the same blue and yellow as his hide. His talons were a darker blue, almost black. His face was dark blue, too, though not as dark as his extremities, and the ridges over his eyes formed a curved boundary on the other side of which was an amber cranium. His jaws, though not as distended as a deinonychus', were lengthy, and his teeth were absolutely terrifying—long, pointed, sharp, and white as pearl. His eyes were large and black, eight balls shifting curiously on either side of his notched nostrils. These, and his nimble fingers, belied his otherwise bestial appearance.

When Bob returned a couple of hours later, he pulled the station wagon up where it had been before he left. He got out, shut the door quietly, and walked over to David.

"What's he doing?" Bob asked.

"Math, I think," David said. "Either that, or something we know nothing about."

"Well, what we *don't* know covers a lot of ground." Bob watched Jekyll warily, but with as much fascination as David. "I got as much meat as I could carry. My Visa will never be the same."

"You've told me yourself how worthless credit cards are," David said as they walked back to Bob's car. "Ruination of the American economy, and all that."

"Tell it to my wife."

"I will, when we see her again."

"I hope we do see her again." Bob unlocked the station wagon's gate and revealed five grocery bags, each brimming with steaks, chops, roasts, eggs, bacon, fish, and hamburger. "Got everything on special," he said.

As they began to pull out the sacks and set them on the ground next to the tent, David heard something that at first made him think of a carnival. It was a loud, distorted voice, amplified electronically. It called his name, and it told him not to move.

"You are surrounded," said the voice through the bull-horn. "Step away from the animal."

"Shit," David said, "I led them right to him."

"I repeat," said the voice on the bullhorn, "step away from the animal."

David looked at Bob. Bob shrugged as though to ask what choice they had. David looked at Jekyll. The dinosaur was alert, cocking his head first one way, then another, as he tried to determine where the sound originated from.

A dozen marines came out of the bushes, carrying M-16s and moving en masse toward Jekyll. A helicopter hove into view overhead, its rotors slicing the air angrily.

Jekyll jerked his head up, took one look at the helicopter, and headed toward the forest. The helicopter banked, moving ahead of Jekyll. It dropped frighteningly close to the ground. David feared that it would crash as vast billows of dust rose from the parched ground. A net dropped out of the bay in its belly.

Jekyll started to bolt, but then he remembered the jacks. He hurriedly scooped them up in his clawed hands. He might have made it if he hadn't stopped for the jacks. The net was on him. He tried to run, but he was caught up. Soldiers encircled the trapped dinosaur, and David recognized Captain Torrance as he stepped forward and gave the signal to troops behind the initial group. These men and women came forward and grabbed lines leading from the net, as Jekyll thrashed about and cried in a keening, frightened trill.

Two marines were standing next to Bob and David, armed but not actually threatening them. There was nothing that could be done to help Jekyll.

"Secure those lines," Torrance commanded his troops. "And see that those men don't go anywhere."

David was outraged, but he was frightened, too. He didn't know how far they would go.

"You bastards," Bob said. "You goddamn, fascist, fucking, holy-rolling bastards."

The soldier standing next to Bob set his jaw, as if he could barely restrain himself from hurting Bob.

"Cool it, Bob," David said. "They mean business."

"So do I, goddammit, so do I."

It was at that moment that the butt of the soldier's M-16 caught Bob in the gut. He doubled over in pain, groaned, and fell on the ground.

"Bob!" David shouted. He went down on his knees to help his friend. He felt a stabbing, stunning pain on the back of his skull. It penetrated his brain and caused everything to go away.

18

David came to with Nurse Jen and Liz looking down at him.

"Welcome back," Liz said, taking his hand.

At first he could hardly feel her touch, but gradually his fingers seemed to come to life. His palm and wrist followed, and the rest of his body seemed to be thawing out at the same time.

"They shouldn't have done—"

"Yes, we know." Nurse Jen handed a clipboard to a stocky doctor who walked airily into the room.

"*You* know better than to play with Jekyll when he's hungry," Liz said. Though her words scolded him, her tone was warm and affectionate.

"Jekyll?" David was confused. And then he realized what was going on. "Did they tell you Jekyll did this?"

The doctor ran a hand through his thinning hair and looked down at David. "Glad to see you're awake," he said. "You got a nasty bump on the head when that animal attacked you, but you're going to be all right."

"It wasn't any animal, and it wasn't Jekyll. It was Captain Torrance and his heavy-handed goons." He tried to sit up, only to feel Jen's gentle but firm fingertips pushing him back into a reclining position. "Where's Bob?" he demanded. "I want to see my friend."

"Now we're going to give you a little something to help you relax," the doctor said.

"No!" David shouted. "You won't get away with this Orwellian shit!" He couldn't hear what the doctor was

136

saying to Nurse Jen, but he thought he heard him say "c.c.'s." They were going to dope him up until he believed that black was white, and he knew it. They intended to blame his injuries on Jekyll, as an excuse to get rid of the dinosaurs.

David tried to struggle, but he just didn't have the strength to resist when two marines were called in to restrain him. Nurse Jen administered the injection as the doctor watched through gimlet eyes. Or so it seemed to David as he spiraled down into unconsciousness once again.

When he began to see and hear things around him again, David slowly came to realize that he was alone with Liz. He tried to speak, but was frustrated to see that he couldn't make any words come out.

"It's all right, David," Liz whispered, stroking his hair where his head was not bandaged. "I believe you."

Her tone was so loving, certain, and supportive that he wanted to cry. It should have been easy, but he simply couldn't summon the stamina required to shed tears. Gradually, though, he regained his strength.

"Jekyll didn't hurt anybody," David said. "Flanagan's just trying to create a situation so he can get rid of the dinosaurs."

"Well, he's too late. Something's happened."

David couldn't tell if Liz was pleased or frightened. Whatever it was that had happened was confusing her. "What?"

"I don't know, but it's big. Special envoys from the White House, Congress—even the UN. Everybody and his uncle has arrived here for some reason."

"The UN? Then they've let the story out?"

"I don't know. It looks as if they might have just moved from covert national to covert international, if you see what I mean."

"Yeah." David felt his spirits sag, knowing that the UN was no more trustworthy than the current administration in Washington, now that it had gained real power in recent years. "I see what you mean."

"I think the best we can hope for is some idealistic soul from Botswana opening his mouth to the media and starting a stampede to get the story."

"It might happen."

A man entered the room. He was dressed in an expensive, tailored Italian suit and wore a gold Rolex on his wrist.

"Ah, I see you're awake."

David thought he recognized the guy from somewhere, but he didn't quite remember where for a moment. He was still groggy. Then it hit him. "White House Chief of Staff Margolis," he said.

"Oh, you remember me," Margolis said, smiling pleasantly. "A lot of people don't."

"Some of us still read the papers," David said. "Is the president here?"

"No, I'm afraid he's too busy with the ozone problem, so I came in his place."

"Busy with the ozone problem," Liz said. "I thought he was still denying that there *is* an ozone problem."

"That's probably what he means, hon," David said, warming to the tone of confrontation. "Thinking up new ways to deny that there is a problem can be a full-time job."

"I can see that you're recovering quite nicely, Mr. Albee," Margolis said. "In fact, you sound as though you're ready for a good fight."

"Always," David said, forcing a grin, "if it's for the right cause."

"Well, all causes, both right and left, just might have to be put on hold for a while, considering what's happened."

David was surprised to hear a politician express such a sentiment. He was suspicious as he asked, "What makes you say that?"

Margolis emitted a deep, weary sigh. "We've received word of an impending visitation."

"Celestial?" David said, hoping that his sarcasm would dislodge the cork from Margolis's rectum.

"Yes, as a matter of fact." He looked at David with new respect. "How did you know?"

"I *don't*. Why don't you fill me in?"

Margolis nodded. "It seems that a signal was sent from the stasis box when it was opened."

"A signal?" David sat up straight and leaned forward, unmindful of the pain in his head. "What kind of signal are you talking about?"

"Whoever left the box here on Earth has, uh . . . gotten in touch with us."

"Our representative will be with you in a few days," Ted Koppel said. "He's on his way to earth from the asteroid belt, where he's been in stasis for several million years. And now this." A detergent commercial played, but the jingle was about the happy union of Earth and alien representative—vague but reassuring, in the classic TV commercial mode.

Liz thought it was pretty funny, the way the aliens had sent a broadcast using the image of Ted Koppel. She supposed they had reasoned that Ted was the planet's most revered figure, since he was displayed so frequently on the terrestrial media, so they had made him their spokesman. Of course, it wasn't really Ted Koppel (at least she didn't think so), but a tricked-up duplicate made of old broadcasts that had been picked up by the alien spacecraft's monitors in the asteroid belt.

The astrophysicists, exobiologists, and astronomers watching the videotape with her and David, who sat next to her on the sofa, were wildly enthusiastic. They speculated endlessly on why the aliens had left their representative in the asteroid belt, and not closer to earth; why they had chosen such a bizarre method of communication; why they had tampered with the dinosaurs' genes in the first place. It was a lively discussion, and wine was served with it, but it didn't solve anything. It wasn't intended to, of course. It was just a lot of fine minds letting off steam before the big event.

David was grinning like a chimpanzee. She hadn't seen him look so happy since that time he claimed to have given her a vaginal orgasm two years ago. She had maintained that it was really a matter of clitoral stimulation, but they *were* having intercourse while it happened, so she wasn't so sure he was wrong now. If she was, it was the only vaginal orgasm she'd ever had. But why was she thinking of that now?

"You say that the dinosaur seemed to be devising some sort of mathematical equation with the jacks," said Dr. Shankaricharia, the noted astrophysicist.

"Well, I don't know," David admitted. "It seemed as if it might be math. Maybe geometry."

"Perhaps the stasis ship was left in the asteroid belt because it's safer there during the periodic comet storms the solar system moves through every few million years," said Dr. Dorleac, astronomer.

"It's possible that the minerals available in the belt are needed for the alien vessel to maintain itself," Dr. Douglas, famed Scottish geologist, put in.

"The results of the dissection of the infant dinosaur were quite interesting," said exobiologist Franken to Liz in an entirely different conversation, "showing a remarkably sophisticated central nervous system, every bit the equal of a human being's."

It was so wonderful to hear this. The government had commandeered the Ramada Inn off Interstate 90 in Billings for the purpose of putting up all these scientists. The cat was out of the bag now, and there was nothing Jaffrey Flanagan could do about it. They had won.

"Dr. Tomlinson," said Franken.

"Liz," she said.

"Liz." He looked at her earnestly. "You observed the

young dinosaurs close at hand. Do you feel that they have
the abilities that David has described to us?''

"Oh, yes, and even if I didn't, I'd know that they had
extraordinary intelligence from what David observed.''

"Oh, I see." Doctor Franken raised his eyebrows and
looked from Liz to David.

The discussion went on, lively as ever. They were waiting for another broadcast, this one promised by Ted Koppel in his kicker to reveal a great deal more. It was due to
go on in just a minute or two. The videotape had been
rewound, and a commercial station was playing on the
television screen when the appointed time came.

Eight minutes into a rerun of "Married with Children,"
the alien broadcast blinked on the screen. This time it
wasn't Ted Koppel. It was Elmer Fudd, complete with
speech impediment and insipid cackle.

"I know you're wooking faw some expwanation," Elmer said. "But aw I'm going to give you is wanding co-
awdinates."

"They're coming!" Franken said. "They're going to
land on Earth."

"My God," Liz said. "They *are,* aren't they?"

David put his arms around her and hugged her. "This
is the most amazing thing I've ever seen in my life."

Liz could hardly bring herself to believe that this wasn't
a hoax. Looney Tunes and ABC collaborating on a gigan-
tic April Fool's Day gag. But it wasn't April, and the image of Elmer Fudd went on in his cartoon voice talking
about signals and stasis fields, and experimental dinosaur
blastoderms, and she knew that it was real.

"What the hell are the folks in Billings making of this?"
David asked no one in particular.

Nobody was listening to him, however. They were busy
scribbling down the latitude and longitude "suppwied" by
the alien Elmer Fudd.

"Well, as an old fwiend of mine always wemawks,"
Elmer said, his bald pate outlined in a generous curve,
"that's all, folks."

And he was gone.

The sitcom came back on the air, and except for the nattering of the insufferable family on the tube, the suite was silent. Dorleac removed a cigarette from a pack in his jacket pocket and lit up. He took a deep drag and exhaled slowly, still staring at the TV screen. "That was certainly well worth waiting for," he breathed.

Liz wasn't sure if the French astronomer meant the cigarette or the announcement; if it was the latter, she concurred wholeheartedly. As soon as he had spoken, the room burst into excited conversation, as though everyone had collectively been holding their breath up to then.

But Liz didn't hear what anybody was saying. One thought overpowered everything else, even sensory input—*They were coming*.

"I haven't seen Burles around," David said, peeking through the window at the confusion in Liz's backyard. "Not that I'm displeased about it."

"Look again," Liz said. "There's somebody else you don't see, isn't there?"

David stood away from the window, looked deeply into her eyes, and smiled. He was so charming when he was like this, she thought, like a twelve-year-old boy. "You mean good ole Jaffrey Flanagan?" he asked.

"The very same."

"I guess the old system of government still has some teeth," David said.

"What makes you think so?"

"Well, the President must have yanked him out of here. Or maybe it was a congressional order, or . . ."

"Or maybe he's just decided to take to the airwaves," Liz suggested, "to combat this latest demonic development."

"Possibly." The smile relaxed on David's face, and he began to look worried. "He might be able to do a lot of damage."

"Even in the face of this?" Liz poured herself a cup of coffee. "I don't think so."

"Really? Why not?"

"It's too overwhelming. I think this is going to break his power once and for all."

"Don't count on it."

"Look, he's been riding a wave that's crested. He's going to land nose first in the sand if he stays on it, David. There is now irrefutable proof that intelligent creatures were on Earth before humans, and that they were *created* by aliens tens of millions of years ago. And those aliens are coming to pay *us* a little visit. And I mean *all of us,* even Jaffrey Flanagan and his admirers."

"People believe what they want."

"Can I quote you on that?" Liz asked, deadpan.

"You might want to take credit for that comment yourself, a little later on," David said.

Liz thought about it. "I hope you're wrong, but I really can't say that I'm sure you are."

David squeezed her hand. He didn't want her to turn into a pessimist, but recent events had her well on the way to becoming the most cynical woman he had ever known. He was suddenly taken with a deep, abiding affection for her that felt almost like physical pain.

"I love you," he said.

Liz moved her fingers, gently entwining them with David's. "I know that, David."

He wanted her to say she loved him, too, but she didn't. There was too much grief in their past, he knew. Even with all that had happened in recent days, she wasn't ready to take him back. Even sex hadn't been enough to make the difference, though it had been fantastic. He felt like crying, but he didn't want to do it in front of her.

"Well, when's everybody heading off to the landing site?" he asked. It was better to change the subject than to push Liz into saying something she didn't want to say.

"Thursday."

"Think we'll get to go?"

"Hope so."

"Yeah." David withdrew his hand from hers and picked up his coffee mug. The hot coffee burnt his lips and tongue, but he swallowed it. At least it took his mind off the dead pain in his guts. He felt very bummed out, and really didn't want to talk anymore.

"Oh, David," Liz said, "I don't want to hurt you. I just can't go through that again."

"I guess not." He couldn't talk to her anymore, because he felt that he couldn't quite trust her now. It was irrational, but that was the way he reacted to rejection. He always had, and he didn't think he could change now.

"Don't do this, David. If we're going to maintain any kind of relationship, we have to talk."

He turned and looked at her. "If you want to talk, go ahead. I'm listening."

"Goddammit, David. We *both* have to talk, not just one of us. You know that you can't just clam up on me like that."

"Flat affect, I believe it's called," David said. This was a reference to her efforts to get him to see a therapist with her. David had resented this, and the issue had grown into quite a bone of contention between them while David's drinking had been at its worst. "I believe that's the mode you used to accuse me of assuming when I wanted to be uncommunicative."

"All right, maybe I shouldn't have thrown that term in your face." She held out her hands in a gesture of submission. "But that doesn't mean you should have refused to see Anne."

"Ah, yes, the beloved Anne. Saver of souls."

"She's helped me a lot," Liz said angrily. "And she could have helped you. Maybe we could have stayed together if you'd agreed to see her."

"Yeah, she would have just waved her magic wand, and all our troubles would have been over. Glory, glory, psychotherapy, glory, glory, sexuality . . ." This last was sung to the tune of "The Battle Hymn of the Republic."

Liz winced and put her hands over her ears in what David perceived as an overly dramatic posture. And then he thought how strange it was that they were fighting like this again. They were on the verge of witnessing perhaps the greatest event in the history of the human race—contact with aliens, for Christ's sake—and here they were acting like poor cousins of John Updike characters.

"I'm sorry," he said. "I guess I've been laboring under a few delusions."

"Haven't we both?" Liz said in a conciliatory tone. "But this is no time for us to be fighting. We should be celebrating."

"Yeah, you're right. Or maybe I should say, I don't know what we should be doing. These are probably the last few days of an era. Thursday will change everything, so maybe we're just clinging to our old behavior, no matter how destructive, for fear of what's going to happen in the future."

"I don't know if the future can be much worse than the present."

"Nobody does, and we're frightened. But I think we're also filled with hope."

Liz managed to smile a little. "It's funny, David, but if you'd asked me a week ago if I wanted this to happen, I would have said yes, more than anything. Now I'm not so sure."

"Me, neither," he said. He reached out and hugged her. "I'm not sure of anything anymore."

19 ———

"It's a wave of mass hysteria," Anne Diltz said. "How else can you account for it?"

"Well, there's plenty of reason for hysteria, mass or otherwise," David replied, leaning forward in the stuffed armchair, not to stress what he was saying, but to look out at the pine trees, "wouldn't you agree?"

Anne remembered the day last week when she'd seen the monster outside with Jill. She could have thought she was suffering a hallucination that day, but she had treated it as if it were really happening. She supposed that those who hadn't discounted the television broadcasts as fakes were going through the same thing now. "This situation requires a reorientation of reality," she said. "But then, we're always reorienting ourselves to reality."

She could see that she was losing David, and so she said, "But you didn't come here to discuss current events, did you, David?"

He looked at her in surprise. "No, I didn't," he said. "I came here to save my relationship with Liz."

Anne nodded. He didn't beat around the bush, she thought. He's going to be difficult. "There are two people involved in that equation."

"I know," he said. "I wouldn't be here otherwise. Liz just won't consider getting back together unless I see you. So here I am."

"Do you want to tell me a little bit about yourself?" Anne asked.

"Sure. I'm thirty-three years old. I'm the son of an alcoholic father, I've never got along with my mother, and I can't finish anything I start. The only thing I'm interested in most of the time is dinosaurs . . . and Liz."

"Is your father living?"

"Nope, but my dinosaurs are."

Anne forced a small, tight smile, to show him that his attempt at a joke had not put her off. "Do you feel guilty about your parents?"

His brow furrowed as he thought that one over. "Of course I do," he said.

"Do you feel powerless?"

He brightened, which surprised her. "I often do feel powerless—about the way the world is, as well as my own life—but now I've been instrumental in the downfall of a very powerful man. Me, just an ordinary, beer-swilling, working stiff, against Jaffrey Flanagan. And I won. It made me click my heels for a couple days, and then I started to feel bad about what had happened to the guy. I mean, he hasn't lost his appointment or anything. He's still Secretary of Morality and all, but his power is broken, on the executive branch level, at least. I'm pretty sure. What the hell is he gonna do now?"

Anne said nothing. This was very interesting, the son of an alcoholic who took the burdens of the world on his shoulders and even felt compassion for his enemies after they were beaten. Messianic.

"I mean," David went on, "I think Jaffrey Flanagan's still dangerous. I don't know what he'll do, but he'll do *something* to reassert his power. That's just the way he is."

"Yes, but let's talk about you a little more, shall we?" Anne suggested.

"I guess that's why I'm here."

"You sound as if you'd rather be somewhere else," Anne said.

"I would. But I'll be going there tomorrow, so I might as well be here today."

"Where are you going?"

"To see the alien ship come down. I've been invited to come, since I supposedly know at least one of the dinosaurs better than anybody else on Earth."

"And what are your feelings about this?"

"I can't sort them out. I'm deliriously happy on the one hand, and incredibly worried on the other. It's like the culmination of everything I've believed in ever since I was a kid, and that makes me happy. But it's also really frightening. What if it turns out badly? Then what? I might be as shattered as Jaffrey Flanagan, as burned-out as my own old man."

Anne made a mental note that he had spoken of Jaffrey Flanagan and his father in the same breath.

"I don't mean that I think they'll come here to enslave us, or anything like that. That's just pulp nonsense. But we don't really have any idea of why they are coming to Earth, do we?"

Anne said nothing. It was best to let him go on talking, now that he seemed willing.

"Whatever their reasons," David concluded, "I hope they don't judge us too harshly."

Amen to that, Anne thought, but she remained silent. She no longer had a clear idea of what she was doing. Her waking thoughts were beset by daydreams, strange thoughts of the creature in her yard playing with jacks, and spaceships landing on the Montana plains.

"I don't think they can judge us any more harshly than we judge ourselves," she found herself saying.

David Albee eyed her curiously, and then lowered his head. To Anne, he looked as if he were praying.

The drive to the landing site was pleasant. Bob, David, and Liz went in one car, Ferd and Charlie in another. Both cars were supplied by the federal government. Credit cards for gas were supplied, too. David was amused when one grizzled filling station attendant grudgingly accepted the card, grumbling that the "damn gummint never pays its bills."

The drive wasn't a very long one. It took them northeast along the interstate to Miles City, and from there a narrow two-lane blacktop heading due east, where the plains flattened the land into an easily negotiated topography. When they pulled onto Route 12, David honked, while Bob and Liz cheered. Ferd and Charlie honked behind them, and then pulled up in the passing lane alongside their car, Charlie rocking back and forth against the steering wheel, while Ferd mugged out of the passenger-side window. Four hours after they left Billings, they turned off the main road, and were soon on a dirt road passing through an arid landscape of brown prairie grass brightened by the occasional green spruce or fir stand.

They passed a lot of cars traveling west, with disgruntled-looking people riding in them. They soon found out why. A long line of cars, all of them being turned away, was stalled at a military checkpoint. Fortunately, David and his friends had been given passes back in Billings that got them through with no trouble at all.

"Just follow this road three miles, and you'll see everybody down there," the marine sergeant in charge said.

The barricade was lifted, and they started the last leg of the journey. David glanced back in the rearview mirror, half-convinced that the marines would come and arrest them, after all that had happened in the past few days.

"Maybe they're zomboid servants of the aliens," he said, "and we're being led into an abattoir."

"Like on the old 'Twilight Zone' episode," Liz said.

"Adapted from the Damon Knight story," Bob said, and then commenced to explain how the original story had been meatier and funnier than the TV adaptation.

"Bob, how did you ever find time to watch television, read science fiction, and fight evil right-wingers all at the same time back in the fifties and sixties?"

"Superhuman strength and nerves of steel," Bob said, smiling slyly. "I used to read a lot of science fiction. Back in those days, it was one of the few media offering any kind of social criticism. It was never quite like this, though.''

They followed Charlie and Ferd down a road that led to an open area extending many miles in every direction. From here it seemed as if you could see to the ends of the Earth. They immediately saw what the marine had been talking about back at the checkpoint.

Trucks, trailers, helicopters, people in civvies and in uniform, swarmed about the prairie. David pulled up near where most of the cars were parked, and the three of them got out. Ferd and Charlie joined them a moment later.

"Where's François Truffaut?" Ferd asked.

"He's dead," Charlie answered for him.

"That's what I thought happened to you guys," David said. "I'm glad they put you to work in the lab, though."

"You thought they killed us?" Charlie said.

"I don't know. They got pretty brutal with Bob and me."

Bob, reaching into the government car's backseat, produced a ten-gallon hat, to the laughter of all four, and to the appreciative smile of a passing technician who was laying cables for television cameras.

"They said Jekyll would be here," David said, "flown over this morning. I wonder how he liked that."

There were thousands of people gathered on the sand, and David and his friends walked among them, looking for familiar faces.

"Nary a C.M. in the entire bunch," Bob observed. "Looks like there's been a *coup de palais*."

"The White House couldn't very well let this happen without appearing to be in control," David said. "Not after the aliens have broadcast all over the planet."

"What will they be like?" Liz asked.

"Huh?"

"The aliens. What do you think they'll be like?"

"Giant slugs," Ferd said.

"Crawling brains," Charlie offered.

"Benign, I hope," Bob said.

"Helpful, I hope," said David.

Liz smiled at him when he said that. "We could use some help, couldn't we?"

Bob said, "Couple of acid rock bands, and this could be Woodstock."

It did look like some immense festival was being prepared for. Carpenters were hammering together a pavilion or stage, from which dignitaries would observe the proceedings—congressmen, senators, the governor, Margolis and other spokesmen from the administration—and perhaps offer a few self-serving comments on the wonder of it all, and why the aliens chose the great state of Montana and the greatest nation on earth, the United States of America, for their landing. Of course, the truth was that they were going to land here because a metal box had been left behind by one of their own sixty-five million years ago—it could as easily have happened in Mongolia—but David was fairly confident that that fact would be given short shrift by the politicians when the spacecraft landed tomorrow.

A red, white, and blue tent offered liquid refreshments and shelter from the hot prairie wind. Fortunately, they were nonalcoholic. David chose a Diet Coke, Liz a passionfruit drink. Bob had an iced tea; Ferd, an Orange Crush; and Charlie, an RC Cola. It was hot, the August sun beating down on the prairie mercilessly.

"Think they'll have fireworks?" David asked.

"This is a pretty upscale group," Bob said. "I guess they just invited us so we wouldn't be tempted to publicly defame the administration."

"After the nice way they've treated us?" Liz said. "Why would we want to do a thing like that?"

"You know how those troublemakers are," Bob said. "But let 'em rub elbows with the big shots, the great, the near great, and the would-be great, and they'll forget the whole thing."

"Sure they will."

Ferd and Charlie had soon wandered off with two young

women, the type who lick envelopes for political campaigns, David thought. Bob continued to wax ironic on the growing spectacle around them, and Liz just kept walking and drinking her fruit juice. That was good enough for David. He was happy about the way things had turned out so far. If the end of the world was coming, then so be it. He'd take these few moments while they lasted. But he didn't really think anything bad was going to happen, not today.

"They picked a good place to land," Bob said, pointing off toward the east, "about the flattest place on the continent."

"Yeah, they've got a good long, flat surface for a landing," David said. "When they came out of stasis, they must have taken a look and decided this was a good spot to come down on. Only a couple hundred miles away from where the eggs were left, which probably doesn't seem like it's all that far if you're looking at it from the asteroid belt."

"Probably not," Bob said.

As the afternoon wore on, and the intense heat tired them out, they began to discuss sleeping arrangements for the night.

"Maybe we'll have to go find a motel," Bob said. "I'm getting too old to sleep in the car."

"I don't think there'll be any rooms," Liz said. "Remember all those cars we saw coming in here?"

"Well . . ."

But after asking a few people, they discovered that tents were being set up with cots in them, so that everybody could spend the night.

"For once the government thought of everything," David said. "Even communal sleeping arrangements. Woodstock for conservatives."

David and Liz slept on cots beside each other. David could hear Bob's distinctive snoring coming from a few cots away. He and Liz were near the front flap of the enormous tent, and every now and then David would awaken and look up at the stars. They were remarkably clear tonight. They seemed closer than he had ever seen them. It was ridiculous, of course, but they seemed to burn his eyes. He felt a tear falling down the right side of his face.

He had everything now: his freedom, his friends, the promise of a new beginning for Earth . . . maybe even Liz. So why was he lying here crying?

Because at eight o'clock in the morning, the world he knew would change irrevocably. That was why. It might be a better place after tomorrow, or it might be worse, but it would not be the same.

And that was something worth shedding a tear for.

In the morning free coffee and croissants were served. David had a cup of coffee, but didn't eat anything. He was too excited. He'd slept very little, but he didn't feel tired. Bob seemed exhilarated, and Liz was hard to read. She didn't seem to be any different than she ever was. Maybe that was why they always fought; she had this immutable core of strength, and he was all over the place.

They ran into Sosnowski, who beamed at them. "Lovely day, isn't it?" he asked in his heavy Polish accent.

"Actually, it's almost a hundred degrees already," Liz said, "and it's only seven forty-five."

Sosnowski, ordinarily quite a serious fellow, threw back his head and laughed. David looked at his watch and saw that Liz was right. They aliens would be here in fifteen minutes.

It seemed like hours as they positioned themselves in the murmuring crowd. There were thousands of people, and it was all pretty hard to take in the heat.

"You know," Bob said, "we'll probably see more if we go back up the road a little way."

"We might see more," David said, "but we wouldn't be with the people, and I think it's important that we *are* with them when the ship comes down."

"I agree with David."

Bob looked at both of them, bemused. "This is even more like Woodstock than I thought. I'm too old to be jostled by these yahoos any longer. I'll see you after it comes down."

David nodded. He understood that Bob wanted to be alone with his thoughts when "the Big Event"—as people were calling it—happened. That was understandable enough. All of them were dealing with this in their own way. Still, he was a little saddened that Bob would not be with them when the ship arrived.

Bob pushed his way back out of the mob, which must have numbered a hundred thousand by now. David and Liz watched as two helicopters swept over the open area to the east and then banked and flew out of sight. David checked his watch: 7:52. Eight minutes to go.

"I hope they're not late," he said.

Liz smiled, but even she looked a little tense now. The crowd was astonishingly quiet for such a huge number of people. They were all feeling the same thing, in a way, but in another way they were all alone in their private worlds, imagining what was about to descend into their lives, into the lives of their children, into the life of their world.

It was 7:55. David watched the second hand sweep around his watch . . . 7:56. The seconds seemed to pass more and more slowly, but at last it was 7:57.

He put his arm around Liz. "I love you," he said.

She put her head on his shoulder. Another twenty-six seconds had passed. The second hand made its agonizingly slow sweep to the top. Two minutes left.

David felt the sweat trickle down his face, and the tears began to well up again. He squeezed Liz tight as it became 7:59.

Now it was so quiet, David could hear the wind blow, even though tens of thousands of people were gathered on the plain around him and Liz. They waited and waited, but nothing happened. David glanced at his watch again. There were still twelve seconds to go.

He'd watched the ball go up on New Year's Eve in Times Square more than once on TV, and these last few moments reminded him of it. The crowd here was surely counting down the seconds to themselves, just as he was. This was the biggest thing that had ever happened, and while the rest of the world would see it on TV, these people were eyewitnesses. *He* was an eyewitness.

A ripple spread through the crowd. It was time, give or take a few seconds. Surely no more than a minute or two could differ on the various watches and the clocks set up in the observation area. He looked at one of the clocks now. It was a minute past the hour.

People began to make exasperated noises. The big clock continued to run. It was two minutes past the hour. Three minutes past.

Where the hell were they? David had never felt so frustrated in his entire life. He'd never had much patience with people who were late, but this . . .

"Three minutes late," he said to Liz.

"Four," she said. "But give 'em a break. They've come forty or fifty million miles."

"Shouldn't radar have picked them up, if they were inside the Earth's atmosphere?" said David. "Seems like they'd announce it on that elaborate PA system they've set up, or something."

He wasn't the only one grumbling. All sorts of people were bitching. And then the speakers crackled into life, and a voice boomed: "Here it comes!"

20

It came so fast that it took their breath away. They were in its shadow almost before the announcement had been spoken. It was immense, but it moved with ineffable grace. It fell so swiftly that the crowd moved back, like a one-celled animal stung by electricity. The vast alien spacecraft dropped down within fifty feet of the ground like a lead weight, and then finished its descent in utter silence, light as a feather, settling on the desert floor without kicking up so much as a single dust devil.

The crowd gasped.

"How is that possible?" David heard himself ask. Everything he knew seemed to contradict what he was seeing. This was impossible.

Now that the alien craft was on the ground, however, it was a little disappointing. It was oddly shaped, and, in spite of its great size, looked a little dumpy. It was pitted and scarred, and seemed blackened in large patches. David supposed that a lot had happened to it in sixty-five million years, even if it was just hiding out in the asteroid belt the entire time.

From somewhere in the crowd, David heard the tinny sound of Elvis Presley singing "Don't Be Cruel" through a cheap speaker. It shut off abruptly. In the ensuing silence, everyone waited to see what the aliens would do next. Time passed, and nothing happened.

"We welcome you in the name of the United States of America," a voice bellowed through the PA.

The aliens didn't answer. Maybe they weren't quite

ready to show themselves, David thought. Or maybe they
hadn't expected a crowd. After all, what did they know
about human behavior, besides what they'd seen on TV?
Humans hadn't even been thought of when they last were
on Earth.

"Not very friendly, are they?" Liz said. But she seemed
amused rather than upset.

"Would you be, if you saw this crowd?"

She actually laughed out loud at that, prompting several
people near them to glance at her in bemusement.

"Nations," the dignitary persisted, "have sent representatives and greetings from every part of our world."

"Do you think he'll vary from his prepared speech?"
David said.

"Probably not. Probably thinks the alien rep really *is*
Ted Koppel."

There was, in fact, an impressive array of the world's
foremost media celebrities, and not only newspeople.
There were movie stars, TV stars, sports heroes, and of
course, many politicians from both parties. Conspicuous
by his absence was the Secretary of Morality. David wondered if this was an unwilling absence, or was Flanagan
protesting this display of international enthusiasm, reject-
ing Earth's first contact with aliens?

An orchestra started playing "America the Beautiful"
on the bandstand. At least, David thought, it wasn't playing "The Star-Spangled Banner," a tune he had never
liked. The patriotic music blared brassily across the wind-
swept prairie.

The music had no discernible effect on the inhabitants
of the spacecraft, however. David and Liz maneuvered so
that they could get a better look at the bandstand. They
saw Margolis among the other politicians, and a lot of
other familiar faces, including Drs. Shankaricharia and
Dorleac, the governor of Montana, both of Montana's senators, and a passel of other congressmen. They were all
struggling manfully to retain their composure, but the heat

and tension were getting to them. The aliens were simply not cooperating.

"They thought it would be like an Asian or African diplomat visiting, I guess," David said. "A little different in customs, maybe, but aware of terrestrial protocol."

More time passed. The alien spaceship sat there like an enormous toadstool. By noon, a few people began to leave. Some of the VIPs followed suit, and were driven away in limousines. The temperature was now well over a hundred degrees. There was very little movement in the crowd, but every time somebody jostled David, he was more irritated than he should have been.

"Maybe they're hoping everybody will leave, and forget the dinosaurs," Liz said.

"Oh, I see," David said. "Then, when there's nobody around to bug them, they can take a look at Jekyll and company in peace."

"Right."

But it looked as if they were going to have quite a wait if that's what they were waiting for. The afternoon wore on. Refreshments began to get low. The Big Event had not been expected to go on for so long, and over half of the spectators had stayed, determined to see the aliens when they first emerged from their spacecraft.

Ferd and Charlie re-joined them about two-fifteen.

"What happened to the girls?" Liz asked.

"They had to go back," Charlie said, "but they gave us their dorm phone number."

"Coeds, huh? How did they get into this show?" David asked.

"Influential parents," Ferd said.

"The Goldwater girls?"

"Not quite." Charlie shrugged.

"So when are these swingin', bug-eyed monsters gonna show their antennae?" Ferd said.

Nobody knew the answer to that, of course. All they could do was wait. The four of them found some crates to sit on as the crowd thinned out to perhaps a tenth of its original size. Even the TV technicians were reduced to skeleton crews. Ferd managed to cadge a few lukewarm sodas for them, and Bob showed up around three. There wasn't much to say, so David stared at the spacecraft, a monstrous anomaly on the flat, brown prairie.

The longer he looked at it, however, the less bloated and bizarre it looked to him. Its odd curves possessed a kind of asymmetrical beauty, if you thought about it. The waning light caught it in an interesting way, too, making it look like some landlocked behemoth. It was miles in diameter, and even more miles in length. It was awesome.

At sunset a dark crisscross shape opened in the side of the alien ship. It happened so quickly and unexpectedly that for a few seconds David wasn't sure of what he was seeing. Then he realized that it was a doorway.

"There is a hatch of some kind opening in the side of the spacecraft!" the announcer said excitedly over the PA. "I repeat, a hatch is opening in the side of the alien space-craft!"

And then the alien emerged.

We should have known, David told himself. It makes sense. It makes perfect sense.

The alien was reptilian. Or perhaps saurian. It was a more mature version of Jekyll, Marie, Franny, and Zooey. At least that was what it looked like from a distance. Its fingers didn't seem to have long claws like the young dinosaurs', and its head, if anything, was even larger, but these details seemed insignificant. This creature was not humanoid in any way.

It stood in the hatch, dwarfed by the immensity of its own spacecraft. The sunset cast a pale orange hue over the plain, the crowd, the spacecraft, and its occupant.

"Is that Jekyll's papa?" Liz asked. "He sure looks like our babies."

"Doesn't he just, though?" Bob said.

David squinted. "That entrance isn't actually open," he said.

"Not open?" Charlie said. "What do you mean, Dave?"

"Something seems to be distorting the figure behind it, almost as if you were seeing the alien through water."

"A force field," Bob said, his voice filled with wonder and excitement. "It's protected by a force field."

"Maybe so, Bob," David said. "Maybe so."

"Jeez, I bet Fine and Sosnowski are creaming their jeans over this," said Ferd.

The shimmering surface covering the alien bulged, and then swelled outward. It dislodged from the side of the spacecraft as if it were a bubble blown by a child. It drifted purposefully toward the bandstand, floating three or four yards above the ground.

"Antigravity!" Bob said. "This is one hell of a well-equipped alien!"

The alien in its clear bubble hovered over the bandstand, and several dignitaries leaped off to the ground and ran away. Marine guards stood by, but their commander shouted at them not to draw their weapons.

"This is too much!" David found himself shouting. He felt giddy from watching the bubble, which now swooped and soared over the crowd. Was it testing them in some way, trying to see what would happen if it did something intimidating? Or was it looking for something?

"Man, this guy is inspecting the fruits and vegetables," Charlie said.

The bubble approached. David noticed, almost peripherally, that everyone had backed away except him and his friends. They formed a little knot a quarter mile from the stage.

The bubble slowed and came to rest above them, hovering in perfect stillness even as the wind buffeted them.

"Astounding tales of super-science!" Bob shouted gleefully. The hooded reptilian eyes glanced down at him. The bubble began to drift again. Only a few hundred stragglers were left now, as well as most of those seated on the bandstand. Car engines roared as people tried to drive back up the road. A traffic jam was inevitable, as dusk soaked the prairie with shadow.

"Look at 'em go!" Ferd shrieked with laughter.

The scene did have a frenetic Mack Sennett quality to it. David saw that Liz and Bob were laughing as hard as Charlie and Ferd. The military, clearly under orders not to harm the unruly alien visitor, were trying unsuccessfully to keep order. Great clouds of dust floated over the sand.

The bubble continued to bob about wherever it pleased the alien to go. It paused over the generators for a little while, followed the cables to the TV cameras and to the stage, and once again intimidated those who still sat there.

"He's just checkin' everything out," Charlie said, "just as cool as you please."

Now the bubble was suspended in the air above some serviceberry bushes. The alien seemed as intent on these as on the humans, which might have relieved some of those in attendance. The camera crew was still shooting, setting up ten-kilowatt lights to illuminate the bubble as darkness descended.

"Okay, switch 'er on," the TV director said.

Unfortunately for him, the bubble was highly reflective. The alien became virtually invisible as brilliant light played over its globular surface. The bubble began to move back toward the spacecraft, not all at once, but sort of dodging and weaving in that general direction. When it was within a few yards of the spacecraft, it seemed to be sucked back into the opening. The reptilian alien looked out at them for a moment, and then vanished. The crisscross pattern formed again, shimmered briefly, and then the opening swiftly closed.

A little while passed before the last of the car horns stopped honking. The orchestra started up a shaky rendition of "Venus, Bringer of Peace," from Holst's *The Planets*.

"Post-Spielberg," Bob said. "Forty years ago it would have been 'Mars, Bringer of War,' but those were the days of alien invasions and big bugs tromping on cities. Now they're going to save us from ourselves."

"Well, you have to admit that was a pretty amazing show," David said.

"And yet it didn't seem calculated to impress us," Liz said. "It was sort of taking a drive through a wildlife preserve, I suspect."

"And we're the wildlife." Charlie looked glum.

"We have been known to get pretty wild," Ferd said. "Not so rowdy and contentious as frat boys, maybe, but we can swing with the best of 'em, given half a chance."

David was pleased to see that his friends were still themselves after this cosmic encounter. Had he really expected anything different? Maybe he'd been just as taken in by the popular UFO mythos as anyone else. Jaffrey Flanagan couldn't win if the religion of the millennium was aliens and spaceships instead of Jesus and the angels. On the other hand, giant lizards floating around in bubbles might cause a resurgence of that old-time religion, at that.

"Please clear the area," an authoritative voice bellowed over the PA. "All unauthorized personnel must leave the area at once."

There were guards with flashlights directing traffic, trying to get everybody on the road with a minimum of fuss. David and his friends started toward their cars.

As they walked through the flattened prairie grass, inhaling the exhaust of hundreds of internal combustion engines, a marine officer approached them.

"Oh, shit," said Bob.

David concurred with Bob's less than enthusiastic reaction. He remembered all too clearly the fun time they'd had with Captain Torrance, and didn't care to have something like that ruin his day again. He took Liz by the hand and started to walk more swiftly toward the car.

"Mr. Albee," the marine said.

"The jig is up." David stopped walking. He turned to face the marine officer.

"Mr. Albee," the uniformed officer said in a stern tone, "I'm going to have to ask you to come with me."

21

"So what have I done, Captain?" David asked as politely as he could.

"Major," the marine officer said. "Major Tom O'Donnell."

"Sorry, Major O'Donnell."

"That's okay, sir. If you'll just come with me."

David looked at him, and saw no malice in O'Donnell's flinty eyes. They matched the close-cropped gray of what little hair showed from underneath the major's garrison cap.

"Please, Mr. Albee," O'Donnell insisted. "It's really very important."

"All right." David squeezed Liz's fingers and let go of her hand. She took a step forward, but David shook his head.

"It would be best if it was just you, Mr. Albee," Major O'Donnell said. His tone made it clear that this was more than a suggestion.

David said to Liz, "Don't worry, they're not gonna kill me," and followed the major to a large tent. It was, in fact, the largest of the temporary structures, with the exception of the bandstand.

Inside, he immediately noticed a familiar odor. He was taken to Margolis, which did not surprise him. What *did* surprise him was the sight of Jekyll in manacles and metal neck brace, chained to a heavy steel loop protruding from a concrete block. Armed guards surrounded the hapless creature, and a meat locker was secured in one corner of

164

the tent, powered through a cable snaking in from one of the generators. Jekyll chirped in recognition and strained at his chain, painfully stretching the wrinkled skin of his throat.

"Hello, Mr. Albee," Margolis said. He was seated at a desk, a fax machine at his elbow, an AT&T viewphone facing him, a secretary seated in a low, folding chair taking notes. He rose and came around the desk to shake hands with David. "Good to see you again."

David nodded. "Thank you."

"As you can see," Margolis said, "we have one of the dinosaurs here, as the aliens requested."

"The aliens requested . . . ?" David was confused. "Does this mean that they've been in communication with you, besides the TV broadcasts we've all seen?"

Margolis frowned. "Yes, it does. Are you disappointed?"

"Yeah, I kind of thought this was for all mankind, like Neil Armstrong said."

"Well, it might be. We'll see how it all turns out. I know you don't like politicians much, son."

"That's an understatement if I've ever heard one, sir."

"Yeah. Still, the breed is part of the human condition, wouldn't you agree?"

"As much as I hate to, yes."

"Well, there were codes sent in different cycles along with the video. These were picked up by our cybersurveillance systems, and translated."

"Cool," David said. "So what do they want?"

"They want to see the dinosaurs, of course. And I believe that little display at sunset was designed to show us the clear physical relationship between the aliens and these fellows."

"You think they're related, huh?" David was pleased that Margolis recognized that Jekyll and the others were *dinosaurs*, and not "dumb animals." That put him one up on Jaffrey Flanagan, Burles, and the other Christian Millennialists.

Margolis smiled. "What do you think?"

"That was my first impression, but when I got a closer look at that dude in his flying bubble, I noticed quite a few differences. I'm not sure they're the same species at all."

Margolis looked dubious, and he swiftly changed the subject. "Anyway, the damn things want the dinosaurs to be brought aboard their spacecraft."

"Great."

"Not so great. What if they just swoop off the planet with the four of them?"

"Well, you've still got the remains of the one that died."

"Not good enough."

David couldn't help wondering why he was being told about this. "So are you going to defy the aliens?"

"No, but we're going to compromise."

"How?"

"We'll allow one dinosaur to go aboard. The others will stay where they are."

"Under armed guard."

"That's correct. Under armed guard."

David thought it over. "Well, I hope it doesn't upset the aliens too much."

"You can explain our reasoning to them, if you would."

"What?" David was pretty sure he'd heard that wrong.

"We're sending you along with that dinosaur, the big fellow over there." He pointed at Jekyll.

David felt a tightening in his throat and chest. When he spoke, the words sounded forced and squeaky: "What did you say?"

"They requested a human go with the dinosaurs, and we think you're the man for the job."

Frightened as he was, David wouldn't have dreamed of trying to get out of it. As he approached the alien ship with Jekyll, he was stunned by the size of it. From a few hundred yards away, it had been impressive, but the nearer he got, the more awesome it became. It must have been over three miles in diameter, and perhaps four and a half, even five, miles long.

"Jekyll, old boy, I hope they've got a lot of grub in there for me and you, 'cause we might get lost inside that thing and never come out."

Jekyll, however, was eyeing a tanager that suddenly popped up from behind a juniper bush. He was on it like a feathered bolt of blue and yellow lightning. The bird was even quicker, though, and fluttered away to safety.

"Guess you aren't all that hungry," David said, "or you would have caught him."

But Jekyll wasn't listening to him. The dinosaur was looking at the strange shape that filled the darkened landscape. Stars shone coldly above its curve as they walked the last few yards. The crisscross shape was faintly visible in the moonlight.

It opened.

David stared at it. He heard an owl hoot in the distance. Taking a deep breath, he stepped inside. Jekyll followed. David felt the hairs on the nape of his neck and his forearms rise, but other than that, there was no sensation.

It wasn't what he had expected. Not that he exactly knew what to expect. There were no blinking lights, or winding walkways above inexplicable machines. No, the interior of the spacecraft was as featureless as a dream.

He felt a peculiar weightlessness, and then realized that he was, in fact, floating. The sensation he had felt as they entered the alien ship was a field surrounding him. He was now rising through the non-light. He looked down and saw Jekyll, also enclosed in a bubble, floating up beneath him.

"Jeez!" was all that he could manage to say. The bubble began to rise faster, and he became giddy with the sensation of flying. He saw that Jekyll was crouching inside the other bubble, tail wrapped around himself in a defensive posture, tongue darting in and out and eyes rolling wildly.

"Don't worry, pardner," David shouted down to Jekyll.

His voice sounded flat and lifeless. "I don't think they're gonna treat you any worse than us humans have."

Jekyll cocked his head and looked at David with his right eye. Apparently the sound must have carried to his bubble. David wondered if it was conducted through the field, or if it would have been audible outside the bubble. If they got to talk to somebody in this damn spaceship, maybe he could find out. So far, though, he hadn't seen anything worth noting. Maybe the guts of the spacecraft were all hidden, but he couldn't see anything in the gloom.

The bubbles accelerated, and then bobbed like corks in water, David's first, and Jekyll's a moment later. There they hung, suspended in air, while a dim glow spread around them like ripples on a pond.

David forced himself to look down. He expected to see a bottomless pit, but there was nothing. He couldn't even be sure he *was* looking down anymore, since the bubble was slowly revolving as it bobbed. A strange smell permeated the place that reminded David of burning plastic, only not so unpleasant.

"I think I'm finally beginning to grasp the concept of *alien* more clearly," David said to Jekyll. "In a vague sort of way, that is."

Jekyll said nothing, but rolled his eight-ball eyes around wildly. There was still nothing to be seen, however, even as light rippled outward from them. David noticed that his short hairs were rising again, and then realized that the bubbles had become the rippling light. The energy fields that had formed the bubbles were spreading outward, and somehow forming a *floor* underneath their feet.

"Some sort of electromagnetic flux," David said. He took a tentative step, and found that new light rippled outward as he put his foot down on the floor that hadn't existed a moment ago. The ripples curved upward thirty or forty feet away, and then ascended out of sight.

David took a few more steps, and felt something touch his elbow. He glanced back to see Jekyll's huge, avian face close to his own. Remembering how Jekyll used to follow at a discreet distance, David was touched by the creature's childish faith in him. But, of course, Jekyll *was* only a child, in spite of his size and implanted knowledge.

David stopped walking, and Jekyll stopped, too. "Where do we go from here?" David said. "I still don't see anything that makes sense to me."

Jekyll made a whimpering sound.

"Are you scared, buddy?" David asked, turning to stroke the bony ridge between Jekyll's nostrils. Oddly, David felt calm; knowing that Jekyll was a frightened child made him feel responsible for what happened to the dinosaur, and he had to stay cool. "Well, it's understandable. I guess I'm scared, too."

There's no need to be scared.

David jerked his head around, but Jekyll gave no indication that he'd heard anything. There was nothing to be seen but the endlessly coruscating rings of light extending outward from where they stood.

"Please show yourself," David said.

Will seeing me make you feel more comfortable?

"I don't know," David said, "but I'd prefer it."

All right.

The alien appeared right in front of them. It just stepped right out of the rippling flux. David felt the heat of Jekyll's breath on the back of his neck. The poor thing was practically clinging to him now, fearful of the sixteen-foot-long creature standing before them.

"Thank you," David said. Now that he got a closer look at one of the aliens, if there were more than one, he saw that it was really not very much like the young dinosaur at all, though it was saurian in appearance. Its posture was more humanoid, for one thing, and its skull was even larger than Jekyll's. Its most telling feature was its eyes, however, gleaming garnets that seemed to contain the wisdom of the ages as they watched David and Jekyll knowingly.

My request was for all the living neonates, not just one.

How was the alien communicating with him? Subvocalization? Or was it actually *telepathic?* David forced himself to answer the alien's implicit question. "The people in charge wanted to keep the others with them."

Why?

"Well, I guess it's because they're scared."

Of what?

"Of you. That you might just leave with all of them."

Nonsense.

"Why do you say that?"

These creatures were designed to live on this world.

"You say you designed them?"

Yes.

"Then they're not your . . . children?"

No, they are genetically altered dinosaurs. They are native to your world, not mine.

David thought of Jaffrey Flanagan, and wondered what the televangelist would have made of *this* revelation. But this was no time for thinking about Flanagan. There were too many important questions that needed to be asked right now.

"Why did you create them?"

The saurian from the stars lowered its great head. It did not answer.

"Was it an experiment?" David persisted. "A way of bringing civilization to a primitive world? Or were you just messing around with chromosomes for the fuck of it?"

We wished only to help.

"Help? By playing God?" David shouted. "Wasn't evolution good enough for you?"

Jekyll backed away from him, and David thought he heard a telepathic murmuring, perhaps directed toward reassuring the frightened creature.

"It's all right, Jekyll," David said. "Don't be afraid."

You must go now.

David felt frustrated. "But I have so many things I want to ask you—"

There will be another time.

"How can I be sure of that?" David cried. He was

blowing this whole thing, and he was beginning to feel desperate. "Please let me stay and talk to you a little longer."

But it was too late. The ripples were receding, and the alien disappeared. In a moment the flux had formed bubbles around David and Jekyll, and they were descending once again toward the world outside.

22

"I'm not sure I believe it," Margolis said, lighting his pipe with a wooden match as he got up from his desk. A man who looked familiar to David sat cross-legged in a folding chair in front of the desk. He smiled at David as Jekyll was taken away and chained up once again.

"Why not?" David demanded. "Do they all look alike to you?"

Margolis scowled. "It just doesn't stand to reason."

"Why not? The aliens left the bioengineered eggs in stasis fields, and they didn't get to pick up one batch because of a natural disaster of unprecedented proportions. We used to think it was the impact of a giant comet that wiped out the dinosaurs, but now we're pretty sure it was a range of volcanoes in India that sent so much crap into the atmosphere that it changed the climate of the earth once and for all."

"But why, after all these eons," Margolis persisted, "did they come back to claim the, um, hatchlings if they're not even their own kind?"

"I don't know the answer to that, not yet."

"Any theories?"

"Yeah," said David, thumbing the spigot on a water cooler to fill a plastic cup. "Maybe they put some of their guys in stasis just to see what was going to happen."

"Sounds a bit farfetched."

"Does it? Well, what if they left the ship in the asteroid belt, where it could easily find the metals necessary to maintain or repair itself, until all of the egg boxes were accounted for?''

''Oh, come on.'' Margolis sucked furiously on his pipe stem.

''Remember that New Testament parable about the shepherd who leaves ninety-nine sheep to search for one lost one?''

''So now these damn lizards are Christians? You've been hanging around with Jaffrey Flanagan too long, Albee.''

David looked at Margolis with new respect. This guy didn't like Flanagan's pieties, either. Still, that wasn't the issue here. ''Mr. Margolis,'' he said, ''do you think it's diplomatically wise for you to refer to our first visitors from the stars as 'these damn lizards'?''

''Just a figure of speech, my boy.'' Margolis gave up on the pipe and set it down on the desk.

''Look,'' said the man sitting in the folding chair, ''if what the alien says is true, maybe they wanted to create a race of creatures that they could mate with, so that they could populate the earth with hybrids.''

David wanted to argue, but he found that he couldn't. This suggestion did not seem unlikely at all. What he did say was, ''Don't I know you from somewhere?''

''This is Dr. Charles French,'' Margolis said. ''Remiss of me not to introduce you two. David Albee, Dr. French.''

David found himself shaking hands with one of the most famous scientists in the world. In fact, he'd heard it said that the telegenic exobiologist spent more time in front of TV cameras than anyone in the sciences. ''How I envy you the experience you've had this evening,'' French said. ''But it's something to hear you describe what you've seen firsthand.''

''Well, I'm afraid I didn't see very much,'' David said.

''Perhaps the next time,'' French said, smiling with great charm.

''If there is a next time,'' said David.

''Oh, there will be a next time, all right,'' Margolis

said. "The aliens want you to go back at six in the morning."

"Really."

"Yes, they sent word before you even left their ship."

The tent seemed huge now that there were only five of them in it. The media had their own, and this one was off limits to them, a rule enforced by Major O'Donnell's marines. Ferd was lying down on a cot, Charlie sat cross-legged on the ground, Bob paced, and Liz stood next to David with her arm around his waist.

"They want us to wait here for you," Liz said.

"So do I," said David. "It's nice to know that people you love are there for you when you go through something this disorienting."

"We'll be here, bud," Charlie said. "Don't you have any doubts about that."

"Thanks, Charlie, but if they change their minds and say you have to leave . . ."

"We'll still be with you in spirit, bro," said Ferd.

David smiled.

"French's theory is essentially that the aliens tried to populate the earth in their own image," Bob said. "But why? If they have their own world, maybe more than one, and space habitats that can function for sixty-five million years, why would they want a backwater planet like this one?"

"Panspermia." French walked into the tent.

"Say what?" Charlie asked.

"One race across the galaxy, or at least variations of one race, at the top of the intelligence chain."

"I'm glad you didn't say food chain," said Ferd.

French laughed, at ease with strangers, in command of the conversation. "A confederation of planets, habitable, lush, sprinkled throughout the Milky Way, all with creatures on it that they have designed to procreate with."

"Then if a disaster happens on one planet," Charlie said, "they just move to another one."

"Talk about any port in a storm," Ferd said.

"Yeah," David said. "Any planet in a storm."

French shrugged. "That's one way of looking at it."

"Maybe you can find out more tomorrow, David," Bob said.

"Yeah, maybe."

Bob and French got into a lively discussion and left the tent. Ferd and Charlie soon followed, leaving David and Liz alone.

"I'm glad you're here," David said.

"Me, too, but I hope Nurse Jen is taking good care of my animals . . . that is, if she's still there."

"Yeah, now that the dinosaurs are gone, they might have all been reassigned to some other duty. Do you think they'll bring the other dinosaurs here, now that the alien has said he's not gonna dinonap 'em?"

"No, Margolis said they're keeping Marie Antoinette, Franny, and Zooey back at my place, just to be on the safe side."

David nodded. "So Jekyll stays as official guinea pig, right?"

"More or less. *You* and Jekyll, actually." She kissed him.

He kissed her back. Soon the kissing became more intense, and they retired to the nearest cot. It was hard to move around on the cot, which made them laugh a couple of times. Soon their passion precluded amusement, and they were so wrapped up in each other that time had as little meaning for them as it had for the alien in its antediluvian spacecraft.

Jekyll was not so hesitant to go in the morning as David had feared. Perhaps it was because he had emerged from the spacecraft unscathed . . . or perhaps his burgeoning curiosity and imagination had been fired by what he had seen and heard the previous evening.

The walk across the prairie seemed shorter. They were at the entrance (hatch?) of the spacecraft now, and neither of them hesitated to step inside this time. David detected the same burnt plastic odor as the bubbles enclosed them, though it didn't seem so unpleasant today. He was eager to continue the dialogue with the alien. More than eager.

The bubbles didn't move in the same direction that they had moved in last night. This time they went up a relatively short distance and then moved forward. They fused together, making an ovoid or tubular shape; it was hard to tell from inside. The motion was not jarring, but it was noticeable. Again, their surroundings seemed featureless, though David did sense a sort of vague funnel shape ahead of them. Or maybe that was just the distortion of the flux bubble.

They achieved a pretty impressive and scary velocity, moving down the dark corridor for a few minutes. At last David began to perceive a widening that emptied into a huge, round chamber, at the center of which sat an alien on a kind of elevated perch.

David and Jekyll were deposited at the base of the perch. Rings of glowing flux emanated outward from where they stood, and the ancient, gray, reptilian alien eyed them with a desultory downward glance.

It is pleasant to see you again.

"Thanks," David said, glad that the alien had made it clear it was the same one who had interviewed them yesterday. "I was afraid I'd offended you in some way."

No.

"But you asked us to leave so abruptly."

I had hoped that your masters would see reason, and permit the other neonates to come aboard.

My *masters*, David thought. "No, they're pretty set on keeping things the way they are."

The alien nodded in a most human gesture, and David thought that he detected sadness in the ponderous movements of the great head.

"I know that things aren't really the way they should be," David said. "I think our leaders know that, too . . . but they're scared."

The alien's tail rustled around its taloned feet. *Why? I have said that I will not take the neonates.*

"I don't know. It's just the way we are. We don't know what you want, or where you come from, or anything about you at all. You've got technology we don't understand, and it's ancient and strange to us. Maybe if you tell me why you're here, I can get them to loosen up a little."

Your world has always interested me.

"Well, thanks, but do you think you can give me some information? I mean, I don't really even know where to begin, but I feel that if we can just open up communication enough to clear away some of the suspicion and fear—"

Observe.

Flux glimmered and reshaped itself, opening an oval window onto a panorama that took David's breath away.

Just a few dozen yards from where they stood was a living world. Cycads and flowering trees flourished in tropical splendor. A miniature sea, complete with a foaming tide, reflected the glare of an artificial sun. Batwinged pterosaurs soared through steamy air on the other side of the vast window. A sauropod stretched its silvery-blue neck to crop some fronds from a curving tree. Water dripped from the crests on top of hadrosaurs' heads as they bathed in a stream. Tiny carnivorous dinosaurs chased rodents and birds. A styracosaur climbed a low hill like a semi in second gear, turned its spiked head and blinked at them from the other side of the flux window.

David could not speak. He was seeing life on earth as it existed at the time the egg box was left behind sixty-five million years ago. Was this some kind of re-creation? No, it was too real. There were living dinosaurs there, not hybrids like Jekyll—who stared at them as raptly as David stared—but dinosaurs as he had always dreamed of them.

"Almost," he said aloud. For, in fact, they were a little different than he had pictured them: the pterosaurs leaner and more like kites, but with lively snapping beaks; the ceratopsian, styracosaurus, fleshier and more leathery; the sauropod (camarosaurus?) somehow more graceful than it had any right to be. And the darting microvenators with their brilliant plumage of red and yellow and blue and purple, like living flowers.

David watched them until his feet ached. He forgot about the alien and the spacecraft, even about Jekyll. He was enrapt upon the sight of this living habitat of the dinosaurs, transplanted through space all these millions and millions of years to be plunked down here on the Montana prairie for him to stare at in silent wonderment.

He was afraid that if he moved, it would all vanish, like a dream of the remote past that can't be sustained by the waking mind.

Birds roosting on a hummock suddenly lifted their wings and flapped away. David couldn't see what had disturbed them at first, and then he thought he saw the hummock move.

It rose, mud and weeds falling from it, as it pushed itself up on its little forelimbs. It shook its massive head and opened its alligator jaws to yawn, revealing bits of rotten meat still clinging to its yellow dagger teeth. It leaned forward menacingly and stalked through the jungle, looking for breakfast.

"Tyrannosaurus rex," David said. It was a living specimen of the most terrible killing machine the earth had ever known. And yet it was like seeing an old friend at the same time.

You enjoy seeing them, don't you? the alien asked.

David sighed. "Yeah," he said, "you could say that."

They are close to you.

Ever since I was a kid.

Before that. Long, long before that.

David glanced up at the alien. Its wise, hooded eyes looked into his. He thought he understood what it meant by that. In a very real sense, dinosaurs were the heritage of the human race. These creatures, varying in size from a chicken to a whale, had once been the rulers of earth. They'd been at the top of the food chain, blanketing the planet for 150,000,000 years or more. They'd had no industry, no nuclear wars, and had not tampered with nature. But they had been destroyed by a volcanic mountain range that kicked up so much particulate matter into the atmosphere that the climate had changed and they were gone forever . . . wiped out . . .

"Almost." David watched these living prehistoric monsters go about their business and knew that their habitat, this living link to Earth's past, would change the way man looked at things irrevocably. Indeed, the process had already begun—with David Albee. "Have they been in stasis all this time?"

No, their environment has been preserved as it was on the Earth long ago.

"And you?"

The alien's red eyes sparkled in the light coming from the dinosaur habitat. *I have been in stasis.*

"Sixty-five million years . . ."

No, four million years.

"Four million years. I don't understand."

Observe. The alien stretched out a hand, and the floor under their feet revolved. Or were the walls turning around them? In any case, they were soon looking at a dark surface, with their backs to the dinosaur habitat. David saw that it wasn't completely dark, however. Points of light glowed and became stars. The Milky Way spun, enlarging until only a section of it was visible. This too was magnified, showing a stellar cluster that David recognized from his astronomy classes as Eridani.

The image focused in still closer, and revealed Epsilon Eridani. This was a star that had long been supposed to have a planetary system not unlike our own, since it was a star almost identical to Sol in every respect. It was pictured in a schematic chart that showed planets at varying distances from it.

David wasn't quite sure when he became aware of something gleaming in the strange, aqueous light rippling around them. He glanced down from the star chart, and saw that Jekyll was playing with his jacks again.

The jacks seemed to be suspended in the darkness between outwardly moving concentric rings of faint light. Now Jekyll set the last one down and stepped back. He looked at the star chart with first one eye, and then the other.

David moved around behind him and looked at the chart. At first he couldn't see what Jekyll had done, why there was such an air of satisfaction about the young dinosaur at the moment.

"Well, I'll be goddamned," he said. There it was. The planets of Epsilon Eridani, laid out neatly in the flux.

It is a memory of our home, implanted in the genes of this one and his siblings, so that one day his ancestors would be drawn to it. We hoped that ultimately they would find their way back to us.

The alien reached down and stroked Jekyll's head. Jekyll seemed indecently pleased with this attention, and very domestic at the moment, but David wondered how soon he would have to be fed. They'd given him a pound of burger and four lamb chops before they set out this morning, and his appetite wasn't what it used to be now that he was full-grown. Still, David didn't want him to do anything weird, like attacking their host.

"Look," David said, "he's got to be fed pretty soon. He gets kind of dangerous when he's hungry."

Yes, that was the problem.

"Problem?"

The problem that we could not solve. It was a simple matter to increase the intelligence of these innocents, but we could not instill the basis of morality into their minds. Their physical needs overpowered any such urges, no matter how carefully those urges were implanted.

"Morality. Why do they need morality?"

There can be no civilization without morality.

"Then you expected them to form a civilization. But why?"

To save them.

"From the natural disaster that wiped them out? Tell

me, was it the volcanoes, the comet, or something we haven't even thought of?''

We thought that the comets your solar system periodically passes through would destroy the dinosaurs. Instead, the volcanoes transformed the climate of the earth forever.

''And so the dinosaurs died out.'' David pronounced this as a benediction while he stood facing these last few lumbering beasts in the habitat.

When we returned to earth sixty-one million years later, we found few traces of your world's former rulers. Birds, reptiles, and mammals were abundant, however, and so we set out to select another species to build a civilization on your world. We decided that there was little reason to accelerate growth and intelligence at such a fast pace. Our choice has proven to be largely successful.

All at once, David knew where this was leading, as surely as he was standing here in an alien spaceship talking to a reptilian Methuselah in front of one intelligent hybrid dinosaur and its countless walnut-brained cousins.

''Your choice,'' he said, looking straight into the alien's red eyes, ''was us, wasn't it?''

23

Margolis looked as if he'd been hit on the head with a frying pan. French, however, seemed to be enjoying himself.

"You're telling me that lizard is God," Margolis said.

"Not really, but his kind did design us—or at least they designed our progenitors, which amounts to the same thing."

Margolis looked at the viewphone. "I don't know if I should call the office or run away from home on this one."

"I suggest you call the office," French said. "This is rather important news, don't you think?"

Margolis frowned. "I don't know what to think."

"Look on the bright side," David said. "Even the Reverend Jaffrey Flanagan should be pleased to hear that we were picked as the creatures on Earth most likely to grasp the concept of morality."

"Jaffrey Flanagan is not likely to be pleased with any of this," Margolis assured him. "In fact, we're lucky he's not in the president's good graces at the moment, but he'll be back before you know it. That, you can count on."

"Like the proverbial bad penny." David frowned.

French smiled. "There are those who think he's done a lot of good for this country."

"Well, I'm not one of them."

"Jaffrey will have the president's ear in no time," Margolis warned. "His constituency are well organized; in fact, they're the most avid group the party has. As soon as he starts preaching fire and brimstone about this, the feces are gonna hit the fan. I guarantee that it won't be a pretty sight."

"Does this mean you'd rather not reveal what's happened? Are you going to try and hide it from the media because you're afraid that telegenic Elmer Gantry might make a fuss?"

"You want to talk to the TV guys, the newspaper reporters, *Time, Newsweek, US News,*" Margolis said to French, turning away from David.

"Don't forget *Mother Jones,*" David said.

"Wise-ass," Margolis said. His thick southern accent gave the rebuke real bite.

"Just trying to make sure this thing receives balanced coverage," said David.

"My better judgment tells me to hold off on this," Margolis said.

"You can't," said French. "This is too big."

"I knew you'd say that," Margolis said.

He sighed and picked up the phone.

"My, how that man can preach," Liz said, feigning great excitement. She sat with her friends in her own living room, watching the ten-o'clock news.

David had to admit that Flanagan possessed a commanding speaking style. He played his audience like a musical instrument, building up to bombastic crescendos that called down the wrath of God on the offending sinners—who were invariably secular humanists and their heathen ilk.

"Was it C. P. Snow who said the new barbarism would fly in on the wings of technology?" David asked.

"I don't remember," Liz said. "But I always blame quotes like that on J. B. S. Haldane."

"No, that's the one about a sufficiently advanced culture being indistinguishable from magic."

Liz made an obnoxious sound in imitation of a game-show buzzer. "Wrong! That was Clarke. Haldane said that not only is the universe stranger than we imagine, it's stranger than we *can* imagine.''

''Oh, yeah. Well, judging from recent events, I'd say he was right about that.''

They both fell silent, and watched Jaffrey Flanagan whipping his followers into a frenzy at the Christian Millennialist Temple in Houston.

''Satan has come to America,'' Flanagan said with what sounded like utter conviction. ''He has duped the weak and the non-Christian into believing that he is God, the creator of man.''

There was so much opprobrium sliding off that last phrase that David felt as if he ought to deodorize the room.

''Now we must be strong,'' Jaffrey Flanagan went on, ''for in a time when this demon from the depths of hell has come to Earth wearing the false face of the Creator, there are those who have proclaimed this foul creature the redeemer, the savior of mankind. Such folly must not go unchallenged, my brothers and sisters.''

The applause drowned out Flanagan's voice. He paused, seeming impatient to get on with his diatribe.

''Boy, he's really pouring it on,'' Ferd said.

Charlie shut off the TV with the remote control. The apoplectic face of Jaffrey Flanagan dwindled to a tiny rainbow point. The room was consumed with silence for one or two blessed moments.

''On the other hand,'' Charlie said, ''we have the Alienation Movement, which the reverend just spoke of with such vehemence that his head almost exploded.''

Television images of crowds in New York, Bangkok, Paris, and Tel Aviv lingered in David's memory. Raving masses of Alienationists, crowding the streets of these cities, proclaiming that *God* had come to Earth at last. The Israeli Parliament, in particular, was having a very bad time of it. Was *this* the Messiah? David wondered if the alien had been circumcised. Come to think of it, he mused, there hadn't even been any evidence of genitalia. Maybe its species fertilized eggs outside the body.

"It looks like we're back to angels dancing on the heads of pins," Liz said.

"Or devils," David said, "depending on how you look at it."

"Well, at least you can sit in your own living room, Liz," Ferd said. "So let's count our blessings. Here we are all sitting around together watching this madness on the boob tube, like one big happy family."

"Except for Bob," Liz reminded him.

"Yeah, but that's just because his wife wouldn't let him come out and play tonight."

"Is she religious?" Charlie asked. "Maybe these new revelations from on high were a little too much for her."

"No, actually I think she just wanted him to stay home and fix the toilet."

"Life *do* go on, don't it?" Ferd said.

"I take it that that was a rhetorical question," Charlie asked, getting up and moving toward the kitchen. "We'll need a couple beers while we mull that one over."

"Bob's coming over with Hiram and Cilla tomorrow," David said. "Which means we'll all get to sit around and talk politics for hours on end."

"And just think," Ferd said. "There's an election coming up next year."

"Think the candidates will be pro-alien or anti?" Charlie shouted from the kitchen. Two beers fizzed as their caps were removed.

"It'll most likely be split cleanly along party lines," Ferd said.

David laughed nervously. He didn't want to admit it, but he was worried. Things were coming together nicely. The alien had changed things on Earth once and for all, but would it be for the better? Already, worldwide religious factions had sprung up to twist what had happened into either a divine or satanic excuse for myth-making. For the first time in his life, the old adage about not rocking the boat began to make sense to him. He had joked with the others about the lunatic images of Alien-ationalists on television, but he privately had felt much the same way he had when, as a kid visiting an aunt in Galveston, a hurricane warning had been announced on the radio. It felt as though a natural disaster were about to occur now, too.

"Got to go check on the kids," Liz said, getting up from the sofa.

David hated to be apart from her even for a few minutes, and so he asked, "Want me to go with you?"

"No, thanks. I'll be safe with all those marines out there."

David watched her go out, and was pleased to think that only four marines had, in fact, been left behind. Even Nurse Jen had been sent back to Washington. Captain Torrance had vanished after the aliens first sent word that they (if there was more than one) were coming, and his jar-heads had mostly gone with him. Those left behind were fairly unobtrusive. Still, David didn't like to have her go out there alone at night.

"Excuse me," he said. He got up, thinking that he might keep an eye on Liz covertly.

"Didn't you hear what the woman said?" Ferd asked. "She can handle it all by her little self."

"Just gonna start some coffee," David lied.

He went into the kitchen and grabbed the coffee pot. Going to the back door, he squinted through the screen at the dark compound beyond. He saw two marines smoking over by the shack with the incubator in it, and Liz standing with a big tray of meat by the transparent cage housing Franny, Zooey, and Marie Antoinette. David wondered idly how soon they'd be mating. There were two females and two males, after all. If Jekyll ever got to come back, there'd be two males, anyway.

Liz set the meat tray down on the ground and lifted the trapdoor on the near side of the dinosaur cage. The door was designed so that it could only be opened from the outside, and sealed as soon as it was set back into a recessed opening. It was barely big enough for a human to climb through. The walls of the cage were smeared; better have them hosed down tomorrow, David thought.

Liz grabbed a raw steak and tossed it into the cage. The three dinosaurs were huddled on the far side, apparently sleeping. The steak flopped onto the floor, and they ignored it.

"That's weird," David said aloud. The hurricane warning feeling came over him again. He'd seen the dinosaurs come out of a deep sleep at the smell of meat before. Was something wrong with them?

Liz waited for a few seconds, and then tapped the side of the cage with her knuckles. The dinosaurs still didn't respond. She frowned, and tossed in another steak.

Still no action from the other end of the cage. Liz turned and called out something to the two marines. They looked up at her, and one of them tossed his cigarette in the dirt and went over to see what she wanted.

David put his palm against the screen as the young marine, Private Lloyd, went to a truck and returned with a long pole. The pole had a pincer on the end, which could be manipulated by a cord fastened to the pole's side. The marine carefully extended the pole through the trapdoor opening and attempted to fish out one of the steaks.

It kept slipping out of the pincer, which apparently wasn't really made for this kind of work. David wasn't sure what it was made for, but this didn't seem to be it.

David watched the slowly expanding and contracting torsos of the dinosaurs as they slept. He saw that Liz was watching them, too. Private Lloyd was busy trying to manipulate the steaks, and wasn't paying any attention to the dinosaurs at all.

Suddenly the three dinosaurs were on their feet. One of them—David thought it was Franny—snatched the pincer and pulled it toward herself.

"Hey!" was all Private Lloyd could say. His arm and shoulder went through the opening. His face was mashed against the clear plastic above the trapdoor. For a moment he struggled with Franny. His free hand fumbled at his holster, but he couldn't loosen its snap to get his handgun free.

"Let it go!" Liz cried.

Marie Antoinette darted across the floor of the cage, came up fast, and caught the marine's arm at the elbow in her powerful jaws. Zooey was right behind her. He gouged Private Lloyd's exposed neck with his clawed hands.

"Oh, my God!" Liz screamed.

David was through the screen door, running toward them. The other marine on duty was running, too. They both saw the same thing. Combat boots off the ground, the hapless Private Lloyd's legs were kicking horribly as he was pulled through the trapdoor into the cage.

Liz grasped his calf, but she didn't have the strength to hold him. David and the other marine arrived a second or two too late. The maimed Private Lloyd was hauled inside the cage with the hungry dinosaurs.

It was hard to see what was happening from where David was, even though he was rapidly moving toward the transparent cage. The Mylar was streaked black with blood in the artificial light. Muffled screams came from inside the cage, and terrible sounds of tearing and crunching. Liz was weeping, pounding her fists against the Mylar wall.

David beat the second marine to the cage by a few paces. He still couldn't see much, but he could see that the four figures inside were paying no attention to him. Private Lloyd wasn't screaming anymore. David took the opportunity to grasp the trapdoor. He glanced in just to make sure that the poor guy wasn't alive.

One of the dinosaurs—he thought it was Zooey—looked up and wiped blood off his jaws with a clawed hand. David got a glimpse of a glistening, exposed rib cage, and knew that there was nothing he could do but close the trapdoor. He slammed it shut and felt it seal with satisfaction.

He turned and almost bumped into the other marine guard.

"We can't leave Lloyd in there!" the kid screamed. David noticed at that moment how young he was, and remembered how young his companion had been. *Lloyd.* They were twelve or thirteen years younger than David, just boys. Now one of them was dead, and the other was in shock. "We can't leave him in there with those *things!*"

David tried to say something, but the marine didn't seem to know he was there anymore. A .45 automatic was in his meaty hand, and he pointed it at the cage. David hit the dirt as the young marine's hand jerked up with a deafening *crack*. Fire blazed for an instant in the warm night air as the bullet spanged off the clear wall of the cage.

"No!" David shouted. "He's gone!"

"No!" Liz screamed. "Don't kill them!"

But the marine didn't hear. He fired again, and kept firing until his clip was empty. Then he pulled the trigger over and over again, clicking it ineffectually. At last he stopped and held the gun up to his grimacing face, shaking it as if it were a living thing that had betrayed him.

David got up and went to Liz. She was crying, her shoulders heaving with emotion. He put his arm around her. Inside the cage, the frightened dinosaurs cowered at the corner, a huddled mass of quivering flesh. The discharge of the weapon, and the shocks of the bullets spanging into their cage, had been enough to drive them away from the half-eaten boy lying on the blood-soaked floor inside. The stench of gore filled the night.

"I didn't know that plastic shit was bulletproof for sure until now," David said. "But you're lucky it was, son. They'd have court-martialed you for sure if you'd succeeded in killing those dinosaurs."

But the marine looked as if he was thinking about shoving another clip into the .45 and blasting away at the dinosaurs again. He might have even shot David, too, he was so furious and shaken by the unexpected death of his comrade. David felt Liz hug him close, as though she would melt into him if she could.

"Shit," the marine whispered. His expression softened into grief, and he holstered the .45. David hadn't noticed that the other two guards had joined them, and Ferd and Charlie were standing in the backyard, too.

One of the other marines, a lance corporal, led the shocked kid away. Lieutenant Franklin, who was in charge, peered through the clear wall in front of him.

"Jesus Christ," he said. David couldn't be sure if it was a curse or a prayer. "Jesus Christ."

The Lieutenant turned away from the gruesome sight. "What happened?" he asked.

"He was . . . trying to help me," Liz said, her sweet face so distorted with anguish that it broke David's heart. "I asked him if he could get the meat off the floor with that pole . . . and they . . . they pulled him inside . . ."

"Yeah, I see, ma'am. Better take her inside," the lieutenant said to David.

David nodded and steered her toward the screen door and the haven of the house where she had lived all her life, where she had carried on her father's work, and where she had been held a virtual prisoner. Now, just when things were looking up, this had happened in her own backyard.

Ferd and Charlie came out to show their sympathy. Liz could hardly walk. She was in shock, and David turned back to say, "I think we're gonna need a doctor, Lieutenant. And somebody to clean up."

"We'll take care of it," he said. "Just get Dr. Tomlinson inside, Mr. Albee."

"Yeah." David steered her toward the door, and for the first time noticed that his legs were rubbery. Charlie must have noticed it, too. He put his hand on David's elbow, as if to steady him. The house seemed to be miles away, but eventually they were at the door and went inside.

"Come on, guys, let's have a drink," Ferd said. He tossed open the refrigerator door and pulled out a six-pack. He popped the tops and handed the foaming beers to everyone.

David accepted the beer without comment. His mind was racing with things he didn't want to think about as he sat next to Liz at the table and held her trembling hand. What would happen to the dinosaurs now, he didn't know.

At the moment, for the first time since this whole thing had started, he didn't much care.

24

Private Lloyd's body was taken away, to be shipped back to the little town in Georgia he'd been born in only nineteen short years ago, in 1980. David, Liz, Bob, Ferd, and Charlie attended a small commemorative service at the local Methodist church. They were besieged by television cameras and photographers as they went in, and they tried to answer questions until half a dozen marines surrounded them and shouldered their way past the media representatives. David was beginning to develop a real aversion to these people, who seemed to swarm around him like insects wherever he went these days.

Lieutenant Franklin and his three charges were already inside the church; there was no need for them to miss the service, since twelve replacements had been sent in, including Major O'Donnell, who was at the little prairie church today, too. David was thankful that none of the boy's family was here. It would have been hard to face them. After the service, David and Liz were stopped by O'Donnell.

"Thank you for coming to the service," he said.

"Least we could do," David said, "after we saw the kid die right in front of us."

"He was a good marine," the major said.

David found a certain amount of irony in that comment, since Major O'Donnell had probably never laid eyes on Private Lloyd while the kid was alive. Knowing that it was meant well, however, he kept his mouth shut.

"I think it's fair to say that he died in combat," the major went on. "He did honor to his country."

"I guess you could look at it that way," David agreed. He bided his time to find out the major's purpose in accosting him with such a barrage of clichés.

"We all have our duty to perform," Major O'Donnell said, "and sometimes it's not all that easy to know what it is in these troubled times."

"Major, are you trying to tell me something?" David asked.

The major nodded. "I guess I am, at that. You see, I was going to come out to Dr. Tomlinson's after the service, to see you two."

"Does Margolis want me back at the spacecraft?"

"Well, no. This really involves Miss Tomlinson more than you, Mr. Albee."

"What is it?" Liz asked. She was wary, after all they'd been through. Her status could change again at any time as a result of shifting government policies, especially after what had happened to Private Lloyd.

"Uh, the visitor would like to come up here."

"What? The visitor? You mean the alien?"

"Yes, ma'am."

"Well, if the mountain won't come to Mohammed . . ." Liz trailed off.

"I'll be damned." David looked at Liz. She seemed excited at the prospect of meeting the alien, but David wasn't quite convinced that this was for real. "How's it gonna get here?"

"It has its own way, I understand."

It has its own way. Now *there* was a comment to stimulate the imagination.

"That is interesting news, Major O'Donnell," Liz said. "How soon can we expect the alien?"

"Tomorrow, if you give your approval."

"Since when does the administration care if I approve or not?" said Liz.

"Oh, it's not the administration. It's the alien. It said it will only come if you want it to."

"If I want it to?" Liz smiled. "Of course I want it to."

"Well, Mr. Margolis thought you would, but we couldn't know for sure—and the alien has made it pretty clear that it has to be this way. It's got a mind of its own, and we can't change it."

"I guess I better go home and do some cleaning," Liz said.

"I guess so." David was pleased. "I'll give you a hand, hon."

"Thanks, Major," Liz said. "But you could have just called."

"No, I couldn't. The alien asked that a representative be sent to ask you personally. Outer-space protocol, I guess."

This was said in such a serious way that it seemed even more absurd than it had to be. David tried to hide his amusement by sticking out his hand and looking solemn. He thought his face would break. "Thanks a lot, Major."

O'Donnell shook his hand. "Well, thank you. Mr. Margolis will be pleased, I'm sure."

He turned and walked off, ramrod straight and stiff. David allowed himself to chuckle. "A born desk jockey, aide to the White House Chief of Staff, and a credit to white people everywhere, I give you Major O'Donnell."

Liz laughed. "Guess who's coming to dinner?" she said, hugging David.

"A friend, as you'll soon see."

"A friend." Liz turned that over in her mind as they walked to the parking lot.

As they piled into the jeep, David wondered if it was really true. The alien may have been the creator of the human race, but that didn't necessarily mean it liked the way we had turned out, he thought as he turned over the engine, revved it up, and backed out of the parking space.

* * *

The helicopter banked high above the Montana plains. Inside it were the pilot, an aide, and Jaffrey Flanagan. The Secretary of Morality was deep in thought, hardly noticing the parched, dry landscape moving past his fierce eyes.

Flanagan knew that he was losing the fight for the hearts and minds of the people. The Beast had swayed them, and now they were damned. Unless . . .

He had come on a personal mission of salvation, and nothing short of his own death could stop him. It was important to remember that. Nothing short of his own death . . .

It was the only chance the human race had. It lay in his hands, waiting to come to life. He clutched it tightly, though he could get another one anywhere. After all, it was only a book of matches. That and an incendiary device, and perhaps a few bullets, should ensure that the job was done.

He had to call back his wife. Sylvia had been calling and calling, which was pretty unusual these days. He would get back to her . . . but only when everything was ready.

Just now, no individual was important enough to distract him from what he had to do for Jesus . . . and for himself.

They didn't have a red carpet to roll out, but they planned to give the alien as much of the royal treatment as they could manage on their humble budget. The trouble was, they didn't know what it liked, so all they could do was wing it. Right now they were cleaning the house. David manned the vacuum cleaner as Liz dusted. He worked his way toward her and shut the vacuum off for a minute to take a break.

"At least it will know our intentions are good," Liz said.

"Maybe the alien likes dust and cobwebs. For all we know, it might eat spiders," David said. "Haven't you heard about hell being paved with good intentions?"

"Uh oh. The old boy's unleashing the aphorisms again. Get out your NoDoz."

He grabbed her and kissed her. In response, she tickled his chin with the feather duster.

"It's really coming to see the babies," she said, "not my clean floors."

"Yeah." David thought it was odd to hear them called the babies after what had happened a couple of days ago, but he supposed that Liz hadn't given up on them yet. The dinosaurs had, after all, only been acting naturally—which was a pretty terrifying thought—and couldn't be blamed for the results of their genetic coding. On the other hand, the alien couldn't be blamed either. Jekyll and his siblings were never intended to live on Earth at the same time as Homo sapiens. "But you never know," he said, returning to the vacuum cleaner. "The alien might moonlight with a column for *Galactic House Beautiful.*"

He snapped on the switch, and the machine's roar drowned out Liz's response.

As he did his housework, David's reverie included a marine division scouring the house from top to bottom. The alien, however, had asked that nobody be at Liz's house when it arrived, other than the bare minimum necessary. Of course, that meant there were still a dozen leathernecks outside, but they weren't allowed to come in. This left the cleaning to Liz and David. He was sure Liz preferred it that way, but he had never liked this kind of thing. His debris-strewn apartment was a testament to that fact.

Come to think of it, his rent was due. If he didn't pay it soon, he'd have to give up his lease. He had no guarantee that Liz would want him to move in permanently once this thing was over—if it ever was over. He had a lot of things to think about besides aliens and dinosaurs.

After the dusting and vacuuming, Liz decided that they had to move the furniture around in the living room.

"I assure you," David said, "that the alien isn't going

to use the furniture. It's simply not built for sofas and easy chairs.''

''That's not the point,'' Liz countered. ''This is a matter of propriety and respect. You don't invite a foreign dignitary into your home without doing your best to make the place comfortable and nice.''

''You didn't invite it,'' he said. ''It invited itself. Besides, how do we know what it considers comfortable and nice? I mean, I've spent more time with it than anyone else, and I have no idea what pleases it, hon.''

''Just give the windows a once-over, and be quiet.''

David grinned. This was the kind of banter they'd always shared when he was living here, and he had missed it terribly. Now they were together, but she had made it clear that they might not end up that way. And yet, he couldn't quite believe that they wouldn't.

''I love you, Liz,'' he said, over the vacuum's whine.

She frowned, not having heard what he said. But then her face brightened, and David smiled, too, until he realized that she was looking past him toward the front of the house.

David turned and saw Bob standing in the doorway, smiling at them both. David switched off the vacuum again, pleased to see Bob and grateful to be relieved of his vacuuming duties. Liz hugged Bob as he came into the room.

''They let me through checkpoint Charlie,'' Bob said. ''I guess security is slipping around here.''

''That means the alien asked for you,'' David said.

''So they tell me.'' Bob sat down on the about-to-be-moved sofa. ''Though I don't know how it even became aware of my existence.''

''The alien must have asked for a complete cast list, from the beginning.''

''Separating the men from the boys. They're doing everything the alien wants, with the possible exception of letting all four of the dinosaurs board the spacecraft with him at the same time.''

"What choice do they have? The alien's technology is so . . . well, alien and powerful that they can't make it do anything it doesn't want to do. Still, they're hedging their bets by holding Jekyll somewhere secret, or so I've heard."

"Oh, I see. They still think the alien will dinonap them. Well, I have to admit that that's a reasonable precaution— in a paranoid, untrusting sort of way. Divide and conquer," Bob said. "Got a beer?"

"Sure do, Prof," David said. He went to the kitchen to get Bob a cold one. While he was at it, he got himself one, too, and one for Liz. When he came back to the living room, he found Bob and Liz engaged in moving the sofa.

"Whoa, hold on," David said. He gently pushed Liz away. "I'll do that."

"Thank you," she said, "And it's about time."

David knew better than to argue. Besides, he felt pretty good. It wasn't every day that an alien came to your former home. He had wondered if he would ever get to visit the spacecraft again. He was still sorting out all that he had seen and heard while he was aboard. It had been pretty confusing, and had sent his view of reality toppling end over end. He had to admit to himself that his religious grounding was solid enough that he felt a little queasy about knowing how the human race had been created. There was no mysticism left, no grandeur. We were nothing more than the result of a genetic experiment carried out by a race of saurian aliens.

"What are you thinking about, David?" Liz asked.

"Guess." He smiled at her. "I'm on tenterhooks about the alien's imminent arrival. What time is it, anyway?"

Liz checked her watch. "Quarter to four."

"He'll be here in less than an hour, according to Margolis. I wonder how the White House Chief of Staff likes being a messenger boy to 'that damn lizard,' which is what he calls the alien." David didn't find Margolis as disturbing as Jaffrey Flanagan, though. Expediency was understandable to him; fanaticism was not.

They finished moving the furniture, and sat down on the sofa to drink their beers, with Liz sitting in the middle between the two men. They were quiet in expectation of the coming visit. The only sounds were the soft stirring of the refrigerator's motor coming from the kitchen; crickets, birds, and the occasional whir of a helicopter's rotors seeped through the windows from outside. Occasionally the sofa would creak with the movement of Bob or Liz.

"They're checking every car that comes within a mile of the place," Bob said. "Just like they did down at the landing site."

This was hardly surprising news, and Bob took the hint from David's and Liz's lack of response. He offered no more conversational gambits. It was time to be quiet.

The late afternoon sun tossed slanted shadows across the living room carpet. David looked around at the room's furnishings: the inexpensive white bookcases; the little table between the sofa and one of the chairs; the colorful painting bought years ago from a struggling artist friend; the chipped armoire that had belonged to Liz's parents. These surroundings had been invisible when he lived here. Now they were poignant and familiar, and yet it was is if he were seeing them for the first time.

The alien was a few minutes early. David sensed its presence before he saw it or heard it. Perhaps it was the stillness of the insects, birds, and other sounds coming from outside that made him realize that it had arrived. No, there was something more. The alien carried with it an air of things beyond the Earth, a hint of the vastness of space, a breeze from its own world orbiting Epsilon Eridani, though it had not been there for millions of years.

Whatever it was, he knew that it was nearby. "It's here."

He felt Liz move against him reflexively, and now that the time had come, she seemed a little frightened. Bob was fidgeting a bit, too. They, after all, had never been in the alien's presence before. They had only seen it drifting over the crowd on the prairie. Nevertheless, they sensed that it was here as surely as did David.

David got up and went past the reception desk, to the open front door. He looked out and saw something that filled him with wonder.

A distorted line formed on the horizon. As it drew closer, he saw that it was more like a tube than a line. It was moving rapidly, and though transparent, it distorted the shape of the land—not only the land through which it passed, but the land *near* it as well.

It was the flux, a tunnel of it extending all the way from the spacecraft. David wondered how it worked. Maybe Fine and Sosnowski would have some ideas. Just now he could only stare at it and marvel as it came across the plain, crossed the dirt road, and extended up the driveway, coming straight at him.

And inside the tunnel, as if seen in a fun-house mirror, was the alien itself, its shape elongated and twisted. Nevertheless, it stood calmly, and it seemed to David with great dignity, at the forefront of the flux tunnel.

"Hello," David said.

Hello.

"These are my friends, Bob and Liz."

Yes.

"I guess you already knew who they are."

Yes.

Liz was standing next to David. He hadn't noticed her getting up. To the alien she said, "Won't you please come in?"

Thank you.

The alien drifted into the room. Around it, the flux rippled outward, obscuring the floor. As it surrounded them, David detected the familiar, musky odor of the alien that he had smelled on the spacecraft. They were all inside the flux now.

"It's really a pleasure to meet you," Liz said. "I'm deeply honored that you have come to my home."

You are very kind. The flux elevated itself under the

alien, and raised the creature up. It sat on its haunches looking down, as it had on its own ship. *The honor is mine.*

David wondered if the alien had learned these niceties from watching old black-and-white British movies. Could it be that such manners were known all over the galaxy? It was pleasing to think that the human race had come up with something good, but it was more likely that the rules of decorum being observed here were only human, and that the alien was merely mimicking them.

"Do you have a name?" Liz asked. Embarrassed, she quickly rephrased the question. "I mean, what is your name?"

My name is meaningless to you, and unpronounceable in your tongue.

"Well, do you mind if I call you something?"

I do not quite understand.

"I mean is it all right if I give you a name, so that I'll have something to call you? The idea that you don't have a name makes me uncomfortable."

Then by all means, call me what you wish.

A pregnant pause followed, in which David hoped that Liz wouldn't come up with something like Dino.

"I'd like to call you Mentor." Liz said this with great intensity and conviction.

You may call me that if you wish, but that name may come to disappoint you.

"Oh, I don't think so. Some people are calling you God, and others are calling you Satan. I think we should establish a name that more clearly defines your relationship to our planet."

I am neither deity nor devil. If it pleases you, then think of me as your mentor. But I am more scholar than teacher.

"You're sort of a caretaker, too, aren't you?" David said. "Or a zookeeper. In a way, you're kind of a pale-ontologist. No, that's wrong, because you haven't been studying fossils, but living creatures."

We had great hope for the dinosaurs, but perhaps our

failing was in expecting too much from a race superficially like our own. Had we developed them to a higher state, as we originally planned, we might have mated with them. As it turned out, the Earth changed too drastically to support them, even in this transformed state, for long.

"So you still thought they might develop a moral system when you left the planet."

Yes, but we soon saw that it was no good. We had designed them to mature at such an accelerated speed that it was impossible for them to comprehend ethics. These advanced dinosaurs died out, all but the five eggs you found.

"And what will you do with the four who are still living," Liz asked, "if the government turns them over to you?"

David Albee has seen the habitat maintained for them. We would put them among their own kind, and observe their interactions.

"Their own kind?" David said. "But these are mutations, not dinosaurs. They couldn't possibly be accepted by the others as they are."

Precisely.

"Then you're going to put them with the other dinosaurs for experimental purposes," Bob said.

Yes.

"Do you think *that's* a moral thing to do?"

They cannot live on Earth for long. Soon the seasons will change, and winter will kill them. Even if you protect them from the elements, they will not survive for very long.

"Good point," David said. "But how do you know they can survive in the habitat?"

We can assume so, but we cannot be certain, the alien admitted. *As time passes, they will become increasingly aware that they are not a part of your present world. In the habitat, they might procreate and prosper. They could never do this on Earth. There is too much danger here for them.*

Obviously the alien had been keeping up with current events. David was impressed by the succinct, elegant way it presented its case. But there was still something odd about it. "Why are you presenting your proposition to us? We have no real power."

More than you think, perhaps. Let me show you.

This, David thought—glancing at the confused faces of Liz and Bob—promises to be interesting.

25

Come with me, the alien said.

Before they had time to reply, the flux closed around them like an electromagnetic snare. They were picked up bodily and spirited through the open front door. The flux tube opened before them, appearing strangely undiminished by distance while they were inside it.

"Where are you taking us?" Liz asked, sounding like a frightened little girl. David had never seen her like this. He glanced at Bob, and saw the usually florid face under the gray beard turned livid.

They were lifted high in the air, the end of the flux tube rising like the head of a snake. From this lofty vantage, they enjoyed a breathtaking view of the Montana steppes and the distant mountains, pale blue in the late summer haze. A helicopter, circling around Liz's property a few hundred feet up, banked to avoid colliding with the extended flux tube. David wondered what an accident like that would mean. He suspected that no harm would be done to those inside the tube, but he had no way of knowing for sure.

Do not be alarmed. The alien must have known they were afraid, and its reassurances resonated with conviction. *No harm will come to us.*

"To us . . ."

Liz looked at David, hearing him speak, and her bright eyes told him that she'd interpreted what the alien had just said in much the same way that he had. It was not holding them captive, and it appreciated that they were at the mercy of earthly social and cultural forces as much as the young dinosaurs were.

Another helicopter buzzed them, and the raised flux tube swooped down closer to the ground.

Observe.

David saw a knot of people, trucks, and banks of what looked like technological equipment. Were these scientists, gathered a mile or more from Liz's? No, all of a sudden David realized who they were as he saw the CNN logo on the side of a generator truck. These were the news media people, exiled from the real story all this time, still lingering as near to the dinosaurs as the government would allow.

Here is your power.

David thought of all the arguments posited against the media. He had found them pretty annoying himself, and had always thought they did a lousy job. Inadequate though they might have been in so many cases, the story of young animals languishing in an alien environment would surely go over well on the six o'clock news.

"Yeah . . ." It might work at that.

Video cameras were hefted onto the shoulders of surprised men and women who dropped their coffee and doughnuts to get some footage of the flux tube for the folks at home.

Bob laughed. "Well, look at that."

Liz giggled.

"Let the good times roll!" David shouted.

They came in low to the ground, giving the media people a better shot, lingered for a moment, and then rose high up into the air once again.

"Wa-hoo!" David hollered. The sensation of the rapidly lifting flux tube made him giddy. He was having a wonderful time. "Ride 'em cowboy!"

Liz was laughing, too, and even Bob looked as if he was coming out of his funk. Somehow this airy electromagnetic contraption gave a sense of security to those riding inside it. David knew that it extended all the way from the alien spacecraft, and he didn't have the faintest idea of how it worked, but he wasn't worried about it. If it did fail them, they would go down in glory as no other human beings ever had.

The flux tube looped over Liz's house, reminding David of the time he had replaced some shingles for her. But the view changed rapidly, and they were descending into the backyard compound, with a complement of astounded marines watching them come down.

For a moment David thought he'd left his stomach about fifty feet in the air. But he was all right, exhilarated by the sensation of rapid falling. They were on the ground, or rather floating just above it, and a flux tunnel opened toward the Mylar cage where Jekyll's siblings were imprisoned.

A marine ran up to the tunnel and tried to break through it. He jumped back as if shocked by electricity, which might be very close to what had happened to him. The alien walked right up to the cage, Bob, Liz, and David right behind him.

The alien turned and looked at David, Liz, and Bob. *I must enter the cage.*

"It might not be safe," Liz said. "Besides, you won't fit through the trapdoor."

David remembered what it had been like on the ship. Jekyll had been well behaved under the alien's influence. He didn't know what power it exerted, any more than he understood how it controlled the flux without any visible apparatus. The alien would be safe enough, but Liz was right about its size. The Mylar cage would have to be partially dismantled for it to get inside, and Lieutenant Franklin probably wouldn't go along with that.

Please help me. At first David didn't know what the alien meant. Then he saw how it was standing at the cage, looking confused as its head bobbed about.

"You don't understand how it works, do you?" David asked it. "It's so primitive that you don't get it, isn't that it?"

The principle is foreign to me.

David squeezed past the alien and tossed open the trap door.

It is so simple?

"I'm afraid so," David said, paraphrasing one of his favorite Tom Lehrer songs: "It's so simple that only a human can do it."

Yes.

David was amused by how quickly the alien accepted that. "The dinosaurs are too big to fit through the opening. It can barely accommodate a human."

David glanced covertly at Liz, remembering the night Private Lloyd was killed. She looked down at the ground, but gave no other sign that she was affected by the horror she and David had witnessed such a short time ago.

The alien reached inside with its right arm and extended its clawed fingers toward the three dinosaurs inside. Franny, Zooey, and Marie Antoinette stretched out their necks, moving their heads closer to the aperture.

The alien changed shape. Or perhaps the flux changed the space around it. The volume of the alien shifted, elongated, and it snaked through the opening, re-forming itself on the inside.

"Did you see . . ." Bob was standing behind him, and David didn't have to turn back to know that Bob was gaping at what the alien had just done.

Liz clutched David's arm so hard that he thought her nails would break the skin. The flux tube still surrounded them, extending into the cage. The rippling forms of the marines outside the flux could be seen, but they might as well have been figures on a television screen, so insubstantial did they seem from where David stood.

Inside the cage, the alien resumed its original shape—if it was in fact its original shape—and stood surrounded by the three young dinosaurs. It stretched out a hand and petted Marie Antoinette's head. Its other hand petted Zooey, and then moved on to Franny.

"Oh, how sweet," Liz said.

David felt strangely moved, too, seeing the obvious affection that the alien felt for its charges, separated as they had been for so many millions of years. He had no doubt that the dinosaurs should be taken to the habitat on the spacecraft, though if that happened, they might never be returned to Earth. Still, they couldn't stay here much longer in captivity. It was entirely possible that they had become so neurotic already that Private Lloyd's death was the result. Who could say that they would have killed him if they had been in an environment more conducive to their health and happiness?

My children, the alien said. *They've separated you from your brother, but you will be together again soon. You will come with me, far away from this bitter place.*

David wondered if the alien had intended for him to hear that. Did it possess some kind of telekinetic power, to calm the dinosaurs so? Virtually nothing was known about the creature. It did as it pleased, flying in the face of the most powerful people on Earth and their self-serving wishes.

The alien didn't communicate with David, Liz, and Bob until it said good-bye to the young dinosaurs. David wondered if it had somehow been talking to Marie, Franny, and Zooey while shielding its thoughts from him and his friends. Perhaps it was telling its creations things that would spur them on to new behavior, by opening conduits in their brains that would trigger implanted genetic traits humans had not yet seen. It was also possible that the alien was communicating with the dinosaurs in a purely physical way—or maybe the dinosaurs were calm because the alien meat just didn't smell right to them.

Whatever the case, the alien shape-shifted again, and came through the opening in an elongated version of itself, emerging to reshape itself inside the flux tube.

"How does he do that?" Bob asked.

"What makes you think it's a he?" Liz asked. Her question was reflexive, but David suspected that the alien was neither male nor female, an androgynous creature whose method of reproduction was completely foreign. Looking at its desiccated skin and its ancient eyes, David could even believe that procreation was unknown to it, something its kind had long since abandoned as they lived longer and longer spans, perhaps approaching—or even achieving—immortality.

"Are you taking them with you?" David asked, for now he was sure that the alien could do so if it wanted to, whether the marines tried to stop it or not. The flux tube affected matter itself, so how could any weapon penetrate it? The flux wasn't just some electromagnetic anomaly, it was a field that transformed the basic stuff of the universe in a *controlled* manner. The alien had come a long way since its days of genetic engineering on Earth during the Mesozoic. Not yet a god, perhaps, but this creature was the closest David Albee would ever get to one in this life.

"You could take them out of here if you wanted to," David said. "Why don't you do it?"

I am not so powerful as you think, nor am I so unscrupulous. Your culture has its customs, and I must respect them. If I were to forcibly remove these innocents from captivity, the fears of many would be confirmed.

David remembered the screaming crowds he'd seen on television, and knew that it was true. The worldwide economic depression that had thrown the world into despair had been obscured by the arrival of the alien. But despair had a way of turning into terror, suspicion, and violence. The alien had said that it was not unscrupulous, but it clearly knew that there were many powerful men on Earth who were. David thought of Jaffrey Flanagan, and knew that if the alien defied the United States government, there would be hell to pay. Maybe the alien could get away with it, but it would leave a wake of disaster behind when it left the planet. Clearly, it wished to avoid such mayhem. David respected it for this, and knew now that he could trust it.

The flux tube looped around and went inside the house through the door in the back. The screen door was closed, but they passed through it like it wasn't there. The house's interior loomed around them as if seen through a fish-eye lens. They were propelled forward into the living room.

"It's as if we never left the house," Liz said. She sat down on the sofa in a daze. Bob sat next to her, looking a little peaked, but David stood facing the alien.

"You say that you're not going to use your power to get what you want," David said, "and I think I understand your reasoning. But you have amply demonstrated how powerful you are. Why?"

I had asked to see the dinosaurs, and this request was not granted. Now I have seen them.

"As simple as that, huh?" But David didn't believe it. The alien had put on a show for them, and for the media. It knew that they would be dazzled, and a little frightened, by what they had seen. Surely the news media would capitalize on this as much as possible; it had already sensationalized it a great deal. The mobs of howling fanatics would be encouraged to ever more extreme behavior by enticing images on TV screens all over the world. The alien clearly knew this, and was prepared to use the media for its own purposes. And why not? This, after all, was the way things were done on Earth in the last years of the twentieth century.

I must leave you now.

"Thank you for taking us on that little junket," Liz said. "It was wonderful."

There are wonders all around you, the alien said. *But they grow tiresome through familiarity.*

What did it mean by that cryptic comment? Was it telling them that happiness was in their own backyard, or was it hinting at some deeper meaning?

"Your control of matter has a simple principle at its core, doesn't it?" David asked.

Of course.

And with that, the alien began to recede through the open front door, the rippling flux gathering around it. David felt the short hairs move on his wrists and neck, and knew that he and Liz and Bob were outside the flux again.

"Good-bye," he said to the alien.

But the flux tube was moving away so swiftly that the alien could barely be glimpsed by now, and it didn't answer. David couldn't be sure it had heard his farewell. He felt a gust of summer heat blow through the open door, and smelled the prairie. Nothing more.

"It's strange to think of that creature as our creator," he said, "as God."

"It isn't God," Liz said. "It didn't create the universe. In a sense, it didn't even create the human race. It just recombined some DNA and made simple mammals into more complex ones. That doesn't mean that it's God."

"The way most people think of God, it does mean *exactly* that," David said. "It probably wasn't even *this* alien who did it. This one is a kind of zoo caretaker, as far as I can see. But it doesn't matter. Those who believe it to be God aren't going to be logically talked out of it."

"And neither can those who think the Mentor is Satan, especially considering its serpentine appearance."

"There are even criminals who are saying the alien made them do it through its baleful influence," Bob said. "People will use any excuse to act like jerks."

"We were created to be moral, after all," David said, "just as religions have always taught us."

"The alien concept of morality may be a lot different than Jaffrey Flanagan's, though," Liz said.

David thought it was interesting, the way Jaffrey Flanagan's persona hovered over them even when he wasn't present. It was as if the Millennialist leader had become the bellwether of the entire schism created by the alien's arrival on Earth.

''I wonder where old Jaffrey is right now,'' he said aloud.

Liz and Bob looked at him curiously. Perhaps, David thought, they had been wondering the same thing.

26

The President, of course, knew where Jaffrey Flanagan was, even if few others did. On behalf of the Secretary of Morality, the chief executive had commandeered a ranch only four miles from the Tomlinson veterinary clinic, and was kept informed of Flanagan's observations. This was only a sop to a fallen public figure, Secretary Flanagan reflected as he stood on the ranch house porch watching the flux tube through a pair of heavy lenses.

A hot wind fluttered his clothing as he swung the binoculars around. The news media were ever in evidence, not quite within spitting distance of the dinosaurs, but close enough to cause trouble, surely.

By now the flux tube had vanished, and so there was little sense in standing here in this blistering heat any longer.

Flanagan handed the binoculars to the aide standing next to him and walked back to the house. He kept in touch with the president by GTE viewphone, a special connection that couldn't be tapped into by anyone. Still, he didn't contact the White House any more often than he had to. He didn't want to overplay his hand, after all. He was working on a presidential order to supersede the position of Charles Margolis, and he was reasonably certain that he was close to his goal now.

"Can I get you something, sir?" another aide asked as he entered the ranch house, a young man named Mark Schechter.

"Just water, Mark. I'll get it myself."

"If it's all right, I'll go to the bathroom, then," Mark said.

"Sure." Jaffrey Flanagan went to the kitchen and opened the refrigerator, taking out a container of ice water. As he poured some of it into a glass, he thought about how easy it had been to persuade the President to approve this covert mission. Just keeping an eye on things, while Margolis was busy. There must have been some reason the alien didn't want the Chief of Staff around, or anyone else of any political or military importance.

That thing was the Devil Incarnate—the Serpent in the Garden of Eden.

Flanagan took a long sip from the glass of ice water. The house had no air conditioning, and it was a hot day: nearly a hundred degrees out on the prairie. The house was sweltering, and there was no escape from the heat outside. A fan seemed to do little but make an annoying hum and plaster his hair to his forehead. It reminded him of his boyhood, listening to his father talk endlessly about Bertrand Russell and Thomas Dewey to his mother. It wasn't until later that he knew these people—his own parents—were atheists. They had raised him to disbelieve, to be different from the other kids. How could his own mother and father have deprived him of the knowledge of God? He had tried to tell himself that they only believed they were doing right by him, but he could never quite swallow it.

It was as if they didn't want him to hear about Snow White, or baseball, or cat's-eye marbles, or all the other things that meant so much to kids in those days. Religion was all of those combined and more, so much more. He needed it; he had needed it as a boy, and he needed it now. He had never caught up with his lack of religious training, not even after all these years.

That was his secret, though. Nobody knew that he was behind, had always been behind, and would most likely always be behind. God hadn't forgiven him for understanding so little, not even after all these years of doing His work.

"Damn them," he said. Realizing what he had said, he looked around furtively. Nobody seemed to have heard him, thank God. One aide was on the front porch, watching the Tomlinson place through the binoculars for Jaffrey, and Mark was in the bathroom. All the security people were outside, and the people who owned the house had been put up at a motel in Billings until he had no further need of their property.

The phone rang. Since there was no one else there, Jaffrey Flanagan moved into the little anteroom where the old black phone was kept on a table. Very old-fashioned and charming, he thought, noting with approval the picture of Jesus above the phone.

"Yes?" he said.

"Jaffrey?" It was his wife. "Is that you?"

He was so surprised to hear her voice that it took him a moment to answer her. "Yes, it is, Sylvia. How did you get through to me here?"

"They put me through. They wouldn't give me the phone number or the address of the place where you're staying."

"Where are you, Sylvia?"

"I'm at home."

Flanagan thought of their brick house on Macomb Street in Washington, D.C. He had never liked it there, and constantly felt restless when he had to stay at home. He preferred going on the road to churches in different states, or speaking at political rallies across the country on behalf of conservative candidates during election years. Most of all, he loved preaching before the television cameras, the virtual reality presentation, and in the sixty-four-frames-per-second films shown in Christian Millennialist temples. He had not been close to his wife for many years; they were still married to keep up appearances only. What did she want with him?

"What is it, Sylvia?" he asked, hoping that his impatience didn't show through.

"It's the tests."

He didn't want to hear this now, but he knew he would have to. There was no way out of it, not anymore. "The tests. Are you through with them?"

"Yes."

"Well . . . what do they show?"

A pause, and then: "I have cancer of the liver."

He had already known. They had both known it, of course, but there was always a chance that it was curable. Cancer of the liver, so far as he knew, was not.

"I'm dying, Jaff."

"I . . ." What good would it do to coo pieties into this old phone? "I'm sorry."

"Yes."

How much time had he spent with her in the past ten years? Perhaps six or eight months. And now she was dying. "I'll pray for you," he said.

"Thank you. You're a good man, a wonderful man, and I still love you."

That hurt him. He knew that he hadn't been a good husband. He had been too busy with God's work, if politics could fairly be called God's work. "Do you want me to come home?" he asked.

"No. Do whatever it is you're doing, and then come home, if you like. I have to hang up now. 'Bye."

The receiver clicked dead, and a moment later the dial tone sounded. She was gone. Just like that.

"Good-bye, Sylvia," he said.

He turned to see that Mark was in the kitchen. Now that Jaffrey was off the phone, the aide spoke: "It's a message on the viewphone, sir."

"The president?" His heart thudded heavily with the excitement of thinking that the time might have come at last.

"Uh, no, sir. Mr. Margolis."

"Margolis? How did he . . . ?" But this young man wouldn't know how Margolis had gotten through, would he? Flanagan walked toward the ranch house's bedroom, where he had set up his office. He heard cattle lowing in the distance. His feet seemed heavy, and he felt awkward and displaced as he walked through the house. He could think only of Sylvia. She was dying.

He thought: *My wife is dying of cancer, and here I am trying to save the world. I couldn't even save her. Save her? I couldn't even help her, couldn't even make her happy.*

Jaffrey Flanagan, feeling lost in a way that he hadn't known since he was a small boy, sat down at a chipped pine desk and stared into the florid face of White House Chief of Staff Charles Margolis, tie loosened and thinning hair unkempt.

"Jaffrey, what's going on over there?" Margolis asked. "That damn lizard just put on a display that is making the boss very, very nervous."

"Yes, I know," Jaffrey replied, "I saw what it did."

"I don't know what the fuck we're going to do about this, but we've sure as hell got to do something."

"Please." Margolis had never had any respect for the ministry, but even so, Jaffrey had never heard him curse with such abandon.

"Please, my ass. We're in trouble, son. The lizard has made us look like a proper bunch of fuck-ups, and it's worse for you than me, Rev."

"How did you break through onto this channel?" Jaffrey asked. "It was only known to the president, as far as I know."

"Guess again, Elmer Gantry. You went behind my back and sweet-talked the boss into setting you up down there near the action."

"It was necessary."

"Sure it was. And you just happened to be in place there to upstage me while the fourth dinosaur is on its way back to Montana, too, right?"

Jaffrey said nothing. This was news to him, but, numbed as his mind was at the moment, he didn't want Margolis to know that he hadn't been informed.

"We figured it would be smart to move him while the alien was away. Now, when the lizard comes back, the dinosaur will be gone, but the lizard won't know it. The only trouble is, you do."

Jaffrey remained silent. The verbal abuse he was suffering at the hands of this vulgarian was worth it, for what he had just learned.

"At the moment," Margolis went on, "I can't put you out of commission, but there's a new day coming, pal, and you aren't gonna like it when it arrives."

Margolis reached forward and shut off the transmission. The screen wavered and the image shrank to a tiny rainbow point. Margolis was gone. The alien was gone.

"But the dinosaurs will all be here," he said aloud. Just a few miles away. And he had clearance. He was, after all, still the Secretary of Morality.

He got up from his desk, and as the late afternoon sun stung his eyes through the open drapes, he understood for the first time that nothing else mattered. God was giving him the opportunity that he had prayed for. For the first time in his life, he knew that his vision was true. But vision was nothing by itself; something had to be done.

It was time for him to act.

"What the hell is going on?" Liz asked.

Rubbing the sleep out of his eyes, David came out into the front yard to see what she was talking about. A convoy of twelve trucks was churning up dust across the prairie. They were standard military trucks with canvas covering their beds, all except for one. This was a semi with no outstanding features, dun-colored, pulled by a diesel driven by a marine sergeant. It was preceded by five trucks and followed by the other six.

"I think I know what it is," David said.

"What?" Liz shielded her eyes from the sun. "Bootleg dope from Mexico?"

"Close. I think that's our boy, come home to be with his brothers and sisters, and Auntie Liz and Uncle Dave."

She turned to him with a quizzical expression. "Jekyll?"
"Who else?"

The first of the trucks roared into the yard, making a distressing grinding noise as the driver failed to use the clutch properly while downshifting. The others pulled up, some of them stopping right out in the road. It didn't matter, of course. They couldn't block traffic, since no traffic could come within miles of the house without government authorization.

"Looks like they're pulling the wagons into a circle," Liz said. "Maybe they're expecting an Indian attack."

"Too bad Hiram's not here," said David.

Indeed, the tractor-trailer was backing the semi into the driveway, surrounded by the military convoy. The hissing of air brakes announced the last truck as it pulled into position at the side of the road, effectively blocking off Liz's driveway.

Marines swarmed out of the canvas-covered trucks, armed with M-16s and looking very businesslike in their camouflage gear.

"Do they think they're in Saudi Arabia?" David asked. He was glad Bob wasn't here. The few marines on duty here disturbed Bob enough; there was no telling how he would have reacted to this gratuitous display of military might. To make matters worse, one of the ubiquitous helicopters flew over the house. No doubt the chopper's crew were armed to the teeth, too.

The gate of the semi was opened, and the driver climbed into the back. Inside were two large objects—a cage containing Jekyll and a forklift—and several smaller ones, which David assumed were food and water for the dinosaur. They must have flown him to the airport at Billings and packed him into the semi there. The airport was only an hour's drive away.

Jekyll was in a real cage this time, with metal bars. Apparently the incident with Private Lloyd had made the brass determined to do things the old-fashioned way. This cage didn't look any safer to David than the other one, but what did he know about security? Just because it seemed logical didn't mean that it was right, did it?

The cage was set on runners, so that the driver could easily maneuver the forklift prongs underneath it. Jekyll crouched in a corner of the cage, eyeing the device suspiciously. He jumped a little when the cage was lifted.

He was brought out into the daylight, and David thought he seemed a little calmer as soon as he recognized his surroundings. It was really hot today and that suited Jekyll, David was sure. The dinosaur seemed enlivened by the sultry air as well as the sight of the familiar house.

He chirped when he saw David and Liz.

"For God's sake," Liz said, "he's saying hello to us, David."

"Yeah, how about that." David was pleased. He lifted a hand and waved at Jekyll as the forklift came down off the ramp and drove past them toward the chain-link fence.

"Welcome home, guy," David said.

"Oh, that's so sweet," Liz said, hugging him.

David was glad that Jekyll had been brought back, but he was still worried. The hurricane warning was in effect again, somewhere deep inside his troubled spirit.

"I don't know what's going to happen next," Liz said, "but I feel like the Cold War has come to an end."

David knew that she was right. And yet a dark wave of pessimism washed over him. He felt certain that Jekyll's return would lead to disaster. He couldn't say why, but he *knew* trouble was coming.

"Liz, let's go in the house," he said.

She looked at him curiously. By now she knew him so well that his moods affected her, too. She sensed that he was disturbed, and couldn't understand why.

They went inside, and David led her to the bedroom. He shut the door behind them, and embraced her, feeling very weak and frightened.

"David, you're trembling," she said.

"This thing is coming to a head," David said. "I can feel it, Liz."

"Come on, David," she said irritably. "Don't rain on the parade."

"Yeah." He knew it wasn't logical, but he couldn't shake the feeling that this was the lull before the storm. And the storm was going to break very soon.

27 ▬▬▬▬▬▬▬

"The helicopter is ready, Secretary Flanagan," the aide said. He was a fresh-faced kid of about twenty-five, even younger than Mark and very personable. Jaffrey didn't want to get him in trouble.

"You stay here with Mark, Robinson," Jaffrey said, cognizant of the helicopter's engine and rotor sounds coming from outside. "I'm going over to the compound alone today."

"Yes, sir." Robinson tried to hide his disappointment. He knew something important was about to happen, and he wanted to be there. Jaffrey couldn't blame him. History would be made today. "Good luck, sir."

Jaffrey shook his hand firmly, picked up his briefcase, and went out the door. The revolving blades kicked up dust as he ran toward the Sikorsky helicopter, which was painted with red, white, and blue stripes in the form of a cross. He climbed up, using a step that was pulled up inside the Sikorsky by the pilot as Jaffrey settled into the passenger seat.

"All set, sir." A moment later, the pilot was taking it up.

The helicopter lifted, wobbled a little, and then rose into the dusky prairie sky. The methodical machine sound of its engine helped Jaffrey to think, to relax, and to plan.

Not that there was much to plan anymore. His world had been irrevocably changed by the events of recent weeks . . . and now Sylvia. They had no children. It was almost as if his life had meant nothing. He would leave

222

no one and nothing behind when he was gone from this Earth. A deep sadness overcame him.

"Where are we headed, sir?" the pilot shouted over his shoulder.

"To the compound."

The pilot's eyebrows lifted a little, but then he banked the helicopter and started flying toward Lizaveta Tomlinson's house. They would be there, Jaffrey hoped, in time to save the soul of the human race from a tale of creation that was a patented, satanic lie.

He felt the tears coming, but he choked them back. He had to go through with this, without a hitch, or his life really would end in a meaningless quagmire of regret.

The helicopter started its downward descent from the sunset sky. It was the first time Jaffrey had landed here since the alien came to Earth, and yet it seemed a very long time ago. He had been watching from a distance, outside the loop, wondering how evil could have overtaken him with such ease and unexpectedness.

That was the way of evil, though, wasn't it? It was seductive, even attractive. It was not something that could easily be resisted. He knew where it lay, however, and he intended to fight it, to burn away its loathsome beauty.

He didn't know what would happen, he only knew what must be done, and he was the only one who could do it.

The helicopter settled onto the ground, and Jaffrey waited for the marines to open the hatch. He searched their youthful faces for some sign of suspicion. He saw nothing. There was no reason to believe that they would find his visit out of the ordinary. They knew nothing of inside-the-beltway politics; all they knew was that the Secretary of Morality, appointed by the president of the United States himself, was coming in for a visit, just as he had several times in recent weeks. He was still in good odor with the president, though Margolis was doubtless working like a beaver to change that at this very moment. The fact that he had broken through the viewphone connection indicated that his efforts had already enjoyed some success.

If his calculations were correct, the President would waver once again after he had heard the Chief of Staff's blandishments, but it would be too late by then. Margolis would have wasted his breath.

"Good to see you, sir," the lieutenant on duty said, saluting as Jaffrey clutched his briefcase and clambered out of the helicopter. "We didn't know you'd be visiting today."

"No, I don't suppose you did." Jaffrey looked officially stern, and the clean-cut marine officer stood aside as he set foot on the ground.

Not looking at anyone, keeping his shoulders back and staring straight ahead, Jaffrey walked toward the front door of the house. He had been here dozens of times, and yet it all seemed oddly unfamiliar. A private opened the screen door for him, and he stepped up into the house.

He felt a tear sting his eye in the reception room, but the shadows of the corridor leading to the kitchen in the back of the house protected him from being seen weeping. By the time he came out into the light, he had his emotions under control again.

He glanced quickly toward the bedroom, and saw that the door was shut. Were Dr. Tomlinson and David Albee in there now? They would try to stop him if they knew what he was going to do. But they wouldn't be able to. If they tried to make trouble, he'd order the marines to seize them.

He paused, but nobody emerged from the bedroom. It was just as well. He had come to like those two, despite all their liberal college sentiments. At least they stood for something, which was highly unusual these days. It was too bad they stood for the wrong things.

Jaffrey passed on into the kitchen. There was a pot of coffee gurgling on the counter. That meant somebody would be out here very soon. It would be best for him to get it over with as quickly as possible; the more time he took, the less likelihood of success he had.

With grim determination, he opened the screen door in the back and made his way carefully down the steps. The shed with the incubator was dead ahead. Its door was ajar, and he could see signs of movement inside. It was probably Dr. Tomlinson. Good. She wouldn't be in the way.

Three marines were smoking cigarettes near the cage. They didn't pay much attention to him. Even if they hadn't recognized him, they had seen so many scientists, statesmen, and politicians of late that one more probably meant very little to them.

He nodded at them. One of them stood at attention and saluted. The other two looked puzzled.

"At ease," Jaffrey said, smiling.

"Sir, I'm a member of the Christian Millennialist Church," the young marine said, extending his right hand. "It's a great pleasure to meet you."

"The lieutenant wants to see all three of you," Jaffrey said, noting the disappointment on the young man's face.

The other two looked dubious, especially the black girl, but the Millennialist kid convinced them to go into the house with him. There was no reason for them not to. He was a good boy, and did what he was told by his elders. Several other marines patrolled the property on the other side of the hurricane fence. The place was still very heavily guarded, although the reasons for this had changed since Jaffrey was superseded by Margolis and his people.

Now was his chance. Jaffrey moved toward the translucent cage. He noticed that water droplets glistened on its smooth sides, and he saw that the ground around it was darkened. A rolled-up hose led to a faucet nearby. The marines must have just cleaned the cage. No matter, the magnesium bomb wouldn't be affected by a little moisture.

It was time. Jaffrey Flanagan squatted in Dr. Tomlinson's backyard and unsnapped the clasps of his briefcase. Inside was a .357 magnum, loaded.

He took the pistol and the bomb out and dropped the briefcase on the ground. A puff of dust rose from it as he advanced toward the cage and clicked off the safety.

28 ━━━━━━━━━━━━━━

David knew they were gunshots right away. They were popping thunder, the unmistakable sound of a pistol being fired. He had heard such sounds all his life, in quarries, on mountain trails, in the woods. Sickened, he knew why the shots were being fired, too. He stiffened as he stopped brushing his hair in the big mirror over Liz's dresser. He set the brush down and stepped back. Looking toward the door, he thought about remaining here in the safety and brightness of the bedroom, but he knew he had a duty to uphold. He had to see what had happened.

He didn't run toward the door at first. But once he got past it, he heard shouts and began to hurry more. He could tell from the commotion that the marines had caught the person who fired the shots. He would have felt a lot better about it if the shots had come from out in front of the house, but they didn't. They came from the back.

A marine ran past, not stopping to look at the unarmed David. He was a healthy-looking kid who had been on duty a little while ago. Maybe he still was. Maybe he had deserted his post for some reason, and now he was paying the price for his negligence. David noticed a glow between the cracks of the venetian blinds as he passed through the kitchen.

David followed the marine private out the back door. What he saw at first seemed oddly festive, bright lights playing on the darkening landscape, people running about.

And then he saw the man at the center, and understood. Jaffrey Flanagan stood with a pistol in his right hand pointed down at the ground. The cage behind him was melting, consumed from within by intense white flames. Feathered limbs twitched inside as the plastic warped and ran, searing the flesh of the world's only living dinosaurs.

The screams were the most purely terrible sounds David had ever heard. The dying creatures inside were trapped, and there was nothing that could be done to save them. Only one of them seemed to be moving. Even so, the marine who had run past David in the house was uncoiling the hose used to wash down the cage. His efforts didn't come to much, though. The burning polymer resisted water; the oddly colored flames seemed hardly affected at all.

It was hard to tell the dinosaurs from the heaps of melted plastic now. Nothing inside the runny, red-hot mass was moving anymore. Jaffrey Flanagan had apparently shot the dinosaurs before he ignited the incendiary device. He hadn't left anything to chance.

Three marines surrounded Flanagan, and one of them, a lance corporal, disarmed him. He put up no resistance, and as they led him away, he actually nodded at David.

"You asshole!" David screamed at him. *"You bloody fucking asshole!"*

But Jaffrey Flanagan either couldn't hear him or didn't wish to hear him. The marines led the Secretary of Morality into the house. Another marine appeared carrying a fire extinguisher, which he put to work immediately.

David felt tears come to his eyes. He stared at the guttering flames until he felt a presence behind him. He turned and saw Liz. She wept copiously. All her efforts to nurture the young dinosaurs had come to nothing but this stinking mass of melted plastic, burnt flesh, and charred bone, nothing but black clouds of oily smoke drifting over the prairie. David put his arm around her to give comfort, but he felt no strength in himself. He felt almost nothing at all, as if not only his emotions had been shut off, but his senses as well. It was as if he was not really seeing, not really feeling, not really smelling, or tasting, or touching. It was as if he were dead.

But he wasn't dead, and he knew he had to force himself to act alive. He gently turned Liz away from the grisly sight and walked with her back into the house. He sat her down in the kitchen, that little haven of sanity in a world gone mad, and watched the coffee finish percolating as the smoke roiled outside the window.

"They were only children," Liz said. She stated this as a matter of fact, not a reproach or accusation.

Neither of them spoke for a long time after that. David got down two coffee mugs, checked in the well-stocked fridge for cream, and searched for the sugar. He could barely see these objects, but their packaging was brighter and clearer than real life, so it was possible for him to locate them and to carry out the almost impossibly difficult task of making coffee.

It was lucky, he thought as he poured the hot coffee into their mugs, that the cage was so far from the house. There was no danger of the house catching on fire. Very little danger, at least. Surely, now that the flames weren't leaping as high, they would be all right, safe inside here with their love.

Suddenly David laughed. It was a high, frightened, unpleasant laugh. He didn't like the sound of it, hated it, in fact, but he just couldn't stop laughing.

Liz looked up at him in horror. She probably thought he was going round the bend, but he didn't care. Just for a moment or two, he didn't care about much of anything. But then he remembered that there was something he cared about. Someone. Liz.

"I'm sorry," he said, sitting down at the table next to her. "I couldn't help it."

Liz, mouth puckered and trembling, eyes red and moist, reached out and gently touched his hand. "I know," she said. "I know, David."

They sat for a very long time.

* * *

"It had to be done, son," Jaffrey Flanagan said. "You see that, don't you?"

"But we've got our orders, Mr. Flanagan," the Christian Millennialist marine replied. Jaffrey saw from the marine's name tag that his name was Millard.

"I'm telling you, those things were the spawn of Satan, Millard," Jaffrey said. "Did you ever hear of an animal that could outthink a man?"

"Well . . ."

"One of them escaped from this eminently well-guarded compound, because it planned its escape in collusion with the other three. How do you suppose they came by such guile?"

But the FBI man who had come up from Billings was firmly forcing Jaffrey Flanagan into the helicopter before the private could answer that disturbing question.

Inside the chopper, which was not the one he had come in—Jaffrey would have to explain that he had acted alone so that the pilot who had flown him to the compound wouldn't be implicated—he found it difficult to sit comfortably. It was because of the handcuffs on his wrists. Yes, he was chained, and yet he saw himself freed, rather than imprisoned. He thought of the holy martyrs, tortured and killed by the Romans because of their efforts to spread the word of God, and he felt a special kinship with them. God's work was done, and Jaffrey Flanagan had done it.

The great plains vanished into the firmament. As the helicopter ascended like some celestial chariot, the melted dinosaur cage glowed blue-white beneath it. Satan was alone now, his minions destroyed. Alone, he would be exposed for the serpent that he was, and the people of Earth would be saved from his evil once and for all.

"Hallelujah!" Jaffrey Flanagan shouted.

The new pilot shook his head sadly. He had no idea that he and the rest of his brothers and sisters had been spared the worst evil since the Garden of Eden; since the creation of the universe by God Himself. There was no way to destroy the devil, who was invincible and immortal, but at least the devil's disciples were gone. The struggle had almost been won by the Evil One, but now the forces of wickedness had been set back, at least temporarily. Jaffrey Flanagan had done it; his life was worth something.

The helicopter soared into the darkness. It occurred to Jaffrey that this was the last battle he would lead against Satan. But there would be others to carry on . . . maybe that young marine private . . . young Millard . . . or Schechter . . . Robinson . . . It would go on . . .

Somebody had to be left to fight evil after Jaffrey Flanagan was gone. Somebody . . .

"I don't know if they've told the alien yet," David said.

Cilla MacDonald and Hiram Walking Bear sat on the couch. They'd come to visit today, the day that the last of the military personnel had left and the scientific equipment had been taken away. Except for the scorched ground in the backyard and the hurricane fence, it was almost as if nothing had ever happened here. Still, it was the first time Cilla and Hiram had been able to see him in weeks, and that was certainly unusual. They had hung out together for years, and yet it seemed strange to have them sitting here.

"I talked to your landlady," Hiram said. "She says you're in arrears on your rent, but if you pay her, you can stay."

"David's gonna stay with Liz from now on," Cilla said. "Aren't you, David?"

"I don't know."

"I'm sure she wants you to," Cilla said, though her tone was a little more dubious than before. "She loves you, you know."

"After all that's happened," Hiram said, "you two can't just separate like it was nothing, can you?"

David was thinking about an answer to that question when the phone rang. Liz was outside, so he excused himself and went to answer it in the kitchen.

"Hello," he said.

"Hello, David." It was the familiar voice of Charles Margolis.

"What do you want?" David asked.

"It's not what I want, it's what our visitor wants."

David felt a glimmer of interest. "It's still here?"

"Yep."

David felt curious about how the alien would view things now, after what had happened to the dinosaurs. He had been sitting around Liz's house for two days with nothing to do; he welcomed the opportunity to speak to the alien again.

"I guess I can leave anytime," David said. "Unless, of course, it wants to come here."

"No, it prefers that you go to the spacecraft. Understandable, I think, after what's happened to the lizard kids."

The lizard kids. This was what this powerful man called the creatures who might have stood in Man's place but for chance. Nothing had changed, it seemed. Margolis had learned nothing—and if he had learned nothing, what about the rest of the world?

"Don't you have anything to say, David?" Margolis asked.

"How soon does it want to see me?"

"Well, it didn't specify, but I'd say the sooner the better."

"Why?"

"Haven't you turned on your TV? They're going nuts all over the world. Half of Benares has been burnt to the ground. There were demonstrations in Moscow today. Los Angeles riots. The place is going crackers. Jaffrey thought he was saving the world, but he just made things worse."

"Of course. If he'd read the Bible less selectively, he'd have known that violence begets violence."

"Nobody reads more selectively than ole Jaffrey. He'll be reading from inside a padded cell from now on, I guess. You know something, though? This is the first time I ever felt that he was sincere. He never really took a risk like that before. It was insane, but he actually tried to stand up for something that wouldn't put him ahead of the game.''

David felt like saying something sarcastic, but he didn't. He knew that it was true. Jaffrey Flanagan had saved his own soul, in a very real sense. But he might have destroyed the future of the human race.

''See you when you get here, David.'' Margolis hung up.

David left in the middle of the night, sometime past two. Liz was asleep, and Cilla and Hiram were long gone. This was something he had to do on his own. He hadn't discussed it with anyone. The only one who knew was Margolis.

David drove for a while in silence. He passed McCullers' Rock Shop and wondered how business was. Maybe things would pick up now. It was hard to imagine that the Christian Millennialist movement could survive to stifle free thinking again, but stranger things had happened in the past. He wouldn't be surprised if Jaffrey Flanagan was back on TV next week, actually.

The drive was quite pleasant. David saw a coyote slinking by the side of the road at one point, and the great plains seemed to stretch right up to the stars, out past where his headlights faded into the darkness.

Maybe the alien would ask him to go with it to Epsilon Eridani. Or maybe it wasn't going there at all, maybe it was going back to the asteroid belt to doze in stasis for another few million years. Maybe it would come back to a future Earth and find things changed for the better, a paradise. David doubted it, but he was willing to allow for the possibility. More likely the alien would want to reduce Earth to a burnt-out cinder.

He got to the checkpoint long before dawn. The on-duty marine had been instructed to let him by, and he was soon on his way to the alien ship.

In the moonlight, the site looked eerie and deserted. The bandstand had been dismantled, and a few temporary structures had been erected in place of the tents Margolis and the others had occupied in recent days. The spacecraft rested on the prairie like some natural object, a mountain that had been here for millions of years.

A small group of military men were gathered midway between the parking area and the spacecraft. A tall man in a suit was with them: Margolis.

"Couldn't wait until morning, eh?" Margolis said, smiling at him.

"It seemed like the right time to come." David looked up at the enormous shadow rising before him, wondering if this was solid matter, or some extension of the alien's will, shaped by physical means unknown to the human race. Would it change shape before his eyes, shrink or grow even larger?

Actually, it seemed the same as the last time he had seen it, as if nothing had happened. He began to walk toward it.

The crisscross hatch in its side opened, and a flux tube rushed out toward him. In seconds it had met him, and he felt the hairs on his arms and neck raise. He was drawn inside the spacecraft. The flux tube turned in on itself, and carried David through the constantly changing interior of the spacecraft. It was quiet inside, and dark. It seemed an appropriately mournful setting, considering what had happened.

The flux tube curved around and shot upward. It moved forward for a few minutes and then opened, leaving David standing on flux ripples all by himself. He waited for the appearance of the alien.

"Where are you?" he asked after what seemed a long time, but which was probably no more than thirty seconds.

Here.

"Please show yourself," David said.

The alien came out of the darkness, floating on a flux bubble as it had the day it landed on Earth.

You are well?

"I'm all right. My heart is broken, but I'm all right."

Yes.

"I guess I'll get over it, sooner or later."

Will you?

David didn't know if this question was meant to mean more than it seemed. Would he, would the human race, ever get over the horror that had been perpetrated in the name of morality? He supposed that they would, that they would soon be back to business as usual.

"I'll never forget them," David said.

The alien bowed its strange, saurian head. *Nor will I.*

David wondered if it had wept, in its way. He doubted that it possessed tear ducts, and yet he was sure that it had been deeply saddened by the murders. He wished now that it had abducted the four young dinosaurs and left the Earth on that first day. All the security on the planet couldn't have stopped it. And yet Margolis had never suspected that the danger lay not in the alien but in the all too familiar form of Jaffrey Flanagan.

"I know this will sound strange," David said, "but I think Jaffrey Flanagan had to do what he did."

Yes.

The alien wasn't surprised by the killings. David didn't know what to say, but he kept talking anyway. "He thought he was doing the right thing, the moral thing. I don't know how much sense that makes, but somehow I understand, and I even sympathize with him. He's crazy, but he—"

—he is a moral man.

The alien was making this easier for him. It understood so much. "In his own blatto way, he is. There are certain things he can't see, though, or refuses to see for some reason. I don't know if he could be any different than he is."

You need not defend him.

David looked down, shaking his head. "I don't know

why I feel compelled to do so. What he did is indefensible, but he is a tortured soul, and in a sick way he represents so much of what the human race is all about.''

The alien listened, and did not speak.

''We've always used morality to do destructive things to each other. The ancient world is full of examples, and so is our more recent history. Cultures have been destroyed, right down to the last man, woman, and child, in the name of morality. We've had inquisitions, reformations, counterreformations, jihads, holy wars, purges, black lists, sacred campaigns against those who haven't seen the light, over and over and over again.'' David paused, wondering if he should tell the alien what was on his mind. Why not? He'd never get another chance. ''You gave this curse to us when you implanted the moral urge in our genetic makeup.''

Yes.

''I don't want you to think that it's all been bad. We've done a lot of good things in the name of morality, too. But I don't think it balances out. I think we'd have been better off without it.''

Without it you would still be rooting for grubs in central Africa.

In spite of his grief and his inchoate thoughts, this statement fired David's imagination. ''What do you mean?''

The moral urge is what drives a species forward. It is fueled by the notion that it is absolutely correct in its moral imperatives, that these imperatives are larger than the individual and must be asserted. Those who stand against it are always *incorrect, though their opponents believe that their version of morality is just as correct. This conflict is the process that culminates in a planetary civilization, and leads ultimately to the stars.*

David thought he understood at last. Perhaps the implantation of morality wasn't just an isolated experiment. ''You've done this before, on other worlds, haven't you?''

On many *other worlds.*

"Then you know if *this* miserable world still has a chance of working things out."

Your world has become too limited. You must reach outward or go mad as a species.

So that was it. The human race had languished in the cradle too long, and was overdue to explore the stars. "We've made a start," David said. "Maybe we can still do it."

There is no other way for you to survive.

David was chilled by the alien's pronouncement. He knew that it was true, deep down inside. Man had soiled his nest beyond recovery, and he had to give the Earth time to heal. In time that would happen, but only if he left the planet. Maybe the alien's appearance here would expedite such a movement. David could only hope so.

"Maybe I can help spread the word," he said. He thought of all the media people whom he had shunned, who would only be too glad to let him spout off to millions about the need for an international space effort to save the planet. He didn't know how long he would have in the spotlight, but he would do as much as he could while his celebrity lasted. It was something to live for.

I must go soon.

"I wish I could go with you," David said.

You may, if you wish. But you will never return to the world you know.

David thought it over. He wished that he could go, but only for a little while. He could not in good conscience leave his time forever, to return millions of years in the future to the possible ruins of the human race. His place was here on Earth, now, trying to make his fellow creatures see the way that they must go.

"I think I better stay here and work on our problems," David said. "I don't know how much I can accomplish, but I've got to try. I've hidden away for too many years already. It's time for me to do something positive."

The alien nodded its massive head in understanding. *Good luck, David Albee.*

"There's one thing you could do for me before you go,"
David said.

Yes.

"Let me see the dinosaurs again." He hoped that there
was still time.

In the flickering light of the flux ripples, it almost looked
as if the alien was smiling. The flux enveloped them, and
together they began to move through the mysterious ship,
gathering speed as they went. After a few minutes, the
flux whorled and eddied around them, and suddenly they
emerged into another world.

The dinosaur habitat was an island of matter floating in
a sea of flux. And yet it was so anchored that the illusion
of standing on solid ground was complete, as the tube flew
away and left David and the alien standing in a Cretaceous
jungle. The first thing that clued David in that they weren't
enclosed in flux anymore was the smell, lush and over-
powering, of growing things, both vegetable and animal.

"Wow!" David hadn't expected to be treated to a trip
inside the habitat, and the absence of the flux tube made
him feel vulnerable, especially considering the big car-
nosaurs he had glimpsed the first time he had been privi-
leged to see this incredible place from the outside. He was
just a country boy who had managed to get through a few
years in college, and all of his life he had been in love
with dinosaurs. Now he was *there* in the Age of Reptiles,
the Mesozoic, when dinosaurs were the dominant creatures on Earth.

The first dinosaur that came near them was an ornithis-
chian unfamiliar to him. Perhaps it was a heterodontosaurus,
but it seemed a little too large, and its odd, cobralike
flared wattles were certainly unexpected. It blinked at David and the alien and then went away, perhaps deciding
that they were too big to mess with. David felt a thrill of
fear and adventure as it cocked its head in the familiar
manner of Jekyll and his siblings. Its hide was the blue of
a gun barrel, and its feathers were varying tints of blue

and green, accented by a touch of orange at the elbows. It ambled away in search of other game.

"What if that had been a tyrannosaurus?" David asked the alien.

Do not be afraid.

David shrugged. He supposed that the alien could summon the flux to surround them at a moment's notice, or that some other, less obvious safeguard might be built in as well. He would just try to relax and enjoy this while he could.

The alien walked ahead of him, swaying from side to side as it made its way through the dense undergrowth. David slapped at an insect that bit him on the arm, noting that the habitat was complete down to such a fine detail. How many generations of these insects had survived in space as the alien slumbered? There were so many things to ask the alien, but it would be gone soon, and he would never have the opportunity. It was more important at the moment to merely be here, to experience the world of dinosaurs as it was sixty-five million years ago.

A sauropod lounged in the tall grass of a clearing ahead. These long-necked creatures were fairly rare by the end of the Cretaceous, David knew, and this one was not among the largest, but he estimated that it still measured a good fifty-five or sixty feet. Its leathery skin was a deep gray with a touch of reddish brown on the snub snout. It rose as they watched it, and a flock of tiny birds flew from their roost on its spine. The sauropod reared back, sat on its haunches, and stretched its long neck up, looking for leafy bits on a nearby treetop.

David saw a herd of ceratopsians a couple of hundred yards away, and started moving toward them, eager to get a closer look. The alien humored him, and together they climbed over a fallen log. David saw that they were not triceratops, as he had hoped, but he thought that they might be chasmosaurs, judging from the lengthy bone frills sticking up from the backs of their beaked heads. Their hatchlings, varying from a yard-long toddler to a

hippopotamus-size half-grown adolescent, were surrounded by the adults, to protect them from predators.

There were hundreds of dinosaurs, pterosaurs, and mosasaurs, all from that last flowering of saurian life before
the volcanoes on the Indian subcontinent had vomited
enough matter into the atmosphere to lower the temperature. Iridium deposits had been much closer to the surface
than they should have been, leading to the comet theory.
The truth was simpler and less glamorous, perhaps, but
volcanoes had wiped out the dinosaurs, nonetheless.

All but these fine examples, kept alive and healthy by
their alien guardian. David wondered about the alien. What
was its life really like? Did it ever get lonely? Were some
of its fellow creatures stored in stasis somewhere on this
vast ship? Or was it created for this peculiar, solitary duty
here in this primitive backwater of the galaxy?

A hissing roar distracted David from thinking about the
alien. He looked up to see a huge figure, head down and
immense jaws gaping, as it bore down on them.

"Jesus!" David shouted.

The yellow-fanged mouth foreshortened as the tyrannosaur charged. David smelled the thing's fetid breath,
and his heart seemed to triple in size. He couldn't get out
of the way in time. He had to do something, though. He
tried to push the alien out of the tyrannosaur's path, and
found that his hands sank into scaly flesh ineffectually. He
couldn't move the alien.

It was just as well. At the last possible moment, the
alien lifted a delicately clawed hand and gestured toward
the monster. Coils of concentric flux shot forward and
engulfed the tyrannosaur. The monster writhed and roared,
startled as it was lifted off the ground. It floated gently
away from David and the alien.

David tried to speak, but the constriction in his throat
made it difficult. His heart was still thudding wildly in his
chest, and he felt weak in the knees, as if he ought to sit
down. He watched the bubble light gently near the shore

of the miniature sea and release the bewildered tyrannosaur. It seemed dazed as it skulked away into the jungle.

It thought we would be easy prey.

"Yeah," David managed to gasp, "I guess it did."

Have you seen enough?

"Definitely."

Flux gathered around them, and swept them backward, out of the habitat and through the dim shapelessness of the spacecraft's interior.

You were very courageous.

"You've got to be kidding," David said. "I was scared shitless."

And yet you tried to save my life. I admire you for that. There is much to be said for a race capable of self-sacrifice.

Before David could respond, the alien receded, almost as if it were shrinking. David knew that he was actually moving away from it, even though the flux tube's interior was virtually inertialess, and provided little sensation of motion.

A moment later, David was outside. The sun was rising, blasting the prairie sky with crimson, violet, orange, and amber, but not tinting the dark shape of the alien spacecraft looming over him.

David stepped back, knowing that the immense ship was not going to stay much longer. He walked toward the knot of military men and media flacks in the distance.

He saw them all react, a human hydra whose heads all raised at the same moment. He could not see their expressions from so far away, but he was confident that they were filled with wonder.

David turned in time to see the gargantuan ship lift from the ground, light as a feather, and rapidly diminish in size as its shadow passed over him. It was out of sight in seconds.

"Good-bye," David whispered.

He kept looking up at the sky. The sun was breaking

over the horizon, but some stars were still faintly visible, as well as the waxing moon.

Media people were all around him, and so were Margolis and the big military brass.

"What did the alien have to say?" they asked. "What did it tell you?"

"It said to keep trying," David said, wondering how he could phrase it without clichés, and realizing he couldn't, he just told them the truth. "It said to reach for the stars."

It was nearly noon by the time he left the restricted area. At the gate he saw a familiar car waiting. It was Liz. He pulled over next to her and got out. She was asleep, so he tapped on her windshield.

She opened her eyes, saw him, and smiled.

"David!" she cried, opening the door and jumping out to give him a hug. "Why didn't you tell me you were leaving last night?"

"I don't know," he said, squeezing her hard. "But I promise I'll never do it again. You're stuck with me, like it or not."

He kissed her, and then they got back in their cars and drove home.

BIO OF A SPACE TYRANT
Piers Anthony

"Brilliant...a thoroughly original thinker and storyteller with a unique ability to posit really *alien* alien life, humanize it, and make it come out alive on the page." *The Los Angeles Times*

A COLOSSAL NEW FIVE VOLUME SPACE THRILLER—
BIO OF A SPACE TYRANT
The Epic Adventures and Galactic Conquests of Hope Hubris

VOLUME I: REFUGEE 84194-0/$4.50 US/$5.50 Can
Hubris and his family embark upon an ill-fated voyage through space, searching for sanctuary, after pirates blast them from their home on Callisto.

VOLUME II: MERCENARY 87221-8/$4.50 US/$5.50 Can
Hubris joins the Navy of Jupiter and commands a squadron loyal to the death and sworn to war against the pirate warlords of the Jupiter Ecliptic.

VOLUME III: POLITICIAN 89685-0/$4.50 US/$5.50 Can
Fueled by his own fury, Hubris rose to triumph obliterating his enemies and blazing a path of glory across the face of Jupiter. Military legend...people's champion...promising political candidate...he now awoke to find himself the prisoner of a nightmare that knew no past.

VOLUME IV: EXECUTIVE 89834-9/$4.50 US/$5.50 Can
Destined to become the most hated and feared man of an era, Hope would assume an alternate identify to fulfill his dreams.

VOLUME V: STATESMAN 89835-7/$4.50 US/$5.50 Can
The climactic conclusion of Hubris' epic adventures.

THE CONTINUATION
OF THE FABULOUS
INCARNATIONS OF IMMORTALITY
SERIES

PIERS ANTHONY

FOR LOVE OF EVIL
75285-9/$4.95 US/$5.95 Can

AND ETERNITY
75286-7/$4.95 US/$5.95 Can

PRESENTING THE ADVENTURES OF

BILL THE GALACTIC HERO

BY HARRY HARRISON

BILL, THE GALACTIC HERO

00395-3/$3.95 US/$4.95 Can

He was just an ordinary guy named Bill, a fertilizer operator from a planet of farmers. Then a recruiting robot shanghaied him with knockout drops, and he came to in deep space, aboard the Empire warship *Christine Keeler*.

BILL, THE GALACTIC HERO: THE PLANET OF ROBOT SLAVES   75661-7/$3.95 US/$4.95 Can

BILL, THE GALACTIC HERO: ON THE PLANET OF BOTTLED BRAINS   75662-5/$3.95 US/$4.95 Can
(co-authored by Robert Sheckley)

BILL, THE GALACTIC HERO: ON THE PLANET OF TASTELESS PLEASURE   75664-1/$3.95 US/$4.95 Can
(co-authored by David Bischoff)

BILL, THE GALACTIC HERO: ON THE PLANET OF ZOMBIE VAMPIRES   75665-X/$3.95 US/$4.95 Can
(co-authored by Jack C. Haldeman II)

BILL, THE GALACTIC HERO: ON THE PLANET OF TEN THOUSAND BARS   75666-8/$3.99 US/$4.99 Can
(co-authored by David Bischoff)